Book One of the Elvenrealm Series

Kerridwyn's Pool

Isaac,
Thank you for all the help. Look
for it in the fifth book.

D. C. BRYANT

First Edition

ISBN-13: 978-1-7339902-0-2

DEDICATION

To Tamsin,

Whose exquisite inspiration and intuition helped to

make this book possible.

CONTENTS

ACKNOWLEDGMENTS

Special thanks to my beautiful wife, who put up with my obsession with Elvenrealm to the exclusion of most of my other obligations. I also would like to thank all the friends and family that read the initial drafts and gave me valuable feedback.

The most auspicious event in the creation of this work was finding one of the most talented photographic illustrators in the nation. Thanks to Kenny Gray for the beautiful cover art.

kgp@kennygray.com

ALSO BY D. C. BRYANT

THE ELVENREALM SERIES

Kerridwyn's Pool

The Goblin Queen

Beyond The Veil

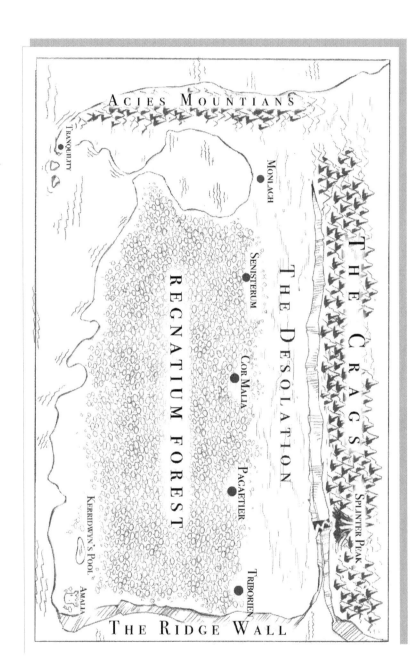

Chapter 1

ELVENREALM

Alone, as always, Sariel sat in the audience chamber of the stone keep when the Great Wolves began to howl. He sat cross-legged in one of the two thrones playing the lute. He never thought of them as thrones; he knew he would never deserve a throne. These were nothing more than copious and uncomfortable chairs as far as he was concerned. The mournful melody coaxed from the fifteen strings echoed throughout the chamber, resonating off the stone walls.

Detecting notes that were not his, he placed the lute on the adjacent seat and went outside. There was no mistaking it. The noble beasts that served as Protectors of the Realm were in the midst of a Great Howling. Something was wrong— whether he was welcome or not (and he never felt welcome) he donned his armour, strapped on his sword, and picked up his spear. Sariel rushed out of the keep and into the darkness.

He ran through the woods and over gentle hills; he

bounded the many small streams and ran down the trail as leaves brushed his face. Despite his haste, the bright, round moon was nearly overhead by the time he reached the Pool of Kerridwyn. Before he could enter the clearing around the pool, he encountered the wolves guarding the perimeter. Three of the beasts barred his way. They snarled and growled, barked and bared their teeth, slobbered and snapped. They resembled a wolf from outside of The Veil with one exception, their size. Their backs stood almost chest high to Sariel, and they could nearly look him in the eye.

Seemingly unconcerned Sariel spoke. "As always, your welcome warms my heart."

One crept towards him. It was a surly beast that the Goddess had named Shade. Sariel simply stood. It pulled up short, growling and baring his teeth.

"I serve as a Protector, like you, and come when there is a call. That is my agreement with Kerridwyn. If you do not approve, then take it up with the Lady. What is happening?"

The beast relaxed a bit and turned to look back in the direction of the Pool of Kerridwyn. *Has the Goddess returned?* Sariel wondered. He had only seen her once; it was when he first arrived and volunteered his services as a Protector. Protector of a realm that was not his. Another place where he did not belong. No matter, he really didn't belong anywhere except for the one place he chose to avoid.

Sariel strode past the wolf, managing to bump his haunches as he walked away. He didn't even look back as the beast snapped in his direction.

In the clearing, there was a large pool of clear blue water. Lotus and lily blossoms of all colors floated in the pool, almost luminescent in the moonlight. Flowers of all kinds perfumed the air. Fireflies hovered everywhere twinkling like tiny golden stars. Trees surrounded the clearing, yet did not encroach upon the pool, as if out of respect. A thick blanket of soft moss formed an inviting place to sit or lie down for many yards back from the edge. And on this moss, there were two figures near the pool.

One was the mate of the alpha male, whom he knew was named Luna. She was the only wolf with pure white fur, the alpha female. She sat straight and regally, even though she was heavy with a litter. There could be no doubt who was in charge when she was around. She sat before the prone figure of a young woman. Sariel glanced around, hoping to see the Goddess, but she was nowhere in sight. Then he noticed another, Luna's massive mate, Thor, standing a short distance behind her. Sariel had been attacked by that one before and bore a few scars from the encounter.

Deciding to err on the side of caution, Sariel placed his spear on the soft moss and slowly moved forward to get a closer look at the young lady Luna was watching over. As he neared the woman, Thor began to move forward, the fur along his neck standing straight up. A disapproving glance from Luna stopped him in his tracks.

Sariel glimpsed a beautiful young woman. Long golden hair lay about her in the moss in gentle waves, the moon reflecting a golden halo. She had delicate features and was small for a human. He had no doubt she was from the other side of The Veil. She wore flannel pajamas adorned with some type of

3

animation characters. The pajamas were ill-fitting, much too tight. Her only other adornment, a long, delicate gold chain, currently lay pooled on the moss to the side of her neck.

He reached down and placed a hand on her chest, just below her throat. Thor growled, but Sariel ignored him. He knew she wasn't dead—his one dubious talent being skilled in the ways of death—but he wanted to confirm she was breathing. That's what Sariel told himself, but the reality was Sariel just wanted to touch her, to see if she were real. She was human, the first he had seen in this realm, and the loveliest he had encountered in the other. Beneath his hand, her pale skin was cool to the touch. She was still breathing.

Sariel looked to Luna. "She is from the other side of The Veil. Only Kerridwyn could have brought her here. Where is she? Where is Kerridwyn?"

Luna just stared at him, sitting straight like a marble statue in the bright moonlight. She didn't know.

"Has she been named by the Goddess?" he asked. Luna looked at the young woman but otherwise remained still.

He gently shook the hand on her chest. "Beautiful woman," he whispered, his thoughts manifesting into words. She stirred but did not open her eyes.

He shook again a little harder. "Lady," he said louder.

Her eyelids fluttered, she opened her eyes and looked at him. Her eyes were large. In the bright moonlight, he could see they were of a deep blue, and they were set beneath eyebrows as gold as her hair. "Ah, good," Sariel said. "You awaken. Who are you? Why are you here?"

The girl gasped and sat up so quickly it startled Sariel, who stood and took a step back. Then she leaned to the side and vomited—traveling through The Veil was never easy for a mortal. It passed quickly, she wiped her mouth with the back of her hand and gazed up at the tall, bronzed figure. Handsome and severe, he appeared to be the type of person who rarely, if ever, smiled. He had, what her friends referred to, as a resting bitch face. Which means when relaxed, he appeared annoyed or angry. He wore his jet black hair close-cropped. He was muscular and lean, too much for her taste, like one of those self-absorbed body-builders. She never met one she cared for in the least. The oddest thing was the way he was dressed. Some sort of black embossed breastplate with armoured leggings. Each scale on the breastplate resembled the tips of feathers. It reminded her of images and drawings of Roman soldiers.

She sat there, staring up at him with her mouth open, so he repeated. "Who are you? Were you sent here by Kerridwyn?"

"What?" She struggled to get up, so Sariel helped her stand on shaking legs to face him. "Who are *you*? Where have you taken me?"

"I am Sariel. I have not brought you here." He motioned behind her. "And these are the Protectors of this realm."

She turned and found herself eye to nose with Luna. Luna sniffed her face. The girl shrieked and backpedaled into Sariel. He held her in place as her feet continued to churn up the soft moss.

"Calm yourself, please, Lady."

Her feet stopped moving, and she stammered. "Are these your … giant dogs?" Luna narrowed her eyes.

Sariel couldn't help but smile a little. "Not dogs, Lady. These are the Great Wolves. Guardians, if you will."

"Are they friendly?"

"Not to me."

"What should we do? Run?"

"That would be unwise. They will catch you."

He released her; she crouched and looked about, like a cat cornered by a pack of dogs in an alley. She saw that Shade and others had gathered around effectively blocking her escape through the forest on this side of the pool. Then she saw Thor, the massive beast, slowly stalking towards her. That proved to be too much. She turned and started to leap into the pool.

Sariel managed to catch a handful of the back of her tight pajama top at the collar. "That is Kerridwyn's Pool! It is sacred," he said.

She spun, lifted her arms, a couple of the buttons popped, and the top came off. She leaped backward into the pool, turned in the water, and swam for the other side, lotus flowers bobbing in her wake.

Sariel looked at Luna. Her ears were back, her neck low as she watched the young woman splash across the water. She turned to him, ears back up and eyes wide. Luna tilted her head.

"I suppose you want me to chase after her?" he asked as the girl scrambled out of the pool on the other side and crashed into the woods.

Luna resumed her stoic appearance.

"Of course you do," he muttered. Sariel jogged back around the pool, picking up his spear. On the other side, he found her prints in the moss and headed into the woods.

She is fast, Sariel thought. He picked up his speed so that the sign remained fresh. She frequently changed directions. This was most likely because she had no idea where to go; however, it made tracking her take more time. A half-hour had passed before he was able to hear her in the distance. There were scuffling sounds accompanied by small, sharp screams. He broke into a sprint.

Sariel broke free of a thicket, skidding to a stop right behind a young wereboar. It had the general shape of a pig, but instead of tusks, bore the toothy maw of a bear. Bird-like talons replaced the standard pig hooves, with thick hide covered in rough, bristly fur. The beast was attempting to climb a tree with the young woman perched on a low hanging branch. She swung at the creature with a small stick when it got close.

Sariel brought the blunt end of the spear around in an arc, striking the beast on the side of the head with a loud *thunk*. The wereboar was knocked to the ground. By the time the boar regained its feet, the point of Sariel's spear rested against its shoulder. It instinctively charged, the blade piercing its flesh enough to cause pain but no permanent injury. It squealed loudly and ran into the woods.

"You! Again?" she cried. "I just got away from you. This is the worst nightmare I have ever had."

"Beautiful woman, are you injured?" he asked, leaning the spear against the tree. Raising his hands, he said, "Let me help you down."

She squatted on the branch, bare chest heaving with exertion, and swung the stick at him. It whistled through the air and struck him on the cheek. He placed a hand on the side of his face and checked for blood. It stung but did not break the skin.

With a sigh, he said, "Very well. I shall withdraw my offer of assistance." He reached into his belt and pulled out the pajama top. "Would you like to have this back?"

She regarded him for a moment then reached down. He promptly took two steps back. "Come down from that tree, and I shall return it."

"I don't negotiate with kidnappers," she snapped back.

"I understand your policy. There is some wisdom in it. However, I am no kidnapper, other than holding your tunic hostage in an attempt to get you to climb down."

"You kidnapped me, brought me to … wherever this is … and chased me with a spear."

"That spear? The one leaning against the tree you are perched upon? It is much closer to you than I. Come down and take the spear if it makes you feel at ease." He took another couple steps back.

"You could still get it before I got down," she said with slightly less conviction.

"I will sit," he said and sat down. "Now, it is not possible for me to reach it first."

She merely stared at him, one hand on the tree trunk and the other still gripping the inadequate stick.

"I only wish for you to descend from that branch and accompany me to a place of safety. However, I am quite content to sit here and admire your breasts until you come down for your tunic. Although they are smaller than some I have witnessed, they are firm and perfectly proportioned. I also think your nipples are quite lovely and located in the proper position on the breast. Not too low or off to one side or the other, but centered perfectly to ensure that they are aesthetically pleasing. I met a sculptor once who I am sure would be quite pleased to …"

"Shut up!"

"Apologies. I understand why you are distraught. I am trying to help. I only wish for you to come down from the tree, and those comments represent my failed attempt to coax you down. You are from the other side of The Veil. You are from a different realm. A realm of cell phones, televisions, and motor vehicles. I am quite familiar with it. This is unfamiliar to you and fraught with dangers, as you have seen. Let me take you to a safe place, where we will try to understand why you are here. Your presence is as baffling to me as this realm must be to you."

"You drugged me. I've been roofied and kidnapped. It's not all that baffling."

"If you had been drugged, you would still feel the effects. Do you feel as though you are recovering from a drug?" She was thinking about what he said. He scooted around to face the other direction, thinking it might make her feel more at ease. "Please descend from your perch. I will not rise until you allow me to do so."

He studied the pajama top while she slowly began to climb down from the tree. It was harder than she thought, and she fell over once her feet hit the ground. She jumped back up and walked towards Sariel with one arm covering her chest.

"Wait!" he commanded, not even looking back.

"Why?"

"You have forgotten the spear. You must go back."

She turned, considered it for a moment then said, "Just give me my top."

"As you wish." He held it above his head.

She snatched it, turned her back, and reassembled her clothing, such as it was, muttering to herself.

"Excuse me?" Sariel said.

"What?"

"Did you just call me an 'asshole'?"

"Kidnapping asshole," she corrected.

"Are you by nature a rude and mean individual?"

"What? No. What difference does it make how I act here? It's my nightmare, isn't it?"

"My dear, beautiful woman, it is quickly becoming my nightmare as well."

"Stop calling me that. Are you making fun of me? I am well aware of how I look. Asshole!"

"I do not understand your statement," he said, then changed the subject. "The images on your garment. What do they represent?"

"It is from a cartoon I used to watch when I was a kid, *My Little Pony.*"

"I apologize. I knew you were young, but I did not think you were still a child."

"I'm not a child! I'm almost nineteen, an adult. Like you're so much older. What are you, twenty-three?"

"I am so much older."

"My Mom got these pajamas for me. She thought they were cute. It would have made her sad if I didn't wear them."

"Then, you did the right thing. It shows that you respect your mother. What is this object? It was in the pocket of your tunic." Sariel held out a small device which she snatched from his hand.

11

"It's a vape."

"A vape? What is the purpose of a vape?"

"You've never seen a vape? It … makes me feel better." She checked the vape and found that there was no charge left, the battery was dry. "Damnit! I need to recharge this. Was there anything else?"

"What do you mean?"

"Did you find anything else? Any small bottles?"

"No, Lady."

"Your armour is stupid, by the way."

"How so?" Sariel asked.

"There are big, open gaps in the back. Your spine is the only thing protected."

"It … allows for a certain freedom of movement," Sariel said by way of an explanation.

"You could be stabbed in the back."

"Then I should not turn my back upon an enemy. Would you please get the spear so that I can stand? We have another hour's journey ahead of us."

"Go ahead, stand up. I think you could probably take it away from me anyway."

"Undoubtedly."

"That doesn't make me feel any better, you know. Look, I

just want to go home."

"Beautiful woman, please listen to me. I do not know why you are here, but the Goddess must have her reasons. I swear to you that I will do my best to protect you from any danger. I will not harm you, even though your rude behavior and hurtful words are straining my patience. I only ask that you stay by my side and heed what I say until we can get you to safety. There I will do my best to answer all your questions. After that, we will follow whatever plan you have for the future. I, Sariel, swear this to you."

"I have a name, you know."

"From beyond The Veil or Goddess-given."

"What?"

"You say that a lot. Shall I speak louder?"

"What? Oh. Shut up! Jenny. My name is Jenny."

"Jenny. Jenny." He mused as if tasting the word. "Shall we be on our way? I hope to get you to safety without further incident."

He turned and headed out through the woods.

"What kind of name is Sariel, anyway? I never heard of it."

"A very old one ... best forgotten."

Chapter 2

THE KEEP

They broke free of the canopied forest. The moon shone upon a fortress nestled against a steep mountainside. The mountain didn't look like any she had seen before. It was more like a long and straight cliff as if a section of the earth had merely broken free and tilted upward, forming a steep cliff of colossal proportion. She imagined that on the other side of those cliffs, she would find a long and gentle slope down. A rampart circled the keep, tall and sturdy. It appeared to run all the way into the rock face. Delicate vines were climbing halfway up the walls—Jasmine. White and purple flowers grew in abundance, and their scent was enchanting. She could only see the crenelated top of the keep itself over the wall.

"Come. The gate is this way."

"Yes, master," Jenny muttered sarcastically in her best 'Igor' voice.

They crossed a small stream of clear water, turned south and walked beside the wall.

"What is this place?"

"This keep is my home while I am in this realm. It is called Amalia. But many simply refer to it as The Keep."

"What does that mean … Amalia?"

Sariel scoffed. "I understand it means something like 'Hope' or 'Last Hope.'"

"Is it a good place?"

"It is safe enough."

"So—why snort like that?"

He looked at her. "I do not snort."

"It sounded like a snort to me. I'm thirsty."

"We are almost there."

The thick, ironbound gates were not locked, Sariel pushed them apart. Jenny followed Sariel inside. He took a moment to close and bar the gates. The wall contained many acres of land, mainly devoted to gardens and fruit trees. She saw one goat in the moonlight, laying in the grass.

The keep itself struck Jenny as odd-looking. It was a round, four-level structure; five if you counted the dungeon. Broad with many narrow windows ringing the first level, each window softly lit from within. Above that level, the keep sported balconies and large, more ornate windows. It was of the same stone as the wall, complete with clinging jasmine on the lower portions.

"I'm thirsty, and I need a shower."

"The keep has no bathing facilities. There is a pool nearby to bathe in. An outbuilding near the back wall serves as a latrine, and there are chamber pots in the bedrooms."

Sariel did not head for the keep. He led them toward the cliff that formed the eastern wall. Small waterfalls flowed directly from the stone. They created a pool, and a stream flowed south from there, only to disappear under the keep wall. Surrounded by flowers, it was quite beautiful, even in the shadowed light.

They approached a tiny pavilion along the stream near the pool. Next to that, a paddlewheel slowly turned in the flow. The wheel connected to a metal spit by way of wooden gears. Skewered upon the spit, the carcass of some animal slowly turned over a bed of coals. A wereboar that Sariel had killed and dressed early that morning.

"What is that? It smells delicious."

As the boar slowly rotated over the heat, the flesh on the outside cooked first. Sariel stopped and cut a thin strip of meat. He handed it to her. It was quickly consumed. From a well, Sariel provided her cold water which she drank greedily.

"Come, I understand you would like to bathe. It has been a long night. I will fetch food and something to drink besides water."

"Wait! You're going to leave me out here? Alone?"

"You are quite safe here. I will stay if you like. I thought you might wish for some food and drink." He waited for a moment. "Shall I stay instead?"

"What about snakes?"

"There are no snakes on this side of The Veil."

"What about alligators, spiders, scorpions, zombies, or other kidnappers?"

Sariel sighed. "Once again, I serve as a Protector, not a kidnapper. I find the accusation to be mean and offensive. There are no creatures within these walls that will harm you. Zombies do not exist on either side of The Veil. The dead do not rise to walk again, trust me, I know of these things. Two goats roam the grounds; they are quite friendly and crave attention. There are chickens, but they keep to their nests during the night. Faeries have been known to fly in from time to time, yet they are essentially harmless if something of a nuisance."

"Faeries? Right."

"Yes, however it is more likely the goats will come by wishing to be pet. Are you afraid of goats?"

"No, I'm not afraid of goats. I think they're cute."

"Shall I stay and keep you company while you bathe?"

Jenny thought about it. "No. I wouldn't mind something to eat. I'm hungry."

"I will join you in a moment. Enjoy the pool."

Sariel disappeared towards the keep. Jenny pinched herself hard on the arm; then slapped herself on the face. *This is the longest dream I've ever had,* she thought. *At least it has improved. No more giant wolf and snapping pig attacks. The only issue left is the kidnapping. But it doesn't really feel like a kidnapping. Shouldn't I be tied up? Chained in the dungeon? Why am I a little disappointed that I'm not? This is some weird shit.*

She tested the water with her foot. It was cool. She sniffed her armpit. She definitely needed a bath. Stripping off her tattered pajamas, she stepped into the pool. It was not too deep around the edges but deepened closer to the cliff. The soft sand felt good on her tired feet.

The water was amazing—refreshing. She swam and floated while looking at the stars. Jenny didn't feel tired, even though she had been up all night. *No wonder why I'm not tired. There is no telling how long I was asleep, or in a coma, or whatever it was before I found myself here.*

Jenny swam towards one of the small waterfalls, climbed up on a rock ledge, and stood beneath the flow. The water massaged her scalp while she removed the few remaining twigs from her hair. *There are twigs … in my hair? Too many strange things. I must be dead. I've gotta be dead. So why am I so hungry.*

Jenny stepped from the flowing water and smoothed her hair. She looked across the pool and screamed, covering herself with her hands as much as possible. Sariel was standing chest-deep in the pool, staring at her.

"I am sorry I startled you. I brought you something to eat."

"What are you doing here?"

"I brought you some food and drink."

"You're staring at me!"

"I was … admiring you."

"Turn around!" she commanded, and he complied.

Jenny slipped back into the pool and stood neck deep as far away from him as she could. Sariel kept his back to her and made his way to the edge of the pool. As it grew shallow, she could see the impressive musculature of his broad back and thick legs. He stepped out, reached down, and picked up a dark cloth. There was a brief flurry of movement, and he appeared to be covered in some clothing.

"I brought you something to wear," he said, still facing the other direction.

"Where is it?"

"There." He turned and indicated a white bundle behind him.

"Don't turn around. I have a big rock."

"Why do you have a big rock?"

"I'm telling you, I will knock you out with it if you try anything."

"You would kill me for bringing you something to eat?"

"No, I'll just knock you out."

"It is more likely that you would kill me. I would suffer a serious injury at the least. It is a more effective weapon than a small stick."

"It wouldn't kill you. You'd just sigh and fall unconscious. Maybe there will be little chirping cartoon birds flying around your head."

"You have never struck anyone in the head with a rock, have you?"

"I have very vivid dreams. So maybe I have."

"This is not a dream. You would have awakened long ago if it were. Yet I will remain here. Bring your rock and take up your clothing … please."

Jenny cautiously made her way to the cloth bundle. It was bright white and folded into a square. Lengths of gold cord lay on top. Setting down the rock, she picked it up and unfolded it, keeping a wary eye on Sariel, whose massive frame stood unmoving with hands clasped behind his back. When spread, it became a rectangle of very soft linen, slightly rounded on the bottom side.

"You brought me a towel to wear? And some string?"

"It is a garment, a stola. I thought it would suit you. It wraps around you. Tie it at the shoulder."

Jenny fooled with the cloth and finally had it affixed as if it were a towel. "Okay," she said.

Sariel turned and chuckled softly, shaking his head. Jenny quickly picked up the rock.

"Let me help you." He stepped up to her. "Hold the fabric in front of you, outstretched, tight against your body just below your arms."

She considered it for a moment then said, "Hold this for me," and handed him the rock. She unraveled the cloth and did as she was instructed. Sariel looked at the stone, amused, then dropped it. He stepped even closer, almost touching her. He reached out and took her right hand in his left.

"May I?" he asked, and she let him take the corner. He kept it tight against her body. "Slide a little more this way." Jenny allowed it, staring up at his face. He brought the cloth up to her left shoulder and pulled the corner up. "Hold this end in place." She did. Removing the opposite corner from her left hand, he wrapped it around her back, enfolding her briefly in his arms. He then brought it around to her front and tied the two corners together, tucking the excess under the cloth. In a short time, she was wearing a dress of sorts, form-fitting, and snug.

He reached down and picked up a section of gold cord. Once again, he wrapped his arms around Jenny and encircled her waist. The rope was evened out in the front and then woven twice more around her waist. He tied it.

"Now, it is secure."

He picked up the remaining cord and grasped her left hand. She yanked it back.

"What are you doing?"

"A simple adornment. May I?"

Hesitantly she held out her hand. Deftly, Sariel placed the center of the cord under her middle finger. Then he wove it back and forth over her wrist and up her arm, tying it at the top. He stepped back.

"There. You look lovely. I think it suits you."

She looked down. It reminded her of a toga. Yet it fit her perfectly … and covered everything. "Thank you. Why is yours black?"

"Because black suits me." His stola wasn't tied as tight, exposing the right side of his massive chest.

He reached down to recover the rock, which he placed in her right hand and led her to a stone bench by the other. A tray sitting in the center contained meat and fruit as well as a decanter and cups which Sariel had hastily gathered on his way out. He led her to one side of the bench. She sat and discreetly placed the rock on the seat beside her, in case she needed it later. Hungrier than she thought, she picked up a two-pronged fork and popped a piece of meat into her mouth. It was tender and savory.

"This is delicious. What is it?"

"I thought you would recognize it. Especially since a young one had you stuck in a tree. It was on the roasting pit."

Her eyes grew wide. "That's what this is? Gross!"

"What happened to 'delicious'?"

"Now that I know what it is, it's gross." She tried some fruit while Sariel filled the cups with liquid from the decanter.

"Here. Take a cup. I think you will enjoy it."

"You first."

Sariel sighed and reached for a cup, but she quickly snatched the one he was reaching for. He looked at her, frowning, then took the other one, finishing it in one draught.

Hesitantly she tried a sip. Then another. It was like nothing she had ever tried. Cool on the tongue and sweet, yet it warmed her inside. She felt a sense of well-being and confidence. She drained the cup.

By the time she had finished her meal, including the rest of the meat, the top of the cliff was beginning to glow with the first rays of the morning sun.

"Let us go to the top of the keep. There you can see the sunrise, and I will try to explain what may be happening to you. Although I may not have all the answers you seek."

Jenny allowed him to lead her back to the keep. Just inside the main door, there was a chamber with another heavy door to the left and another, to the front. The door ahead of her was open, the audience chamber. Jenny saw tables and thrones. To their right was a broad stone stair, which circled around the inside of the keep wall. He offered his arm and led her up the stairs. They circled around the perimeter of the structure. On the way up they passed other landings with similar heavy doors. He promised to show her around after the sunrise.

Other than the covered stairway, the top of the keep was nothing more than an empty circular structure surrounded by crenelated walls. Sariel led Jenny to an opening between the stone crenellations on the southern side. Jenny thought she caught the faint scent of the ocean, although she had only been one time. She stopped before the edge and held his arm tight. The cliffs stood out in a stark silhouette against the brilliant orange and yellow of the quickly rising sun.

"You have many questions," Sariel stated.

"Yes. Will you tell me the truth? Will you tell me everything?" She looked up at him.

He looked thoughtful. "In all that I tell you, I promise it will be the truth to the best of my knowledge."

That seemed to satisfy her. "My first question. Am I dead?"

That caught him by surprise, but his answer was quick. "No."

"How do you know?"

"I am considered quite expert in that matter. You are certainly not dead."

"How much is the ransom?"

"The ransom?"

"Yes. You are a kidnapper, so I assume there is a ransom. My parents don't have much money."

"There is no ransom. I am not a kidnapper. How many more times shall I be forced to say this?" He didn't look pleased, so she decided to change the topic.

She reflected a moment. "Where am I, and how did I get here?"

"Ah, good questions. I can answer the first, the second I can guess at."

"Okay."

"This is Elvenrealm. It is a realm protected from view and trespass by a veil. This is where the original creations of the God and Goddess yet live. Beings believed to be creatures of myth on the other side of The Veil, where you are from. The Gods love them and have ensured their safety from the outside world. Here dwell the first creations of light and beauty. A manifestation of what was to represent all that is fantastic and good in the world. Collectively, these Creatures of Light are known as Elven, although there is a race commonly referred to as Elves—the Wood Elves. Man hunted these creatures, so the Lord and Lady made them safe here, lest they be lost to the world."

"And you're one of those creatures?"

"No."

"What are you?"

"I … was without a home. An outcast of sorts. I offered my services as a Protector, and the Lady graciously took me in. She gave me the use of this place, where we now stand. Now I have a home and a purpose."

"So you are not one of these 'Creatures of Light'? You're just some good guy who found his way here? And this is why I should trust you?"

He looked away toward the dark cliffs. "I am not. And I beg of you not to trust me."

"I don't," Jenny flatly stated, although she still held on to his arm.

"Then, it is settled. What are your other questions?"

"Why doesn't everyone know about this place? What kind of 'veil' could protect it from satellites? I think everyone would already know about it by now."

"I know not. I do not presume to understand the ways of Gods and Goddesses. They created it and only they could explain it. Although you may not understand their explanation."

"What about the other creatures? What are they?"

"You have already met the original Protectors, the Great Wolves. There are Faeries and Brownies, Wood Elves, Sprites and more. The drink you had earlier is nectar distilled by the Water Sprites. It is quite rare, I was fortunate to find a few bottles in the keep."

"Faeries and Elves. Right. I suppose there are unicorns as well."

"It is rumored so, although I have not seen one."

"Of course not. You have to be pure of heart," she said.

"That may explain it."

"Let me guess. The unicorns slide down on rainbows, and the pink one is named Princess Cadance."

"As I have explained, I have not seen one, nor do I know of their names. I have been told that they are white."

The sun began to explode into view. Sariel led her to the south-western side, where she could see how the sun slowly revealed the terrain as a line of light from the sun broke free of the restraining cliff. She remained silent as the land brightened and came to life. The morning light moved closer and closer to the keep, as the sun rose.

"Come nearer to the edge for a better view," he said.

"I'm quite close enough. I can see from here. I'm not fond of heights."

To the south was the shoreline with blue water and white sand. Waves cast lines of white foam. The tropical foliage was found between the beach and the rolling hills. From there it blended into a dense forest, double canopied where the two vegetation's met.

"So you and the wolves are Protectors?"

"All of the original Creatures of Light will protect themselves when pressed. The wolves and the Elves were given that task from the beginning."

"And you, right?"

"I came much later. But yes."

"And they can talk to you? They're talking wolves? I heard you speak to them."

He smiled a little. "I am alone here. I find myself talking to things that do not exactly speak back. I suppose they do communicate in their way if one is willing to listen."

"You are so weird." Jenny thought for a moment, then said, "I have a dog. It is trained to do all sorts of things for me. He's very smart."

"And did you ever talk to it?"

"Yes, I suppose I did." She giggled. "I suppose I'm a little weird too."

"That would be understating things."

"Hey!"

"Apologies."

"Why am I here? How do I get back home?"

"Ah, these are the harder questions. I know not why you are here. Although I do not believe anyone other than Kerridwyn herself could have brought you to this realm. You were found near her pool. She was not present when I arrived."

"Who exactly is Kerridwyn?"

"The Lady. Kerridwyn and her consort, Lord Cernunnos, are the Gods who created this land and all of the Creatures of Light. I met Kerridwyn only once when I first arrived. I understand that Cernunnos has been absent from this side of The Veil for quite some time. This has concerned Lady Kerridwyn. He has not answered her calls, and she believes there is a grave problem. She is often absent from the realm searching for him. In any event, I have not had the pleasure of meeting him."

"Why do you think I was brought here ... by some goddess supposedly?"

"I know not."

"Then, I need to find her so she can send me back."

"There will be a Great Howling upon her return. We will return to the pool to speak with her at that time."

"When?"

"I know not."

"There must be another way."

"Why, beautiful Jenny, are you in such a hurry to return?"

"I told you to stop calling me that! Do *you* like being mocked? You ... overgrown stupid sack of ... muscles!" She grew angry.

Sariel held up his hands. "I apologize. Jenny, why are you in such a hurry to return?"

"I was ... I was very close to ... graduating. And my ... education was causing my family great financial hardship. And they will be worried about me. I miss them, especially my little brother, Samuel. I need to get back. That's all."

"I do not completely understand your situation. However, I will consider the alternatives. I do expect the Lady will not be absent for too long. She has yet to reveal her purpose for bringing you here."

"Can't you just call her back?"

"She is a Goddess. No one can command her. She will return in her own time."

Sariel continued. "I do know one thing for certain. The first time you return to the world beyond The Veil, you will return to the exact time and place you left it. No one will know you were gone."

"What, like time travel? They are all frozen in place while I'm gone? You are so full of shit!"

He shrugged. "I know not how. But that does not make it less true or your words less offensive. Come. Let me show you to your room."

"I have my own room?"

"Yes."

"So you knew I was coming?" She eyed him suspiciously.

"I did not."

CHAPTER 3

THE MIRROR

The main living chamber was the next level down, the top floor. A massive canopied bed stood against one side with a balcony opposite. The room was expansive, circular, taking up the whole level. Wardrobes and various other furnishings packed one side near the bed, they were currently covered in linens. On the opposite wall, there was one lonely wardrobe and a small cabinet with a pitcher and bowl resting on top, uncovered. Near the balcony, Jenny saw a sizeable and well-ordered desk. There were many narrow bookshelves on either side of the windows. All the furnishings were of intricately-carved wood. The center held a stone fireplace, clean with neatly stacked firewood and two chairs.

Sariel moved to the covered furniture and started removing the linens, throwing them into a pile against the wall.

"You may have anything you find here. There are many female garments within. I hope some will fit. I was curious when I first arrived and looked through them." He finished removing the linens from a vanity and full-length mirror. "I need to see to the goats. Feel free to explore the keep. It is your home for as long as you choose to remain here."

"Even the dungeon?" she asked.

Sariel nodded as he walked away. "Yes, Lady. Even the dungeon."

She watched him go. She thought, *He is so strange. Good looking ... too good looking. But there is something terribly odd about him.*

She looked through the first wardrobe. She found linens and gold braid in the same manner in which she was currently dressed. There were soft leather items; leggings, tunics, and the like. She found leather boots and sandals with leather straps that crisscrossed up to below the knee. She tried on a pair of gold-colored sandals and found they fit. Everything was either gold or white, except for the leathers which were natural—tan colored.

The other two wardrobes contained beautiful dresses and gowns of fantastic quality. Some of the gowns were even adorned with sparkling gemstones. A blue gown caught Jenny's eye. The fabric was soft and delicate. It glimmered as if each thread held the light captive and shimmered luminescent. She couldn't resist. She carefully took it from the wardrobe and pressed it against her. *It might fit!* she thought with some excitement and gently placed it upon the large bed. She hesitated before taking off her stola. It seemed a simple thing to fasten together, she thought she could do it again. So she removed it to try on the dress. It was something of a halter that plunged to just below her navel, much farther than she had first thought. It was floor length with a provocative slit up her right leg. A belt of fine golden mail accompanied the gown. She felt its weight and thought it might actually be gold. *If this is gold, and the gems on some of the dresses are real, then these gowns are worth a fortune!* The belt was about two inches wide and had the effect of accentuating her narrow waist, drawing attention to her hips, and hiding the last bit of the neckline plunge, leaving the rest to the imagination.

Jenny bounced over to the mirror to see the dress but stopped at the vanity where she spied a circlet of golden leaves—sapphires set as if they were sprouting flowers evenly spaced about. She placed it on her head where it sat comfortably on her brow.

She stepped in front of the mirror, gasped in fear, and spun around. *There's someone else in the room!* Yet she saw no one. Slowly she turned back to look in the mirror. And the person she had glimpsed turned to face her.

The young woman that looked back at her with wide eyes had golden hair, flowing in gentle waves to her breasts. Eyes as blue as the sapphires stared back between long lashes set under lush golden eyebrows. Her skin pale and flawless, her lips full and soft. Jenny gasped again and placed both her hands over her mouth. So did the woman in the mirror. She barely recognized her own features. Slowly she began to understand she was looking at herself. Or at least how she may have looked if things had been different. It was too much for her to bear. She fell to her knees and wept. And the young woman in the mirror did the same.

Jenny sobbed on the floor until she noticed the sound of music drifting up from below. She left the room and descended the staircase to the first level. All the doors were open, so Jenny followed the music to a large chamber, the audience chamber. On the opposite end, she saw a raised dais with two massive carved thrones. Two long tables set with many chairs filled the space between the door and the dais. Sariel sat cross-legged on the throne to her left with a lute in his lap. The room reverberated with a slow and somewhat mournful tune coaxed from the fifteen strings.

She crossed through the light from one of the windows and Sariel looked up. He stared at her, and the music stopped. To Sariel's eyes, she was radiant in her beauty, even though her eyes were swollen and her nose runny from the tears. He saw her as luminescent in the glow of the sun. The blue dress and sapphires only served to draw attention to her eyes. He slowly set down the lute on the adjacent throne, never taking his eyes off of her. Lastly, he noticed that she appeared very angry and had a stone in her hand, probably the same one. He stood, the sight was breathtaking, even for him. Despite the anger, Sariel thought her to be the personification of beauty. For the first time in ages, he felt helpless, undone.

She was taking deep breaths, her lips set in a frown. "How do you explain this?" She said gesturing to herself, then wiping her nose with the back of her hand.

"You look …," he began.

"If you say 'You look beautiful' or 'I know not,' I swear I will throw this rock at you. And it's a big one."

"I see that," was all he said.

"Well?"

"I do not understand."

"What kind of mirror did you put in my room? What was the purpose of doing that to me?"

"The mirror?"

"Yes! What is it for?"

He thought carefully before speaking. "It is simply a mirror. For a lady to see her reflection."

"Her reflection?" Her voice caught in her throat.

"Yes. I do not understand. What happened?"

She grew angrier. Her knuckles white as she gripped the rock. "And the wardrobes? All the dresses fit! Everything in there fits *me*! I suppose you don't know anything about that as well?"

He remained silent, concerned.

"Say something!"

"I fear to say the wrong thing."

"Do something, then. Anything." Tears began to fall down her cheeks.

Sariel hesitated but a moment, then turned to where his sword rested against the throne. He drew it from its scabbard but held it by the blade with his right hand. He began to walk slowly towards her.

"Oh? You're going to stab me then? Go ahead, see if I care." She stood defiant, regal. Beauty incarnate.

Once Sariel was a pace away, he dropped to one knee, his left fist on the floor. He placed the silver sword at her feet and then put his hand behind his back, bowing his head. "I am yours. I yield to your mercy."

Jenny looked down. "What are you doing?"

"I have failed to help you. I am confused and do not know what to say. I yield to you."

"You are the weirdest man I have ever met."

"I am no man." He looked up at her, concerned.

"You see? You say stupid things like that. How am I supposed to trust you?"

Sariel stood and took the stone from her hand and dropped it. Then he held her hands in his. "You should never trust me. And I would never ask that of you. However, I do not know what to do or say to ease your pain. Please, Lady, tell me what happened with the mirror."

"It's just … it's just that with so many other things going wrong in my life, now I know for a fact that I've gone insane," she replied, and the tears began to flow in full force.

Sariel closed the gap so that he could hold her in his arms. She sobbed against his chest. "May I be allowed to speak?" He felt her nod.

"You are many things. In the brief moments that I have known you, I find that your beauty gives me strength and leaves me helpless at the same time. There is something within you that compels me, yet there are times when you are so mean of spirit that I wonder why the Goddess brought you to this realm. You confuse and sometimes offend me, yet I cannot walk away. You are many things that I do not understand, but you are not insane."

Moments passed while he held her. "I'm not a mean person," she finally whispered. "I'm just afraid."

"I know."

Jenny pushed away and turned, heading back up the stairs. Soon Sariel heard the door close to the bedroom.

It was early afternoon when he approached the door and knocked softly.

"Go away!" Her voice sounded strained.

"I have brought food. I will leave it outside the door."

"Go away," she repeated.

Sariel complied but was a bit amused when he heard the door open and close again before he was to the end of the stairwell. She had apparently succumbed to her appetite. And then the first wisps of an idea began to form in Sariel's mind. And possibly, this idea just might work. He smiled to himself as he descended the stairs.

Chapter 4

THE PLAN

For the first time since Jenny's arrival, Sariel had a plan. He knew what might help. He was sure of it. With that realization, he thought he could relax and take a nap. He felt that he was in need of a little sleep, although he never required much rest. He laid down on the cold stone floor before the dais, folded his hands across his chest, and slept.

Jenny alternated between looking in the mirror and crying on the bed. By late afternoon, she decided to run away. Jenny thought that maybe she could find a phone and call her parents. She gathered the soft leather tunic and leggings from the wardrobe and donned the leather boots. She quietly descended the stairs and made it to the first level. *All the doors are open,* she thought, *maybe my luck is changing.* She saw the open door ahead of her and realized she hadn't been in there yet. Her curiosity caused her to want to take a look. *No, he may be sitting on his stupid throne again and will see me. Better to just run out the door and take my chances.*

Jenny took a quick peek around the corner. She glimpsed the throne but didn't see him. Her heart beating rapidly now, she took a more extended look. Jenny saw him lying on the floor. He appeared to be asleep. She thought, *I'm in luck,* and crept out the main door and headed to the gate. She moved slowly so she wouldn't make much noise. One of the two goats stood between her and the entrance. It began walking towards her. *What if it starts barking or making goat noises or whatever?* She began to fear she would be discovered.

The goat quietly walked up to her, its short tail wagging and shook her floppy ears. Jenny couldn't help herself. She stopped for a moment and pet the goat who seemed grateful for the attention.

She was petting the goat when she realized that there may not have been any other bedrooms. She hadn't yet searched the keep. *Perhaps he was sleeping on the floor because I was given the only place with a bed?* she mused. *If so, then that is unlikely behavior for a kidnapper. But he told me not to trust him. He looked at me while I was naked. And then he gave me clothes and food. He chased off the pig-thing, which was nice. But then he made fun of my boobs. What if there are more pig beasts? I don't have a spear or really know how to use it. Well, he actually said sweet things about my boobs.*

While she was debating with herself, she heard the soft bleat of another goat. It wanted attention, as well. She realized that her idea may not have been thoroughly thought out. The goats were nuzzling her, competing for her attention. They were cute and funny, and she laughed at them.

"Ah, Jenny!" Sariel called out from the keep. "You are up and properly dressed for a short adventure. Good. I will be right down. Shall we meet in the kitchen?"

"Okay," was all that she could think of to say. *Well, so much for that escape attempt.*

Jenny thought that the kitchen was the door to the left of the entrance. It wasn't. A small landing led to stairs which wound down into the earth. *This must be the dungeon!* The thought was more exciting than frightening to her. All those many nights spent watching scary movies with her father got the better of her. Along the stairwell, there were glass jars set into stone recesses which held what looked like some type of porous rock. The rocks gave off a dim glow that allowed her to see. These were also found on the stairs to the upper floors, and scattered throughout the keep. On the lowest level, there were rooms, most of which held food stores and grain. She found a well-stocked wine cellar.

Finally, she opened a door which may have met the description of a proper dungeon—but barely. There were two large cells which did have metal rings hanging from spikes embedded in the walls. Outside the cells was a room which held a massive table. There was a chest with chains and shackles. She found no apparent implements of torture. Everything was neat and clean.

She heard Sariel calling her name and returned to the first floor. He was in the main hall when she returned. She felt like she had been caught doing something naughty.

"You found the wine cellar! Did you pick out something you might enjoy?"

"No, should I go back?"

"If you like. However, I have something prepared."

"Your dungeon seems to be lacking the proper implements of torture."

Sariel looked up, concerned. "Is that something you enjoy doing?"

"No. I just thought all dungeons have such things."

"I do not."

"But there are cells. For prisoners."

"I did not build this keep, and I do not take prisoners."

There was an uncomfortable silence while he stared as if appraising her character. Jenny spoke. "You said you prepared something?"

"Yes, in the kitchen."

The main hall was squared off along two walls, leaving a rounded wall and its many narrow windows behind the dais. A door in one of the walls led to the kitchen, which narrowed at the ends due to the circular nature of the outer wall. Narrow windows were found here as well. Shelves and large tables lined the walls. All filled with spices, pots, pans, and utensils. Everything needed for food preparation.

He indicated a small table with two chairs already set with food and drink. While they were eating, he told Jenny of his idea.

"I do not understand everything that distresses you, but I have a couple of ideas that I think might help."

"What is this? It's wonderful," Jenny asked wiping a creamy white mustache with the back of her hand.

"It's milk and honey," he said, handing her a linen napkin. "It is delicious. By itself, it can sustain your body almost indefinitely. This," he held up his cup, "is why I keep goats."

"Goat milk?"

"As I was saying, I think I should introduce you to some of the various Elven folk. I thought if you saw some of them, it would help you see that you are actually in a different realm, and not at all insane. Within the keep, there are Brownies and Dryads. Since Faeries can fly, they intrude from time to time. Dryads are uninteresting and, I am fairly certain soulless creatures. They carry out specific tasks such as cleaning the keep. If you manage to see one, they will appear as shadowy forms only. However, they normally work while no one is around. If you do happen upon them, they will quickly disappear."

"Dryads?" she asked dubiously.

"Yes. Very helpful and uninteresting."

"And you have Brownies? Do you have Girl Scouts too?"

"The latter, no." He continued, ignoring the sarcasm. "Brownies are Elven. They are intelligent woodland creatures, especially fond of gardens."

"Gardens."

"Yes! A large portion of the grounds is devoted to gardens. There are many Brownie holes to be found within our walls. They mainly come out at night, so I thought we might go to the garden at twilight and sit quietly until they come out. Then you would see them for yourself and know that you are absolutely not insane."

"Did you ever think that if I did see them, I might feel more insane?" she asked. She could tell by the look on his face that he had not thought of that.

She could see that he appeared quite pleased with this idea, that is, before her last comment, so she stifled an observation about his own sanity.

"Have you seen them—these Brownies?"

"Yes, many times. They tend to the gardens. I have no need for most of the produce, they take the rest. To me, they appear similar to large … squirrels."

"Squirrels? Really?"

"Not exactly, of course. Brownies are small, with large round heads, big bellies, and black eyes. They are quite capable of running on four legs or standing like a man. They have long fingers that end in retractable claws … similar to a cat."

"They look like a squirrel? A squirrel cat?"

"I am confident you will see for yourself soon. Brownies are also covered in short brown fur, except for their tails. The tails are hairless."

"And what do you and the Brownies talk about when you see them? Gardening?"

"Well." Sariel cleared his throat. "They usually scream and run into their holes."

"Really?"

"Yes. And they bite if frightened so do not stick your hand in their holes."

"Oh?"

"Just some advice."

"Don't stick my hand in a Brownie's hole. Got it. Any other advice?"

"Yes! I have one other idea."

"Is it better than *not* violating Brownie holes?"

"I believe it is equally as good," Sariel replied with a big smile ... his first big smile.

"Let's hear it."

"I think I should take the mirror outside ... and destroy it! Or you could destroy it if it helps."

"Destroy the mirror?"

"Absolutely."

"Absolutely not."

"Why not? It has caused you distress. And destroying it

seems a simple solution. We destroy it, and your fear of mirrors will have been efficiently dealt with."

"No."

"I do not understand."

"It is a beautiful mirror, and I will not destroy it or allow you to destroy it. Understand?"

"No. I do not understand, but I will respect your wish." Sariel seemed a little disappointed.

Jenny could see she had disappointed him. He was only trying to make her feel better, she knew that, so she changed the subject. "Sariel, I believe it should be dark enough to catch some Brownies raiding the garden. Shall we go?"

He visibly brightened. "Yes!" He pulled out her chair for her and offered her his hand.

Sariel grabbed a tablecloth, and they headed to the gardens. The gardens were extensive. However, there were no neat rows of vegetables. There were paths but no discernable planting pattern. In the center of the garden, Sariel spread out the cloth and offered her his hand to help her sit.

"So what's the plan?"

"Keep quiet and still," he whispered. "I believe they usually work at night."

"Okay," she whispered back.

They waited, and nothing happened. A breeze rustled leaves. Birds chirped. They could hear the waterfalls flow into the bathing pool. The moon began to rise. And that was all.

"What about Faeries?" Jenny asked, feeling rather bored. "What are they like?"

"They are a nuisance, really. Faeries have wings, like a dragonfly, and are very small."

"How small? Do they look like bugs?"

"Only a few inches long at most. They resemble a human, can speak, I am told, and will glow if they desire to."

"They glow? Really?" Jenny didn't sound convinced.

"They do not have to, but yes, they have that ability. You may see something that resembles a firefly, and then discover it is actually a Faerie. There are many fireflies here, so it is hard to tell from a distance."

"Why would they be a nuisance?"

"They only mate while in the presence of some other creature mating. Faeries have the ability to ... stimulate someone's thoughts to the ... well, erotic. Thus coercing others to do things they would not have done otherwise. By inciting lascivious behavior in others, they are able to mate and reproduce." Sariel did not look comfortable with the conversation.

"So Faeries make you horny?" she asked.

"If you mean sexually aroused, yes."

Jenny yawned and scooted close so she could lean her head against him. Sariel flushed. For him, this one moment was worth the wait, and yet he did not wish to disappoint her.

"Jenny, I have reason to believe that Brownies are fond of wine. I will fetch some and be right back."

"Okay," she said and yawned again.

As soon as he was out of sight, Jenny heard the rustling. She sat up straight and listened. There was no mistaking it, something was moving around the garden. Suddenly frightened, she stood, causing a rustling in many directions. She glimpsed movement. Small shadowy forms. *They are all around me!* she thought. *Sariel, why are you taking so long?* She couldn't tell how many of them were out there, a dozen perhaps, or more?

Now she could hear them, hear them talking. It was a fast and high-pitched sound, but it was definitely some kind of language. The shapes were moving closer. *Moving in for the kill?* she wondered. Heart pounding, she slowly started backing up towards the gate.

"Awww." The sound came from right in front of her. There was no mistaking the tone of disappointment.

Jenny stopped backing up. "Hello?" she said softly, tentatively.

A high pitched response came from the same place. It was too fast to understand and possibly wasn't English.

"Hello?" she repeated and was greeted by another string of gibberish. At least it was gibberish to her.

"I sure hope you're friendly."

The diminutive creature stepped out of the shadows and stood before her, its hands behind its back. It appeared very much as Sariel had described. However, he left off the round, furry ears on the sides of its potato-shaped head. Its mouth seemed to be small, considering the relatively large head and it began to chatter away amicably.

"Oh my! You are the cutest thing ever. I'm sorry I don't understand what you are saying."

It turned and spoke to the others in the darkness. They began to creep towards Jenny. She slowly went to her knees while the Brownie watched her cautiously.

"Hello, I'm Jenny."

The creature squealed in delight and danced around. In its high pitched voice, Jenny was sure of it, the Brownie was repeating her name. Jenny laughed and clapped her hands.

The Brownie smiled ear to ear, literally. Its small mouth spreading across its face, revealing for a moment, rows of sharp teeth. She was startled at first, then he walked solemnly forward and held out his hand. He held out a big, perfect strawberry.

"Oh! Is that for me?"

The Brownie nodded.

"Thank you so much." Jenny reached out and took the strawberry.

The Brownie stood and stared at her. Several others came close. They all were still, watching. Confused, Jenny looked at the first one who nodded at the strawberry and looked at her.

"Oh, may I eat it?"

He nodded eagerly.

She took a bite and found it sweet and delicious. The brownies remained quiet, almost enraptured until she had finished it.

"That was the best strawberry I have ever tasted," she said, and the garden erupted into high-pitched woohoos and hoorays. The Brownies danced about, and most of them came even closer.

She looked to the first Brownie, placed her hand on her chest, and said, "I'm Jenny." She pointed at him. "What is your name?"

It said something.

"I am so sorry. Could you repeat it? Perhaps a little slower?"

It did.

"I heard Bleek. Is your name Bleek?"

He nodded vigorously, and more chattering ensued. Bleek climbed up onto her lap. As he crawled up, she was aware of tiny claws, like a kitten. It caused her no discomfort through the soft leather leggings. It stood on her leg using its tail for balance.

Jenny reached out and stroked his head. Bleek purred. She held his cheeks softly in both hands, then bent over and kissed the top of his head.

Bleek squealed, went stiff, and then fell off her lap, over onto his back. The garden erupted in laughter, there was no mistaking it.

"Bleek, are you ok?"

He grinned, stood up, and hugged her leg.

Jenny gently picked him up and hugged him against her breast. A collective "Awww" rose from the crowd.

Suddenly the Brownies went silent, tense. A high pitch scream rang out from the small pack and they all, including Bleek, ran off into the night.

"Jenny? Are you well? What was that sound?" Sariel stood behind her, arms laden with bottles of wine and bowls. "Did the Brownies come out while I was away?" He sounded disappointed.

Jenny knelt motionless for a moment, eyes closed. Slowly she stood and faced him. Jenny placed her hands around his neck and coaxed his head down. Then she kissed him on the cheek.

"Thank you," she said and headed back towards the keep, leaving Sariel looking about, quite bewildered and staring at her retreating form in the moonlight.

Chapter 5

RAPHAEL

Jenny awoke refreshed. Oddly enough, she felt healthy and vital from the moment she arrived in Elvenrealm. Even so, her new surroundings had confused and frightened her. Yet this morning, after her incredible encounter with the Brownies, she felt joyous.

As always, since she arrived here, she had an appetite. It was another odd feeling for her. She headed for the kitchen to find something to eat. Sariel wasn't around, so she found fruit and milk. Before long, Sariel arrived with a fresh pitcher of milk, and they began talking. She recounted her encounter with the Brownies with delight.

"So one actually climbed onto your lap?"

"Yes! It was so cute. I think it had a name, Bleek." Jenny beamed.

"I am sorry I wasn't there. I would have liked to see that."

"I think you scared them off," she said, then added. "Don't worry, it will be okay next time. I'll introduce you. What can I meet today? Can we meet the Sprites or Faeries? Where are the unicorns?"

Sariel sighed. "I know not where to find unicorns. Sprites are elusive but found near water. Faeries have been known to flit about the keep yet can be elusive as well."

"What about the Wood Elves? You said there were Wood Elves."

"Ah, I know where to find them. However, they are far to the north, nearly a three-day march. The Elves and the wolves guard the northern border."

"Guard against what?"

Sariel considered this before speaking. "Lady, nature exists in balance. At least it should exist in a state of balance. There is female energy, and there is male energy. Nighttime and daylight. Creatures of Light and, unfortunately, creatures of darkness. Creatures of darkness are jealous of the Creatures of Light. They seek to destroy all that exists in harmony and love; they seek to destroy and corrupt beauty."

"Why would Kerridwyn and Cernunnos create such creatures?"

"I do not believe that the Lord and Lady created them. They found their way into this realm. This is why we need Protectors. They, all the dark ones, are found in abundance far to the north, within The Desolation and the mountains beyond, and they try to spread their corruption to our lands.

The Elves guard the northern border, and keep the realm safe."

"What kind of creatures?"

"Goblins mainly. There are ogres, trolls, and more."

"Like wereboars."

"No, Lady. A wereboar is just a beast. It eats roots and plants or the occasional prey, but it is just a beast. A creature of darkness is much worse. The Wood Elves and the wolves guard against them. I have assisted the Elves on many occasions, but it is difficult for me to deal with them."

"Why?"

"The Wood Elves are a matriarchal society of fierce warriors. They are strong and follow a complex code. Very particular rules of honor."

"Matriarchal?"

"It means that women lead their clans. Men are relegated to more … household chores. There are very few males, so they are kept protected. They have no say in the governing of their society."

"So because women make the decisions you don't like them?" she said, crossing her arms. "I think I would very much like to meet them."

"No. It is not that. I find it difficult to get *them* to talk to *me* since I am a man."

"But you're a warrior, right?"

"I am. However, even that concept is something of an abomination in their eyes."

"When can I meet them?"

"You are not ready."

"Oh, so now you are making decisions for me? I think I might like to meet someone that respects *my* decisions. Women running things—sounds good to me," Jenny said, feeling like it was an appropriate time to be stubborn.

"They are warriors. You are not a warrior."

"You couldn't get the Brownies to talk to you, but they had no problem talking to me."

"They are nothing like Brownies."

"I'm bored here, waiting to see if this Goddess ever returns. Maybe they know how to send me back. I miss my family, my little brother. Tell you what, I'll go see for myself. They're in the north. I'm going to head north. It's not that hard."

Sariel looked down and rubbed his temples. "It is not that simple. You would never make it there on your own. You would be killed by the beasts or the dark creatures that made it through the border. And even if you did find them, you will find yourself in a difficult position. As I said, they have a very strict code, and will not give you any special consideration because you are from the other side of The Veil."

"I think you're afraid of them."

"I have some deep reservations, of that there is no doubt.

You should know that they are completely free with their sexuality, and possess no inhibitions in that regard. You are modest. You would not fit in with their society."

"I think I'll head out this morning," she stated.

"I believe you have not listened to anything I have said."

"What? I wasn't listening." She stood up. Sariel buried his head in his hands. "Out there in the woods, when you first found me, you swore to follow any plan I had for the future. This is my plan." Jenny stared at him triumphantly, as if she had just won a round of Jeopardy.

"I did swear it."

"There you go, Bucko."

Sariel sighed. "This plan of yours, it distresses me. I have an old friend. A very close friend. I would like to speak to him before we go."

"Sure. Whatever. As long as it won't take too long."

"Jenny?"

"What?"

"If you happen to meet him, please be respectful."

"I'm always respectful." Sariel raised an eyebrow as she turned and left the kitchen.

Jenny returned to her room and brushed her hair before the mirror. She smiled at her reflection. Glimpsing a quick movement, she looked towards the bed and caught a wardrobe door closing. A white dress with a short collar rested on the freshly-made bed. She walked over to see it. *This must be the Dryads he talked about,* she thought. *He said they were helpful.*

"Thank you," she said to no one in particular.

She tried it on. The top of the dress was form-fitting with a modest plunge and long flowing sleeves. The dress hung just past her knees. A small gold leather corset which accompanied the dress lay on the bed. It was only about three inches wide. She laced it tight around her waist then turned it to the back. She admired the look in the mirror, smoothing out a few wrinkles caused by the corset. She laced up the gold sandals and placed the circlet on her head. The circlet did a marvelous job of holding back her hair. And she thought it was pretty.

Once she opened the door, she heard the voices from below. There was a new voice, loud and booming. It definitely wasn't Sariel. After spending so much time with no other company than the stuffy Sariel, she felt apprehension and a little bit of fear about meeting the newcomer. But her curiosity was stronger. She descended the stairs.

She stepped into the room. Sparkling green lights danced about the fellow like fireflies or sparks. A large man in heavy white robes sat on the throne to her right. He had long, curly black hair braided down the back. Unlike Sariel, he had a medium-length beard of the same black hair, neatly trimmed. He was taller than Sariel but plump with a pronounced belly.

He saw her and boomed, "GADZOOKS!" Dropping the apple he was eating.

Startled, Jenny took a step back.

He looked to Sariel. "THIS? This beautiful and delicate creature is the woman causing you so many problems that you called me here? Absurd!"

"My dear, come closer." He stood. "Sariel, I thought you were a gentleman. Where are your manners?"

Looking embarrassed, Sariel began the introduction. "Jenny, I would like you to meet an old friend of mine, this is ..."

"Raphael!" he interrupted. "*I* am Raphael. Surely you have heard of me?"

"I have heard the name before."

"Of course you have."

"Raphael is my favorite Ninja Turtle," Jenny said.

Raphael went silent, mouth agape. Sariel appeared appalled. All was silent for a moment, then Raphael exploded with uncontrollable laughter. It was deep and loud and echoed off the walls. His laughter became contagious, and Jenny started laughing as well. Even Sariel smiled a little.

He caught his breath and held out his hand. "Dear Jenny, do come closer."

Smiling, Jenny walked forward and took his hand. "Where did you get such a name? Jenny. It simply doesn't suit you. It is like calling a rose a plant, or the Aurora Borealis a glow. It does not do you justice."

Jenny giggled.

"How is this charming creature the source of any problems? Her presence causes me no distress whatsoever. Quite the opposite." Raphael spun her about, and she turned as if ballroom dancing, her dress flaring. "I am enraptured, captured, and pleased to be your favorite turtle," he said with a bow and broad smile.

Jenny could only giggle.

"My dear, what have you done to cause my friend to call upon me for advice?"

"She is newly arrived and has demanded to see the Wood Elves," Sariel answered for her.

"THE ELVES?" Raphael boomed. His face assuming a suitably shocked visage. "Is that true?"

Jenny looked unsure of herself. In a small voice, she could only say, "Yes."

"Ha! Then you should meet them." His eyes twinkled. "They are wonderful creatures! Most interesting, I am positively in awe of them."

"Raphael, they are harsh, difficult, and demanding. And … extremely provocative."

Raphael looked at Jenny. "Do you believe you are strong enough to handle a brash and provocative lot?"

"I think so."

Raphael looked to Sariel. "Well, there you have it. I am at

your service to solve problems. Problem solved."

Jenny smiled triumphantly.

Sariel was not as satisfied. "They dwell far to the north, it is dangerous for her to travel there."

"He has a point there. Will you promise me that you will not go alone? Sariel here can escort you, although you may find his company a bit dry, I'm afraid."

"I promise," she said with a beaming smile.

"Then it is settled, you will soon meet the Elves, and I will be on my way. Obligations, there are always obligations." He looked to Sariel once again. "You understand, don't you?" Sariel gave a solemn nod.

"Young lady, would you be so kind as to accompany me to the gate?"

Jenny nodded. "Of course."

Once outside, he said, "Sariel is my friend. He is a troubled sort, but you can trust his judgment. This is a beautiful and terrible place. He will try to keep you safe."

"He told me not to trust him."

"Of course he did."

At the gate, Raphael turned and said, "Jenny, may I give you a gift before I go?"

"I suppose."

He placed a hand upon her chest, and there was a burst of

blue light. She briefly felt flooded by a warm glow.

"Green is my color, but I think blue is yours. It matches your eyes." He gave a conspiratorial wink and stepped through the gate, closing it behind him. Jenny heard a loud snap, the sound of a sail catching a strong wind. She opened the gate and looked about. He was nowhere in sight.

Chapter 6

PUPPIES

Jenny removed the dress and placed it in the wardrobe. Her encounter with the jovial Raphael had left her feeling content. She decided she would head out to see the Wood Elves another day. Maybe tomorrow. She chose to wear the comfortable stola and head to the pool for a swim.

Even with the help of the mirror, she was having difficulty getting the stola to fit appropriately.

"Jenny," Sariel called through the door, then he knocked softly.

She flung open the door, holding the stola over her body with one arm, and exclaimed, "I can't get this right. It seemed so simple when you did it. Will you come to the mirror and show me again so I can do it for myself?"

"Certainly."

Looking in the mirror, Jenny held the garment stretched out in front of her, like before. She didn't think about it, but it left her backside exposed to Sariel's gaze, and he could not help but look. While he was instructing her, he said, "It is getting late to be heading north. I would feel better if we started at dawn and traveled fast. Even so it will take three days if we make good time."

"Okay."

"You do not mind? I thought you had firmly decided."

"It's fine," she said. "I like your friend."

"Everyone does. Raphael is quite gregarious."

"He didn't seem to think it was so bad to visit the Elves."

"He isn't responsible for your safety."

"Who made you responsible for me?"

"I did, Lady. When I swore the oath to you. But I would do so without it."

"Raphael said you would. What you are doing, it's a sweet thing. Thank you."

"You are welcome."

"I'm going to the pool. Care for a swim?"

"Yes. I will be there shortly."

Sariel brought wine. They swam and drank and talked about inconsequential things for a time.

"Jenny, I have been thinking. Maybe I should begin to train you in the martial skills. There are dangers here, of that there is no doubt. Many of which should not be met with small sticks and rocks. Is there a specific weapon that you might be interested in mastering?"

"I'm not much of a fighter."

"That is inconsistent with my past experiences with you."

She laughed. "Okay, if I had to choose, I choose the bazooka."

"There are no bazookas here. And if there were one to be found, they are quite heavy."

"I dunno, how about a bow? That way, I don't have to be too close."

"An excellent choice. I am considered to be an expert with one. Sadly, I have not found a bow or arrows within the keep. It is somewhat ironic that the Wood Elves are without equal when it comes to the bow. When I take you to them, I will see if I can obtain one."

"So they're all archers?"

"I would say that they all demonstrate some skill with the bow, although they utilize a variety of weapons. However, some of them do specialize as archers. Those specialists far exceed my ability. They can make incredible shots, even at long distances. But every warrior seems to gravitate to the weapon of their choice. Often, they are taught the weapon their mother is comfortable with. There is a common weapon they use, especially for their trials of combat, called The Trial

Pit. That would be the staff."

"A staff?"

"Yes. Generally, it is slightly shorter than the wielder is tall. We could begin with the staff as a weapon. From there it is effortless to transition to a spear. Many of the movements are almost identical."

"Well then, since we find ourselves without a bow, let's start with the staff," she said.

"Another excellent choice."

"Can we start tomorrow?"

"Certainly. However, if we are not immediately setting out for the northern border, I would like to check in with Luna, near the Pool of Kerridwyn. I suspect that she has had her litter by now, or will very soon."

"Awww, puppies! Let's go see the puppies!" Jenny exclaimed.

"I will admit to being pleased that you are not pressing for a trip to the northern border."

"After I spoke to Raphael, I feel like there's no rush."

"Ah, so he advised caution?"

"Nope. He said to go see them."

"I do not understand."

"You rarely do."

After a moment of reflection on her last statement, Sariel said, "There are a few things you should know. New life here is very precious. They will not allow you to touch the puppies. The last time I tried, Thor attacked me quite vigorously. I suffered injuries trying to get away."

"Then why do you want to go?"

"Well, they are puppies. They are … cute, I suppose."

"You are the weirdest man I've ever met."

"You have said that before." Sariel continued. "There is also a good chance you may get to meet the Wood Elves there. The Du Shar Clan warriors ride the wolves if they are lucky enough to bond with one. Du Shar is their chieftain. Her young warriors will frequent the area until the pups are weaned, hoping one will form a bond, an imprint. If there is a bond, a spiritual and visible connection between the two, it will last a lifetime. If no bond forms by the time they are weaned, the Elves will never be allowed to ride them."

"The Elves can ride them? That is so cool,"

"Yes, it is quite fascinating. Unlike similar creatures in your world, these pups grow rapidly, yet take many months before they are fully weaned—before they are ready for The Bonding. The Elves always seem to know the right time."

Jenny awoke before dawn the next morning. She returned to the room to find the bed made, and her leather gear laid out neatly. "Thank you," she said to the room. "You are very kind. I do appreciate all the things that you do for me." There was no response. Jenny was beginning to have doubts about the nature of the Dryads. They seemed too intuitive to be the soulless creatures that Sariel described.

The light was still spreading towards the keep when they left for Kerridwyn's Pool.

"We will head north here. If I remember correctly, there is a copse of Wax Wood trees a short distance away. They make the best staves."

"Why is that?"

"They are strong, yet will bend without splintering."

It did not take long before they were in the midst of a small Wax Wood grove. The trees were tall and narrow, most branching out initially in a two-pronged fork higher up the trunk. She held his spear while he looked about, selecting several trees. She kept back as he felled three trees of differing widths with his sword. All but the thickest staff cut just slightly shorter than she was tall.

"The thicker, heavier staves will be the first ones you will use for training. Their extra weight will serve to strengthen you as you learn the basic moves. You will finish with the lighter one. That will be the one for combat."

"Wouldn't the heavier one be better for combat?"

"It is not as fast. You will learn there is more power in speed. You will also learn that combat quickly saps your strength. A minute of fierce fighting may leave you completely exhausted." He handed her the thinnest staff. "Carry this one with you. Get used to the feel of it. We will retrieve the others on our way back."

66

"Your spear is heavy."

"Yes. You may gravitate to a heavier staff as you gain in strength and endurance. However, you may still decide against that. As I said, you can use speed to your advantage. You are naturally fast. I think you should capitalize on that. We shall see in time what works best for you."

Near the pool one of the wolves leapt from behind a tree, knocking Sariel to the ground. It was Shade. He found himself pinned by the large paws and the weight of the beast. Its bared teeth mere inches from his face.

"Stop that!" Jenny yelled. "Bad boy! BAD dog!" She ran right up to it. It looked at her, confused.

Holding the small staff in both hands, she shoved on the wolf, but it did not budge.

"Get off him!" It continued to stare at her, bewildered.

Jenny dropped the staff and began to push with both hands. "GET! OFF!" she yelled. "Down, boy!" And it took a couple of steps back.

"There, that's better. Good boy." She stood directly in front of its nose. "You're supposed to be one of the good guys. Aren't you? You should be ashamed." The wolf looked down, abashed, as Sariel regained his feet.

She reached both hands up and began to scratch it behind the ears, her cheek against its muzzle.

Quietly, cautiously, Sariel said, "Jenny, that is not a dog."

She continued as if speaking to a poodle. "I know that.

You're a Great Wolf, aren't you? You're one of the Protectors. You're such a good boy." His tail actually began to wag.

She let him go, picked up her staff, and started up the path, patting her thigh. "Come on, boy. Show me the pool. Show me the puppies. Let's go see the puppies. Come on."

The beast gave out a short bark and bounded up beside her. They started up the path, with Jenny's hand resting on its back, gently scratching its fur.

Sariel stood still with his mouth open, staring after them.

Luna lay upon the soft moss, her head near the pool. Thor stood nearby. Two pups were already feeding while a third struggled to break the amniotic sac it was born in.

Softly, almost reverently, Sariel spoke, "There are many differences between Elvenrealm and your world. The pups must face their initial trial on their own. They must break free of their birth sac or suffocate. Also, they take many months to be fully weaned and prepared for Bonding with the Elves. But they grow at an accelerated rate from what you may be used to. They will be the size of a large breed dog from across the veil by that time." The third pup fought its way through the membrane and took its first breaths of air. Eyes shut, small head bobbing, it located its mother and began to crawl. Luna bent around, sniffed the pup then started to clean it with her tongue.

Soon there was another effort of labor and another pup.

"I'm going to pet one."

"Do not. I cannot defend you from this many wolves. Thor alone is a difficult match for me."

"Fine." She didn't sound happy.

Luna began another labor. Her body racked in spasms of pain. The pups fell away from their milk. Jenny moved as if to go to Luna, she thought to comfort her, but Sariel's firm grasp on her shoulder held her at bay.

Luna whined and howled in pain as the last pup was born. It was bigger than the others and squirmed within the amniotic sac. Small paws pressed against the membrane repeatedly. It wriggled back and forth, yet the sac did not rupture.

"What's wrong?"

"It cannot break free. It will soon suffocate. This is very sad."

"Then, we have to do something."

"No. This is the way of the Great Wolves. We cannot interfere. The pup faces this trial alone."

By now, only small, spasmodic twitches were to be seen. The pup was near death.

"This is stupid." Jenny broke free of Sariel and headed to the trapped pup.

Thor leapt in front of her, stood over the pup and let out a bark like a thunderclap. Jenny realized how he got his name as the startling sound caused her to fall over onto her butt.

A determined look came over her, and she flung herself forward, arms outstretched. She grasped the sac and pulled it apart. The pup lay still. She was vaguely aware of movement around her, but her focus was absolute. She scrambled forward and lifted the puppy, knelt and cradled it on her lap and wiped away the remaining membrane revealing the animal within. The fur was pure white. She vigorously rubbed its belly, and it gasped, then began to breathe and squirm.

A white muzzle intruded and lifted the bundle of fur from her lap. Luna carried it by the nape of the neck and plopped it down with the others. Sariel knelt down and lifted the young woman, now sobbing in relief. He carried her off down the trail. They said nothing to each other and Jenny went to her room as soon as they arrived back at the Keep.

Chapter 7

HALLELUJAH

The next morning, Jenny ran into Sariel as he was bringing in a pail of milk. He didn't say anything, so she followed him into the kitchen.

"I'm sorry," she said.

Sariel filtered the milk through a cloth into a large jar. He didn't answer.

"Do the wolves hate us now?"

"They let me retrieve the weapons."

"I'm sorry. I should have listened to you." Her eyes began to water.

Sariel looked at Jenny. "I am not sorry. Upon reflection, I am unsure that what you did was the wrong thing. I am only sure of one thing."

"What?"

"It was the right thing for you to do. It is your nature. I believe you are kind. It shows with so many of the things that have happened since you arrived. The Brownies loved you; Brownies run from me. You tamed a wolf; wolves despise me. I understand all their reactions to me. Now I am trying to understand you, and I believe that if you had done nothing, it would have hurt you, damaged your spirit." He looked back down at the milk jar. "Though I would, if I could, keep you from harm."

"I know that."

"My distress comes from the fact that I know with absolute certainty, there are so many creatures in this realm that will not be tamed. Creatures that will harm you in unspeakable ways without regard for your charm. I fear for the day I must avenge you. I am afraid there will be a day when ..." His voice trailed off, and he stopped speaking.

He's not worried about what the wolves think, she thought. *He's concerned about me.* "So you will train me. You will teach me. And I will listen to you. As your friend would say, 'Problem solved,' right?"

"That sounds like something he would say," Sariel said.

"You went back for the weapons?"

"Yes."

"Was the white puppy still alive?"

"Yes, he was. Very much so."

"Then grab your staff and follow me. Time to get your butt kicked."

The training lasted all day. They took frequent breaks for rest and refreshment. Jenny took it seriously and made some progress with the basic moves.

That evening Jenny found Sariel in the audience chamber tuning the lute. "Why don't you use the ballroom?"

"The ballroom?"

"Yup. The giant room on the next floor up? The one with the high ceiling and the musician's balcony? The one with all the pretty stone carvings? You really didn't know it was a ballroom? I'm betting the acoustics are amazing."

"I suppose that may have been the intention."

"Ya think?"

"I knew there was an empty room. I never found a need for it."

"It never occurred to you that the balcony would be for musicians? Or that it may have been designed to enhance sound? Duh."

"I did not give it much thought."

"Did you ever think that the third floor has guest rooms, and maybe you don't have to sleep on the floor in here?"

"I can sleep anywhere."

"Okay Eeyore, grab your banjo and follow me." She

headed up to the second level.

He arrived with the lute. The massive chandelier and wall sconces were lit. Jenny knew it was the intuitive Dryads at work. She stood by the door and pointed, directing him to the low balcony, no more than three or four feet high. The rear half was raised, so she told him to sit there. "Strike a chord. I want to see if it was designed to be closed or open."

Sariel did as he was told. She shut the door and told him to do it again. He did.

"It doesn't seem to make much difference. I'll leave it closed." She sat next to him on the balcony and nodded at the lute. He began to play, and the acoustics proved to be spectacular.

"Hold on!" Jenny said. "What is that?"

"It is Tombeau sur la Mort."

"Don't you know anything from my world, you know, from 'beyond the veil' and all that?"

"I am familiar with the modern world, which is where I heard this piece."

"How about something *more* modern? Something you can sing to?"

"I do not sing." He paused a moment and looked up. "Can you?"

"I used to sing all the time when I was younger. Had lessons and everything. Some people thought I was pretty good. Especially my Mom, but that doesn't count. It's been a few years, so I probably suck."

"I know of a poet and composer by the name of Leonard Cohen. The song is entitled *Hallelujah*. Are you familiar with him?"

"I dunno, the name sounds familiar. Play the introduction." She scooted closer to him.

Sariel strummed the lute and adjusted two strings. He began to play.

"I know this one!" she said excitedly. "Keep playing while I remember the words."

After a couple more times through the introduction, she looked at Sariel and nodded, indicating she was ready for the first verse.

Her first couple of lines were good, it was obvious she had training. By the fifth line, Jenny had found her full voice, clear and powerful. Suddenly the room wasn't empty at all. Every space filled with mellifluous resonance. Each 'Hallelujah' of the refrain reverberated in perfect synchronization with the lute. Jenny and Sariel were one in harmony.

Sariel's fingers danced upon the lute. With each new verse, Jenny's voice grew in intensity and filled the room. The poet's passion and pain transformed into soulful and melodious sound. Behind them, glowing lights began to fill the window glass as Faeries were drawn to the melody. Jenny's voice penetrated deep within Sariel, tearing down barriers he spent centuries building. Emotions flooded to the surface, head bowed, he wept as he played.

As in all things, the song finally came to an end. The last echoes of 'Hallelujah' bounced from the walls, and all was silent. He set the lute against the ledge and kissed Jenny on the forehead. Into her hair, his unsteady voice whispered only one word. "Amazing." Then he walked out of the ballroom.

As he walked away, he must have brushed the lute. It slowly slid from the ledge to the floor with a small discordant *clang*. Sariel refused to look back.

Jenny sat for a few minutes, still absorbed in the moment. When she bent to retrieve the lute from the floor, she saw an object resting against the stone balcony balustrade. It sparkled like a perfectly cut diamond. She reverently set the lute upon the platform and picked up the object. It was a gem of sorts, smooth and egg-shaped with a milky-white center that somehow managed to catch the light in a cascade of reflections. *Sariel must have dropped it,* she thought *I'll give it to him later.*

Chapter 8

FAERIES

Jenny found the pool, with its many waterfalls, serene and relaxing. Tonight she felt the need for some serenity and headed there. Jenny was not surprised to find Sariel sitting waist-deep in the water. She was surprised to see the air above the pool filled with fireflies.

"Oh, look! The lightning bugs are out tonight," she said as she released the cord around her waist and began to work on the knot at her shoulder. Each one would glow in the starlight, then go dark. Some would reflect from the surface of the water to double the effect.

"Have a care. These are not fireflies," he said, "They are Faeries. I think they were attracted by your voice." He swatted at one that came nearby.

"Faeries! How wonderful!" she said as the stola fell away. She strode unabashed into the pool and felt his gaze upon her. She felt safe with Sariel and had lost a lot of her prior inhibitions regarding nudity. There was, after all, only one place to bathe.

Many of the creatures appeared to be perched in the branches of a young willow tree. Its limbs bent down to reach the surface of the pool. Jenny went over to get a closer look. As she neared, the bright flashes grew faster until it was a steady golden glow.

Up close they appeared to be beautiful golden humans with delicate wings. She could see that the creature, a female, was smiling at her. She held up a finger, and the Faerie flitted there without hesitation. The tiny creature bent over to peer at Jenny.

Jenny giggled in delight. She turned towards Sariel carefully so as not to disturb the tiny Faerie. She sat down, the water barely covering her breasts. Others began to light on the branches behind her, several landing in her hair. She was murmuring to them, but they did not answer, other than with their tiny smiles.

She fell silent, as if in contemplation. "Do you hate me?"

"No!" he responded quickly. "Absolutely not."

"So many of the things I do upset you. I can see it. And you said you would tell me the truth."

He thought a moment before answering. "You are naïve to the dangers here. I fear for your safety. And you can be quite stubborn at times."

"Why have fear. If something bad does happen, you would

be free of me. Things would go back to normal."

"Free?" he said and drew in a deep breath. In a soft whisper, as if he were speaking to himself, he added, "I would be destroyed." But the water carried the words to her. She looked at him, sitting alone on the other side of the pool.

"Is there anything you like about me?" she asked tentatively.

"Many things, Lady."

"Like what?"

"I love that you are quick to smile, and when you do, it fills me with joy. I love that you are so kind that the Creatures of Light are drawn to you. Although it causes me concern at times, I love that you are quick to protect others. I love the wonder in your eyes when you discover something new. I love the sound of your voice, especially raised in song."

Jenny stood, the faerie on her finger flew into her hair. "You called me beautiful before. Do you really find me attractive?" She stood and began to slowly walk towards him. He arose and started to back into the deeper water as if he were a mouse, cornered by a housecat.

"Yes, I have told you many times. You are most beautiful. I am truthful when I say that I cannot describe it. You are so beautiful that it hurts in a way, to look upon you. Now, with the Faerie glow about your golden hair, I am undone, unable to draw a proper breath."

He did not back away fast enough. Jenny put her arms about his neck. Buoyed by the deeper water, she easily drew herself up and kissed him, legs wrapped around his waist. He succumbed to the kiss, and the two remained in that embrace for a time, suspended by the pool. They kissed again and again, only separating to draw ragged breaths.

Then Sariel took her by the shoulders and held her far enough away she could not reach his lips. "I cannot take this advantage," he said through ragged breaths.

"You can," she replied. "I want this, and I know you want it too. Your body betrays you." She bore a seductive smile as he walked them near one of the many small waterfalls, her legs wrapped around his waist.

"I do. However, only if I am certain of your desire." He continued. "Do you remember what I told you about the Faeries?"

"I'm not thinking about Faeries right now. I'm thinking about us—and how badly ..." she said right before he plunged her head into the stream of water. Tiny Faerie voices screamed in frustration, flying off in a golden cloud as the water dislodged them from her hair.

He quickly pulled her free of the spray. She still clung to him, her breath in ragged gasps. At first, she looked surprised, then confused. Sariel began to walk back towards the shallower water.

She unwrapped her feet and stood, her arms still about his neck. Sariel looked down and sadly asked. "Do you still want me?"

Jenny kept her head down, forehead against his chest,

regaining her proper breath as the effects of the Faerie glamor dissipated. Finally, she looked up and whispered. "I think so." She kissed him, then turned and walked towards the keep. She didn't bother to pick up her stola.

Sariel stared after her, watching her wet body glisten in the starlight. He observed the sway of her hips as she disappeared into the night.

Sariel arrived soon after. He quietly climbed the many stairs until he reached the bedchambers. The door was closed. He hung his head and retreated back down. Jenny never knew he was there.

Chapter 9

WOOD ELVES

The next three weeks were much the same. They would train in various places, rest often, and go to the pool in the evening where Sariel would rub her sore muscles so that she would be able to train again the next day.

One evening Sariel stood close behind Jenny, locating and smoothing out the knots in her shoulders and neck with practiced hands. Jenny cleared her throat and said, "Sariel, there is a rather ... *pressing* matter that I would like to talk about."

"What?" he cleared his throat. "Yes, what matter?" He sounded distracted.

"You're starting to sound like me." She was smiling, but he couldn't see that. "Remember that time when I said your body was betraying you? Well, it's betraying you again—against my back."

"Oh!" he exclaimed and stepped back. "I apologize. Truly. My mind was elsewhere."

Jenny turned to face him and saw a male Faerie sitting on his head, wearing a mischievous grin. Her smile grew a bit naughty, as well. "So ... what exactly was your mind on?"

Sariel looked so embarrassed that she pointed to his head. He glanced around, and the Faerie held on. She closed the gap and waved her hand near his head. The Faerie flew off. Sariel saw it and immediately went into an arm-waving dance that you might expect when someone has disturbed a beehive.

"Horrible creatures! They are nothing but an annoyance!"

Jenny burst out laughing and soon so did he. Once his passion had subsided a bit, they walked from the pool.

Jenny picked up her stola and exclaimed, "Race ya back!" Then swatted him on his bare backside. It startled him, and when he jumped, Jenny screamed and ran laughing all the way back.

It was at that moment when Sariel realized something. Or rather, he finally admitted it to himself. He was genuinely in love with her. He could not imagine being without her. That momentary joy quickly faded with the thought that there was no one more unworthy of being with her than him. He thought of the countless lives he had taken, the sea of grief he had left in his wake. This was the burden he was cursed to carry—and it was a heavy burden.

At dawn the next morning Jenny asked if they could see the

puppies.

"Before you say anything, I won't touch them. I do listen to you. So you don't have to worry about anything like that."

"I think …" he began.

"Maybe it's a bad idea." she interrupted. "What if they're still mad at me?"

"I think it is a wonderful idea."

"Really?"

"Really. Get dressed," he said, heading up the stairs.

They met no wolves on the way to the pool. Once they entered the clearing, it was apparent why.

Jenny gasped when she saw them. "Elves! Those are the Wood Elves, aren't they?"

Sariel frowned. "Indeed, they are."

A group of a dozen young Elves stood near the litter of puppies. There were six of them now, all feeding. The Elves noticed their arrival but did not seem interested. What they were interested in were the puppies, especially the larger white pup.

One other Elf did notice them and was intensely interested. She sat mounted on her wolf. Her hair soft brown and straight was braided tight. Two small braids hung on either side of her face, the rest bound in a larger braid that started at the top of her head and ran down her back. The braided hair exposed her long, pointed ears. She wore leather corseted armour, cut low to reveal the cleavage and tops of her large, firm breasts. There was a tattoo of sorts above her left breast, a paw print. The younger warriors were similarly dressed but without any tattoos.

She sat straight and tall. Looking directly at Jenny, she asked, "Are you a warrior here for The Bonding?"

Jenny looked at Sariel for guidance. She was determined to obey all the proper protocols. He whispered, "This is their chieftain, Du Shar."

Louder, he said, "Du Shar, may I present …"

"Silence!" She held up a hand, not taking her eyes off Jenny. Sariel acquiesced.

"Are you a warrior here for The Bonding?" she repeated to Jenny.

"No, I'm not a warrior," Jenny said. "I'm just here to see the puppies."

As soon as she spoke, the white pup looked up, saw Jenny, and started moving towards her, stumbling over its own feet every so often. "What do I do?" she whispered.

"Nothing, do not move," Sariel whispered back.

The Elves all stared, their expressions either astonished or a little angry. Only Du Shar remained impassive, interested, yet expressionless. She dismounted in one fluid movement and began to walk towards Jenny. The other wolves watched but did not move. "Sariel, she scares me," she whispered urgently.

"Stay strong," he whispered back to her.

Then the puppy arrived, tail wagging. It had grown fast and was bigger than the rest of the litter. It put a paw on Jenny's leg. It barked in a high pitch. "Can I pick it up?"

"No!" Sariel hissed.

She knelt down to talk to it, but Luna was there to carry it back. However, she only made it a few feet when it wriggled out of her jaws and headed back to Jenny. It jumped into her lap and started licking her face. Jenny touched it, even though she had promised not to. It was too cute to resist.

"Look at you, you are so cute! You're white as a ghost with little black eyes. Like a spooky Halloween costume. A little Halloween spook. That's a great name! I'm going to call you Spook."

Jenny saw the leather boots and looking up, the smile left her face. Du Shar was standing next to her, watching. The puppy, now bereft of the attention it craved, jumped up, placing both paws on Jenny's chest and began to lick her face.

Jenny turned her attention back to the puppy. "Ow! Spook, watch the puppy claws." She grimaced. "Ow! Ow, ow, ow!" She gently pushed Spook away with shaking hands. She grasped her chest and sucked in a deep breath. She rocked back and forth and peered under her leather tunic. "IT BURNS!" she screamed, her face contorted in pain. Spook collapsed to the ground.

Sariel moved to aid her, but there was a silvery flash. Du Shar held a long dagger to his chest. Sariel looked at the deadly blade and froze. The other warriors gathered around. Never taking her eyes off of Jenny, Du Shar said, "Move again, male, and die."

Jenny now lay on her side, the cords in her neck standing out. Her face turned a bright red. Sariel couldn't stand it. "We need to help her. We must find her wound. She could die."

"She may die. Many others have. Stand back and be silent."

The other warriors formed a ring around Jenny, keeping Sariel outside. Spook appeared to be asleep, unmoving. Jenny writhed in agony, her breath in short irregular gasps, or screams of pain. Then she went silent and still.

"We will know soon, Sisters," Du Shar said. They waited. Du Shar moved to Jenny's side, then pushed on her shoulder with her foot. Jenny flopped onto her back, eyes wide and bloodshot, unblinking she stared at the sky. Helpless, Sariel was filled with grief and loss. If there was one thing he knew, it was death.

Du Shar gave Jenny a sharp kick in the hip. Jenny gasped, Spook gasped, and they both sat up. Jenny stared around her, breathing fast. Then she was hit with another wave of pain and cried out.

"Help her up," Du Shar commanded, and two of her warriors pulled Jenny to her feet as she sobbed in pain. Jenny found herself face to face with Du Shar.

Although the chieftain was shorter than Jenny, she possessed the most commanding presence she had ever known. She spoke with confidence and radiated the authority of one who knows she has nothing to prove to others. She was lean, muscular, and moved with animal grace. She was also pretty, even with many visible scars, including a thin one that started above her right eyebrow and ran down her cheek. However, she was definitely feminine in all aspects, voluptuous with large breasts, small waist, and pronounced hips.

Two of the younger warriors were supporting her by the arms. Jenny was in too much pain to protest as Du Shar untied the laces on her tunic and forced it apart. Above her left breast was a paw print, now red and swollen, still blistering. The mark of a Wolf Rider. The warriors all began to talk at once.

"Behold." They heard. The voice was soft and yet carried around the pool. All fell silent. "Behold she whom I have named Bright, The Elvenstar." Kerridwyn stood in their midst. The young warriors all took a knee, Du Shar and Sariel acknowledged the Goddess with a bow of their heads.

Kerridwyn continued. "Her spirit will shine as a beacon to all of Elvenrealm. She will give us hope during the dark times that will surely come. Bright is now and forever Elven. I bid you, welcome her."

Du Shar stepped aside as Kerridwyn moved to stand before Jenny, now named Bright. A Goddess-given name. She smiled at Bright as she pulled the laces of her tunic tight and tied them.

"Walk with me, Child of Light. We have much to discuss." Kerridwyn took her hand, lacing her fingers through Bright's. Bright felt peace with her touch, although there was no lessening of the pain she felt. Hand in hand, they walked to the western side of the pool, away from the crowd.

From this moment on, Bright was often asked to describe the Goddess. Everyone wanted to know what she looked like, but Bright could never precisely define Kerridwyn. Always she is exquisite in her beauty. Her features change in subtle ways, from one glance to another. At times Bright felt there was some connection between how she appeared and her mood. If speaking of light and happy things, she may seem to be an exuberant young woman; when speaking of more pressing matters, severe and matronly. Her long gown of gossamer overlapping green leaves, the circlet of flowers in her hair, and her green eyes seemed to be the only constant. She radiated an aura of peace and calm. Bright felt she may be all things, all women. The embodiment of what was pure and noble.

Kerridwyn led her to a fallen log away from the others. The wood was covered in soft moss. Kerridwyn indicated she should sit, then sat beside her. The movement of Bright's leather tunic against the wound sent a stab of pain. Bright lifted the edge, and gingerly touched the wound. It was hot, angry, and swollen.

"The mark is a blessing, you will see," Kerridwyn told her.

"It really, really hurts!" she said, looking at Kerridwyn. "Is there something that will stop the pain? Some herb or something?"

"I could take away your pain with a thought. I will not. In life, there are milestones, rites of passage. The only ones that will be meaningful to you require hard work or pain ... or both. The Bonding is one such rite. You will endure it like your sisters before you, then you will understand."

Bright nodded, and Kerridwyn continued. "I have not been forgotten beyond The Veil. There are those that still practice the Old Religion, and I am their Goddess. It was there that I became aware of you while searching for my consort—I felt your resonance. And I brought you here. I knew that Elvenrealm needed you, and I thought with all that you had gone through in your world you might welcome the opportunity to help us. Your destiny is here if you have the will to fulfill it." Kerridwyn squeezed her hand. "So my question is, is this what you want?"

"You can send me back? Sariel told me that my family is stuck, frozen in time or something."

Kerridwyn laughed. "There are many timelines. In one, everything is still. Every leaf halted in its fall, every breath held, awaiting your return. In another, your family has moved on without you. In yet another, you did not exist on that plane at all. Everything is happening at once. The people in your modern world are just beginning to understand this. But yes, I can send you back, and I will if you ask me to. There are many ways to go back. Sariel is not of your world and has the power to return you."

"Wait. What? He could have just sent me back? He told me he couldn't. That only you could."

Kerridwyn furrowed her brow. "That does not sound like him. He does not lie. Is that what he said?"

Bright thought about it. "Well, not exactly. Sariel said that you could and that you probably brought me here … and he would consider the other options."

Kerridwyn brightened. "Ah. So he did not lie. He 'considered the options.'"

"I suppose so, but why wouldn't he just admit it?"

Kerridwyn giggled like a young woman. "You really don't understand. Sariel loves you. He would be eternally miserable without you. But if you pressed him, made him see you could not be happy here, he would send you back. He would do it for you, even though he would be devastated. Sariel will place your happiness over his own, I know this."

"Sariel loves me? Really? He has been kind to me, even when I do stupid things." Bright looked up. "What do you mean, he is not of my world? What is he?"

"Sariel is a fallen angel."

"Fallen angel! He fought with Lucifer against God and was cast out of heaven and all that?"

"No," Kerridwyn said sharply. "That entire story is nonsense. A tale made up by religious leaders across The Veil to cause fear. Fear they exploited to gain political control. I know of no angel named Lucifer that caused a war against a god. Gods do not rule in the angelic realm, and no angel could challenge a God. There is no truth in any of it."

Kerridwyn continued in a softer voice. "A fallen angel is one who has chosen to become mortal for a time. One who has given up their rank and stature and fallen from their realm. Sariel was a Dominion. He held authority over a host of angels, second only to the archangels themselves. Angels have obligations. He was the Angel of Death, Vengeance, and Protection."

"The Angel of Death?" Bright asked, shocked.

"Yes. And death and grief weigh heavily upon him. His empathy for humans caused him to feel responsible. He feels their pain and loss. He bears the weight of those obligations every moment. It tortures him. But death is part of the cycle of life. So is grief. I will talk to him about this today."

"I haven't seen any wings. Aren't angels supposed to have wings?"

"Not all of them. Only Dominions and Archangels have wings, a mighty symbol of their authority. He has wings, but only while in the realm of angels. Here he retains power over the mists, but is essentially mortal." Kerridwyn paused for a moment. "I believe you have something from him."

"I have something from him? I guess everything I have is from him."

Kerridwyn placed her hand over a small pocket in her tunic.

"Oh! You mean the gem I found. I am going to give it back, I forgot."

"May I see it?"

Bright didn't hesitate, she extracted the gem and placed it in Kerridwyn's hand. She admired the jewel. It gleamed in the sunlight. "I do not doubt that this is from Sariel, but he will not want it. It is yours now, I think. May I ask how you got this?"

"I was singing while he played. When the song was over, I found this gem on the floor. It might be some sort of diamond."

"You must sing for me sometime." She smiled. "Your voice must be exquisite to have coaxed a tear from an angel."

"What?"

"This is no gemstone. It is an Angel's Tear. It holds great power, I could sense its presence. With this, you can call any angel in their realm to your aid. Hold the Tear in both hands and call aloud for aid when you have great need. It can be used only once, then it will be shattered. Others will covet the tear so it should be hidden."

Kerridwyn left her seat and found a small flower. She sat back down and freed Bright's long gold chain from within her tunic. Placing the gem within the flower, she wrapped the petals about it, then grasped the chain. When she released her hand, Bright found that a golden bud, as if about to bloom, was attached to the chain.

"Now, it is hidden. Only you know what it truly is. Keep it a secret."

"I will. Thank you," Bright said.

"My consort and I made this place to keep our creations safe. His name is Cernunnos, and he has been long absent. Far too long, I am worried about his delay. I must find him, and the search leaves Elvenrealm frequently without my aid.

The creatures of darkness are pressing the borders. They seek to destroy our creations."

Bright interrupted. "Why would you create creatures of darkness?"

"We did not create them, they found their way here. As I said, there are many ways to move between the realms. They are jealous and seek only to corrupt and destroy. I found you and thought you may help balance the scales in my absence."

"I can't do what you do. Or what Sariel does. Or Du Shar, I imagine. I'm nothing like them."

"You are not. You are Bright, the Elvenstar. You can only do what you do. I speak plainly, there are great and terrible dangers to our realm. Nothing is safe. So tell me, do you want to stay, or shall I send you back?"

Bright considered it. She rocked back and forth, holding the pendant while the mark burned. She looked across the pool at the others where they were gathered. She glimpsed the small, white bundle of fur sitting at her feet, staring up at her. She thought of her family.

"This is so hard! Elvenrealm is fascinating, and I feel good here. But I miss my family. What if I stay, and then change my mind? Sariel tells me you aren't here very often. Will you be back soon, in case I change my mind?"

"I will instruct Sariel to send you through The Veil without delay if that is your desire. All you have to do is tell him that you want to return."

Finally, Bright decided. "I will stay and do what I can."

Kerridwyn smiled, but there was sadness in her eyes. She kissed Bright on the cheek. "Very well. Would you ask Sariel to join me here?"

Spook barked and stumbled, following Bright as she approached the small crowd. Bright felt uncomfortable with all eyes, even the wolves, upon her. Spook whined and looked up at her, so she picked up the large puppy. She winced and immediately adjusted his position so that he did not press upon her left breast. She walked up to Sariel.

"Kerridwyn would like to speak to you."

"Of course," he said, then added, "I can make ointments at the keep. They will ease your pain."

She quickly replied, "No. Let it burn." Du Shar actually smiled a little and approached her. Sariel nodded to Bright and headed around the pool.

"I do not like being lied to. A warrior should not lie," Du Shar accused.

"I didn't lie to you."

"You said you were not a warrior. That ..." She pointed to Bright's chest, then to a similar mark proudly displayed on her own chest. "Is the mark of a warrior, a Wolf Rider."

"I'm not ... or I wasn't. I don't know what happened. Some kind of mistake?"

The young warriors started murmuring amongst themselves. Du Shar shouted, "There are no mistakes!" The warriors went silent. "A Bonding is *never* a mistake."

Du Shar moved uncomfortably close. *She scares the crap out of me,* Bright thought. "The Lady has declared you are Elven. She has named you, giving you a title. And asked us to welcome you." Du Shar turned to face her coven of warriors. "And we, my sisters, had the honor to bear witness to it. We now have another great story to tell our ancestors once we are slain. The story of how we few stood at the Pool with Kerridwyn. Of how we were here when the Elvenstar was named." The warriors nodded, eyes wide.

Du Shar took Spook from her arms and set him on the ground. Bright felt exposed without the pup between them. "Sisters, look at the size of this one!" As imposing as Du Shar was, the top of her head barely reached Bright's nose. And Du Shar was taller than most of the coven. "I hope to have a daughter this size one day!" The warriors nodded approvingly.

Du Shar looked her up and down, appraising her. "What weapon have you mastered?"

"Well … I haven't mastered any weapon."

"An honest answer. Which weapon do you favor?"

"I dunno, the bow?"

"Are you asking me?" Shar demanded.

"The bow," Bright said in as firm of a voice as she could muster.

The chieftain nodded. "The bow is a fine weapon. We are all skilled, but few are its master."

She began to squeeze Bright's upper arms, her shoulders. She wrapped her arms around her to probe her back with her fingers.

"You are too soft. Can you even draw a bow?" Du Shar asked.

"I've never tried."

"Sir Leesee," Du Shar called out, and the shortest of her small band ran to her side. She was adorable, almost childlike. Her hair was braided back into two ponytails. "Sir Leesee has mastered the bow. Leesee, let her see what an archer's back feels like."

Leesee moved at once, pressing right up against her so that she might wrap her arms around. She looked up at Bright with a big smile.

"Go ahead," Du Shar commanded. Bright did. While she was probing her back, Sir Leesee hugged her. The motion flexed the muscles in her back.

"Holy cow! You're hard as a rock." Leesee giggled. Once Leesee stepped back, Bright could see her arms were just as well-defined.

"You will need much training and conditioning," Du Shar stated and looked to Sir Leesee who was nearly shaking with anticipation, pleading eyes looking up at Shar. "Sir Leesee will see to your training for now."

Leesee leapt into the air. "Yes!" she exclaimed and hugged Bright around the waist. "We're going to have so much fun!"

"Do not underestimate this one. Sir Leesee will no doubt be challenging me for chieftain soon." Shar said with a stern glance at Leesee.

"Very soon," Sir Leesee agreed.

Du Shar laughed and kissed her on the top of the head. "You see why I am so proud of my warriors?"

Bright seemed confused. "Sir Leesee will see to my training? She's coming to the keep?"

"Absolutely not. You will train with the Clan. But now, you must meet your sisters."

Bright met the rest of the coven. They were all young warriors that had attained the rank of Knight of the Realm. Some, like Leesee, appeared almost childlike, too young to be warriors. Many expressed disappointment that the white wolf was no longer an option, but they were friendly and called her "sister."

Bright learned that a knight was addressed as 'Sir,' a knight who was bonded with a wolf received the title 'Ahn.' The chieftain's designation was 'Du.' Bright also learned that Spook was the youngest wolf to Bond, and she was the first to experience a bonding that wasn't already a knight. Du Shar dismissed the issue, stating that with training, it will all soon be remedied.

Bright learned that they thought of themselves as sisters, regardless of rank. And it appeared they actually meant it. They stood close and were quick to touch; to hold a hand, lean their head against you, or wrap an arm around your waist. Two had already kissed her cheek, Leesee was one of them. Leesee was also the one excitedly pushing people in front of her to introduce.

"Bright," Leesee said as she pushed a particularly stocky elf in front of her. "This is Pyper! Her mother is an artisan and a knight. She creates our weapons and armour. Isn't that interesting? Pyper, show her your axe! Her mother made it for her. She gave it to Pyper when she was knighted. I wish you could have been there. I cried."

Pyper produced her axe and handed it over for inspection. It was unlike any Bright had seen before. A thick semicircular band of metal was affixed to the haft only at the bottom. The top portion came to a point at the end. It was definitely an axe, but swung in reverse would prove an equally deadly spike. Bright was drawn to the intricate carvings along the blade. A string of roses, but upon close inspection, the stems were skeletal, like a spinal column. The veins of the leaves, bony fingers ending in claws.

"It's beautiful," Bright said, "You have the most awesome axe I've ever seen."

"Thanks," Pyper replied. "Yours isn't bad either. But what do you think about my weapon?"

Another warrior, slender and almost as tall as Du Shar made an exasperated sound and swatted Pyper's shoulder.

"She always says that. She thinks it's funny," Leesee said. "This is Willow. Willow doesn't talk, but she's very sweet."

"Very sweet." Pyper agreed with a wink. Willow appeared

embarrassed and looked down while trying to suppress a smile. "My mother named it The Wicked Rose. That's what mother calls the axe, not Willow."

Leesee said, "They're always together. The Ahns gave up trying to send them out on separate patrols." The long, two-handed sword strapped to Willow's back was hard to miss.

"Sir Dahni?" Leesee called out. "There you are. Dahni is another archer, like me. I'm a little better shot, but she's way prettier. I wish I were as lovely as she is. Don't you think she's pretty?" Sir Dahni was the only Knight with her hair cut short in a pixie cut.

Sir Leesee grabbed the tallest Elf in the group by the hand and drug her in front of Bright. "This is Sir Elaine. She's wicked smart, and so fast with the staff that it's nothing but a blur. Elaine, you can help with Bright's training, can't you?"

"If Du Shar gives me permission, I would be honored to," Sir Elaine replied.

"They're coming back," Pyper interrupted. "The big male doesn't look very happy." Du Shar motioned for Bright to come to her.

"Don't worry, Bright," Leesee said. "If he gives you any trouble, I'll kill him."

Dahni said, "Bet I can kill him first."

"Stop! Neither of you is going to kill him, Okay?" Bright said. Not convinced she added. "Promise." They did but looked disappointed.

"Are you still in pain?" Sariel asked.

"I'll be okay," Bright said.

"Bright, I want to talk to you. There are some things that I want to say," Sariel began. "However, I have learned that many raiding parties have gotten through the border. The goblins are pushing hard. If I do not try to stop them now, it may soon be too late. They could cause a lot of harm."

"I thought the Elves and wolves stopped them at the border?"

"It is not possible to stop them all when they are determined. I try to find the ones that get through. I have not been on patrol for many days, and now it is important for me to find them. I would like for you to wait at The Keep. Kerridwyn can send Thor to Amalia to watch over you. I would like to speak with you as soon as I get back."

"The Elvenstar is coming with us," Du Shar stated flatly.

"To the border? No, absolutely not," he replied.

"You would have her stay alone and do nothing? She is a warrior of the Du Shar Clan. She needs to be with her sisters. She needs to be trained if she is to survive."

"She is not a warrior. She is not a member of your clan. And I can train her."

"Bright is bonded, so she is a warrior. She is a member of my Clan if I say it is so. And you are not capable of training anyone, you're a male."

"She needs to be kept safe!" Sariel's anger began to show.

"Are you trying to suggest that I cannot keep her safe? Just say those words, male," Du Shar said, definitely angry, her knuckles white from gripping her twin daggers. Her warriors were close now. Leesee and Dahni had arrows notched.

"Bright," Leesee called out. "Can we kill him now?" Dahni stood beside her, eagerly nodding her head.

Bright turned and shouted. "NO! I said no killing." Leesee and Dahni looked a little hurt from the admonishment.

"Hold." Kerridwyn had spoken. "Be at peace. We will not prevail broken. Our only chance is to work in harmony."

"Sariel, your skills are sorely needed. You may be gone for a long time, perhaps weeks or more. It would be wise to let Bright train and prepare while we yet have time. Most likely the clan will return here soon to check on the young wolves, and they must return for the bonding when they are weaned. You will see your Bright again. Shar will see to that. And she will see to her safety. You will have time to speak your heart."

Kerridwyn continued. "Shar should take The Elvenstar north. She will be with her sisters, and they will keep her safe." Kerridwyn looked to the small group of warriors. "You will keep her safe, won't you?" They all nodded with most saying, "Yes, Lady."

"Thank you, Knights of the Realm. That is not only my request to you. It is the Holy Quest I give to all my knights before the dark wave comes. Keep her safe. Help her to become a knight worthy of the wolf." There was a small pause as Kerridwyn's words sunk in, then Leesee cheered first, and the others joined her.

"Sariel, Shade will join you. You can use his keen nose, his sharp ears. Find the bands that infiltrated and end them before they can join forces and become formidable. Go now, he will soon catch up to you. Know that my thoughts go with you." Sariel nodded. He approached Bright, placing his hands on her shoulders.

"I will worry about you every moment," he said.

"Don't worry, I'll be fine. We'll be back at the keep soon, and everything will be like it was," Bright said, and it looked like she meant it.

Sariel kissed her and walked away. But he knew it would not be as it was. Nothing will ever be quite like it was. The border and the Elves would have an effect on her. She would return a different person. She would see him differently. If he only had more time alone with her, if only he dared to tell her how he felt before this moment. He could not shake the feeling that he had already lost her.

"Shar, your task is great. Prepare your clan, your defenses. Prepare for the worst. I fear even your husbands may soon be pressed to battle." Du Shar paled slightly at Kerridwyn's words.

"And Bright, learn everything you can, train well, and never lose the wonder you feel for all that is Elven. There is much to fear in the creatures of darkness. But you have one advantage, they have little capacity for love. Listen to your heart. Never let the darkness lessen the love that makes you who you are." Kerridwyn embraced Bright, then walked away.

Du Shar moved to Rend, her mount. She put an arm over his shoulder, rested her head against his neck, and thought about what she had heard.

Bright moved to the coven of Knights who stood in a tight knot. Leesee was crying, and it looked like she was beginning to affect several others.

"Leesee, are you okay?"

"Oh, Bright. Did you hear? Did you hear what she said?" Leesee was waving her hands as if it would fan her face.

"Yes … but what …"

"We have a quest! A Holy Quest! Given to us by the Lady herself. How wonderful. Isn't it amazing? She looked right at us and gave us a quest. I think I'm going to die! Oh, what if I do? What if I actually die while defending you from slobbering goblins or something? What a great story to tell the ancestors! The first quest given to the Knights of the Realm since the ancient times. Can you imagine? I have never been happier." Now Willow began to cry; Pyper put a strong arm around her waist.

Leesee smiled right before she was overcome with another sobbing fit. Bright hugged her while the rest gathered around. Everyone wanted to reach out and touch Bright, perhaps to believe the quest was real. Bright felt overwhelmed, she felt loved and very, very concerned.

"I don't want anybody to die." She whispered.

Chapter 10

THE ROAD TO COR MALIA

The knights refilled their water skins, and left the Pool, heading north. Bright said a tearful goodbye to Spook, and Luna had to pick him up to prevent him from following. Du Shar sent Rend on ahead to scout while she walked with the rest of the sisters. Four knights formed a diamond formation close around Bright. Pyper in front, Willow bringing up the rear, with Leesee and Dahni to her flanks. The other eight moved along a wider perimeter. Bright found they all seemed to be able to walk with a silent grace through the trees. She had difficulty spotting any of the others, even when she concentrated on finding them.

Along the way, Dahni and Leesee chatted incessantly. She learned many things. A defined rank structure existed. Some Elves served as laborers, gardeners, gatherers, or worked for the craftsmen. They had warriors, some of which had attained the rank of knight, and knights that had bonded with wolves, the Wolf Riders. There were some that earned the title of knight mainly due to their skill as artisans. However, they were still required to participate in some kind of trial or rite of passage. Pyper's mother, Sir Mahri, was one although initially, she began as a warrior, then found she had considerable talent as a smith. Another was the bowyer who crafted their bows and arrows, the elder Sir Rhaine. Some highly skilled masons and carpenters had also achieved the same status.

The men were few. This was because only about one in ten births produced a male child. They were protected in the household, and tended to the more domestic chores, along with being responsible for providing more children, children especially needed as warriors since many were lost to combat. Men choose the women they would be husbands to. If their mate fell in combat, they would typically either select one of her close friends with whom they were familiar, or one of the more influential women such as Du Shar or Mahri, so they would be adequately provided for. For this reason, it became a symbol of status in the clan to have many husbands. The women cherished the males for all the things they did and for the gift of children, which was a rare gift indeed.

Women seldom could become pregnant, no matter how hard they tried. If they had any sign, or feeling, or even a slight desire for a male, it was common for them to ask the wife if they could bed them in the hope of producing a child. It was considered common courtesy to allow it. Every thought was to create more children, especially daughters. The survival of the Clan depended on it.

To her horror, Bright was told that their sleeping quarters were constructed in the top branches of the tall trees found along the border. In this manner, they could sleep in safety from the all-too-frequent goblin raiding parties. Many buildings were constructed on the ground, such as the Great Hall and Mahri's forge. Mahri and her husbands stayed there, but most sought shelter in the safety of the branches above.

"What am I going to do? I'm afraid of heights," Bright confessed.

"What do you mean? How can you be afraid of heights?" Leesee asked, then stated. "I'm afraid of trolls."

"There are trolls?"

"Yes, horrible creatures. Do you want to hear all about them?" Dahni asked.

"No, not now. I'm worried enough about climbing to the tops of giant trees. Sure, I've climbed on low branches, but not much further. And then only when I had to."

"Are you afraid of clouds? Clouds are higher than trees," Leesee asked.

"Not clouds … well, I would be if I were somehow on one. I'm afraid of being in high places, and of falling from them, I suppose."

"I wouldn't be afraid of falling, I think that would be like flying. I'd be more afraid of smashing into the ground," Dahni said.

"Sisters!" Du Shar overheard the conversation and moved near. "We all have our own fears. I have many. We must recognize them in ourselves. Accept that we have them, then you can take control. Your actions in the face of fear are what defines you as a knight. We will be kind and help Bright face hers."

"What are your fears, Du Shar?" Leesee asked.

"Yeah, what are you afraid of? Are you afraid of trolls? Or ogres or dragons?" Dahni asked.

"Many things. I fear for the welfare of our Clan. I fear we have too few children. I am afraid for every patrol I must send out into the night, and that fear remains until I see them safely return. But ..." Shar lowers her voice. "... one thing I fear most of all."

"What?" Dahni asks.

"Is it worse than trolls?" From Leesee.

"Yes!" Du Shar speaks ominously. "Worst of all, I fear the slow, agonizing torture of being talked to death by Leesee and Dahni."

It took a second to sink in. Leesee and Dahni looked at each, mouths agape in shock. Then Leesee shoved Du Shar's shoulder and said, "No, that's not true. That's not a real fear. Is it?" Du Shar just laughed.

A few paces later, Bright asks, "There are ogres? Dragons?"

"Oh, yes!" Leesee said. "Hideous. Awful. Want to hear all about them?"

"No, I'm good."

Late afternoon the knights caught up with Rend who

seemed to be on point, alerting them to something. They stalked a young wereboar of about the same size that Bright had encountered on her first day. They removed the hams, the back two legs, and cleaned it. Shar decided it was safe enough for a fire and it was soon roasting on a wooden spit. Du Shar's wolf, Rend, busied himself eating the rest of it raw.

Shar posted a triangle of sentries to stand watch around the perimeter. The rest gathered near the fire, slicing thin strips of meat as it cooked. Shar brought out a decanter and made a toast. "To my knights, to those gathered 'round, and those soon to be." Du Shar said, indicating Bright. She took a sip and passed it to Leesee.

Leesee grinned and said, "We now have a Holy Quest! To Bright and the Holy Quest!" She sipped and passed it. The example had been set. Everyone drank to the quest and to Bright.

When it came to Bright, she raised the bottle and said, "I never had a sister, now I have many. To my Sisters!" Everyone approved. In another place, they may have cheered, but this was not the place.

She took a sip and recognized the draught as Water Sprite spirits. She immediately felt warm, confident, and self-assured. "I've had this before. Sariel had a bottle. He said it was very rare."

Shar scoffed. "It is rare if you don't know where to look. Is he your mate?"

"Sariel?"

"Yes, the large male." All the knights were listening for her answer.

"I guess not. I'm really not sure what he would say. I'm finding it a difficult question. I guess it should be easy, but it's not." Bright shrugged.

Shar said, "I don't like him. He makes my skin crawl. But I find myself frequently thinking ... thinking about what a strong warrior he would make. I imagine the daughter we could create. A warrior of legend."

Bright smiled. "Yes, I can see that."

"Is he big?" Leesee asked.

"Yes, you've seen him."

"No, I mean, you know. His thingee. Is it as big as he is? Does it match his size, or is it tiny."

"That's an embarrassing question, Leesee."

"Have you seen it, or not?" Dahni pressed.

Bright hesitated, but everyone was waiting for an answer. "I have seen it. I would say it is quite proportional," Bright said then covered her face with her hands, embarrassed.

"So how does that work? Would it even fit?" Leesee asked. Shar looked amused.

"It wouldn't fit. If it were forced in there, you know, pounded into place. It would probably hurt. A lot. Maybe even cause some serious damage," Dahni said, then added. "Did it hurt? When you bedded him?"

"That's absurd," Shar interrupted. "Of course it would work. You would accommodate it." Bright was relieved that she interrupted.

Leesee wasn't as satisfied. "Well? Did it hurt when you bedded him?"

"We never ... I've never ..."

"Why not. Did you think it would hurt?" From Dahni.

"My mother does it all the time. She likes it a lot. My fathers all seem very content. Even when they get all bruised up," Pyper added to the conversation.

"I know, right?" Leesee said. "Husbands seem to flock to her. I thought her new husband, the young one, was pretty. I told her that, and she said I could ride him if I wanted to."

"No. Sir Mahri said you could bed Alred only if you promised not to break him," Dahni corrected her.

"That's right. Sir Mahri told me that males are delicate creatures, and I had better not break him. Dahni should probably come to watch so that I don't get too rough." Dahni solemnly nodded her agreement.

"Males have their purpose, and are pleasant in their way, but cannot satisfy like a woman. A woman knows what a woman needs," Du Shar stated.

"I know, right?" Leesee started in again. "Bedding males are somewhat satisfying, but what is most exciting about men is that chance, that little chance, that you might get a child. But when it comes to being totally satisfied, I'll take a sister.

Dahni does these things and you just ... you just feel like your head is going to explode! I mean, actually explode." Leesee stood up so that she could gesture the event properly while Dahni giggled. "Then it keeps feeling so good that my eyes roll back in my head until I can see my brain ... it looks like sparkly lights. And then it builds and builds until—POW! It's like my head actually explodes. Blood and brains all over the bed, my eyeballs rolling on the floor until finally ..." Leesee stiffens falling to the ground on her back. "Whoa! Pure ecstasy. And then, I fall asleep." Dahni clapped while the sisters laughed.

"Leesee?" Bright asked. "Do you have *any* boundaries?"

The morning of the third day, Leesee and Dahni were braiding Bright's hair as the rest were breaking camp. Leesee said, "You should take off your top. I would. I'd walk in without my top so everyone would see the mark."

"I think I'll leave my top on."

"I think she's right. Take it off and show the mark. You're a Wolf Rider now!" Dahni said.

"Do you agree with everything Leesee says?"

"Nope. Only when she's right."

"I'm right a lot. It's a curse," Leesee said with absolute sincerity, and Dahni nodded.

"Du Shar!" Leesee called out. "Do we call Bright 'Ahn' now?"

"Not yet. Bright must pass all the Trials of Knighthood

first," Shar answered.

"You have to pass the Trials of Knighthood first," Leesee repeated.

"I heard, Leesee. Thank you," Bright said.

Chapter 11

GOBLIN SIGN

Late that afternoon, the forward scouts came back with Rend at their heels. Sir Elaine stepped in front of Du Shar and said two words. "Goblin sign."

"What's goblin sign?" Bright asked.

"Signs of goblin movement; Tracks, crushed or disturbed vegetation, broken twigs, and that sort of thing," Sir Elaine said.

Shar made a hand signal that was repeated by everyone. Soon the rest of the perimeter guards started rallying on Shar.

Elaine cleared the leaves from a spot on the ground and started making marks with a stick. "About a hundred paces north of here I bisected a trail with goblin sign heading from west to the east. After calculating the width of the trail versus the average walking pace of a goblin, I've isolated the differing prints and have determined that there are ten of them, fully armed and armoured judging by the depth of the track. My margin of error is estimated at one. The sign is extremely fresh, if we were making slightly better time, we would have run right into them."

"We will make an ambush." Shar began. "Sir Elaine, you are the senior knight. You will take the warriors at a run as far as you can up the trail without being discovered. Spread them out evenly on either side. Archers take to the trees if possible. Sir Pyper and Sir Willow will set up farthest down the trail, let them pass, then come up behind them while the rest closes the flanks. Rend and I will ride up as if stumbling into their camp. I will do my best to get them to pursue. Once they are between the two forces, and in the zone of destruction, Elaine will give the signal, and the attack will begin. When you hear the signal, attack with speed and violence. Let's get this over quick. Pyper, will you be able to keep Willow under control and quiet until the signal? I can move you two to the far end if you don't think you can do it. You two are my heavy hitters, I'd rather have you cut off their escape."

"Willow will wait. She can do anything," Pyper said. Willow didn't acknowledge the statement. She was already trembling slightly.

"Dahni, Leesee, take Bright with you but keep her out of it. She will get her chance soon enough. Let's go."

As they started off at a jog, Bright asked Leesee, "What did she mean to 'keep Willow under control'?"

"Pyper can keep her from going berserk … sometimes."

"Berserk?"

"You know, keep her from going wild, like batshit crazy."

"Our quiet little Willow?"

Dahni snorted. "You'll see."

Sir Elaine began to place the knights in position for the ambush. Leesee and Dahni found a copse of bushes near the tree they had selected and told Bright to stay hidden. They scrambled up the limbs until they found the one that gave them the best view. The two archers laid down on the branch to reduce their silhouettes. Sir Elaine made one final glance around the area, making sure everyone was hidden. Du Shar mounted her wolf, Rend, and ran off down the trail toward the goblins.

Du Shar and Rend disappeared from view. Long minutes ticked away and they saw nothing, heard nothing. Bright thought that she heard something move in the brush behind them, but when she peeked through, she didn't see anything. She felt alone. Bright felt like it had taken too long. Her limbs were aching, and she needed to move. She worried about Shar. Something must have gone wrong. She thought the others must have sensed it too, that something was wrong. She knew they could move almost silently. Had they left without her? Had the knights reached the same conclusion and already departed to find Shar, forgetting where they told her to wait? She couldn't see or hear anyone else.

Bright heard panicked, frantic breathing on the trail. Rend ran by, tail tucked between his legs. Next, Du Shar came into view. She appeared frightened. She tripped and fell down, screamed, and ran again. Bright was about to go to her aid when she saw them. Goblins. Sickly-looking light green skin, oily or slimy it reflected in the evening sun. They wore armour and bore cruel looking weapons. Rounded helms reached down the nape of their necks yet left an opening for their large bat-wing shaped ears to stick straight out of their heads. Wrinkled faces, long downward-hooking nose, and large mouths full of sharpened teeth. Most of the males were bald, but the hair they did have on their bodies was blood red. The stuff of nightmares.

Pyper sat in front of Willow. She held both her hands, softly whispering, "My love, look at me. Just look into my eyes. Breathe, I know you can hold on." Willow kept her gaze on Pyper's eyes, but her red face was pure rage. She was hyperventilating, the blood veins on her temples stood out. Her hands were trembling and causing Pyper pain as she held on too tight.

The goblins were closing in on Shar fast, they were shrieking with anticipation. It appeared that it took all of Du Shar's effort to keep a little distance ahead of the goblin pack. Then, all of the goblins were within the ambush, Du Shar's zone of destruction.

Sir Elaine gave the signal, and everything happened at once. Pyper pulled Willow to her feet and yelled, "GOBLINS!" Then backpedaled out of her way. In a flash, Willow drew her long blade, let out a blood-curdling scream and leapt onto the path. Willow was a dance of death, a ballet of steel and blood and rage. She spun and leapt, rolled and swung, screaming, her maniac frenzy cut into their ranks, leaving bloodied limbs in her wake. The screaming continued one breath after another.

The archers on both sides stood on their branches and rained death down upon the goblins, who were starting to panic and look for ways to escape. Du Shar ceased her panicked ruse and turned on her pursuers with both daggers whistling through the air. Rend had turned and slammed full speed into the goblin in the lead, sending it into somersaults. The rest of the knights charged in and the goblins were purely on the defensive, trying desperately to avoid death. But they had nowhere to go.

Bright realized that there was another movement. The sound she heard earlier was, in fact, another goblin, now standing very near her position and looking up at the backs of her new friends on the branch. The goblin curled his lips into a smug grin and lifted his bow, notching a heavy arrow.

There was no thought, no moment of preparation. Bright sprang from her cover, ran forward and smashed her small staff into the bow and the goblin arms that held it. Her momentum left her nearly leaning against the goblin. Up this close, she realized it was taller and heavier than she. It backhanded her with a strong, wiry arm and sent her sprawling backward. When she first hit the ground, she could see only a bright white light caused by the blow to her cheek. It cleared quickly, in time for Bright to see the leering goblin standing over her with a crudely forged blade raised for the strike. She heard several wet thudding sounds, and the sword fell from its hand. The monster fell beside her, with a half dozen arrows sticking out of its back. Dahni and Leesee stood on the limb, each with another arrow drawn and trained on the now dead goblin.

When the trio approached the trail, Shar took one look at

Bright's swollen eye and cheek, then turned on Leesee and Dahni in anger. "I thought I told you to keep her out of it."

"We did, but there was another archer, and she attacked it," they began. Bright saw Willow at the other end of the ambush site and headed that way, leaving the pair to their long explanation with the chieftain. An explanation that must have required lots of arm-waving and hopping around.

Willow was chopping on the body of a long-dead goblin. It was a mess, and Bright was hit by a wave of nausea at the sight of it. Willow was clearly exhausted and could barely raise her sword for the next strike. Her screams were now nothing more than a hoarse exhale.

Pyper said, "She has to wear herself out. Then I'll be there for her."

"Willow is lucky to have you."

"I'm the lucky one."

Bright stepped up to Willow after her last strike and placed her hand over hers, still wrapped around the sword. "Willow," Bright said softly.

Willow looked towards her, eyes unfocused. Bright gently took the sword from her grasp. Pyper was right there and picked her up and carried her a short distance away from the others, Willow's hands went around Pyper's neck, and she buried her blood-splattered face in Pyper's shoulder, and began to cry.

Bright held the sword away from her as she rejoined the group, refusing to look at it with her now queasy stomach.

"Ewww!" exclaimed Leesee. "We've got to get that cleaned up. Look at the chunks. Goblin pudding."

Dahni reached for the sword. "Goblin pudding is Willow's specialty. Here, I'll take care of it."

"Most of the kills belong to Willow," Leesee stated proudly. "We have to keep an eye on her in battle and stay out of her way. And most of the severed limbs are Willow's doing. We could go count them if you want. It's always interesting to wager on how many there will be. I love to watch her fight, it looks like a dance. A screaming rage dance."

"I can't believe our quiet, sweet Willow did all this," Bright said.

"When she was really young, a group of goblins took her and her family captive. We really don't know all that happened, but when they found her, she was standing over a goblin doing what you just saw. The only difference was it must have gone on a lot longer, all the goblin bodies looked like red goat cheese. She was completely covered in blood. They could tell that her family had been tortured until they died, probably right in front of her. No one ever said what the goblins probably did to her, but I know they did things. Horrible things, I'm sure. I guess she might have talked before that, but she hasn't said a word ever since."

"Oh, my God!" Bright exclaimed.

Leesee and Shar looked around. "Your God is here?" Leesee asked. "I wanna see."

"No. It's an expression, sort of an exclamation."

"Strange expression. Anyway," Leesee continued, "when Du Shar brought her for training, Pyper saw her and fell in love that very moment. POW! Like getting hit in the face with a rock. They fell in love with each other, and they've been together ever since. Isn't it romantic?"

Chapter 12

COR MALIA

With the delays, it was well past midnight when they arrived at the edge of the town. Du Shar had ridden into camp earlier. Now she met them with another Wolf Rider, only to be seen as a shadow sitting upon her beast. As they spoke with Sir Elaine, the other wolf sniffed the air. Then the dark rider headed straight for Bright. The warrior actually leapt from her mount to land in front of Bright.

She stood before her, long black hair unbraided, and allowed to fall over her face. She was holding a spear. She sniffed and slowly raised her head. Bright could see her eyes, but her face was shadowy, indistinct. Her voice a harsh whisper, Bright heard her say, "What is this?"

Bright was suddenly afraid when she realized the other knights had stepped back, all except Leesee and Dahni who remained on either side.

Leesee spoke up first, as always. "This is Bright. She's The

Elvenstar. Kerridwyn named her. You know what else? Kerridwyn even gave us a ...." The dark warrior shoved Leesee to the ground.

"Alanna, we have much to discuss. For now, let's allow the young ones to get some much-needed rest." Du Shar had ridden up and interrupted the encounter. "Pyper, would you see if your mother will allow Bright to stay with you for now. It is too dark for her to learn to negotiate the trees."

"Of course, Du Shar. Mother will welcome her."

"Sister Bright, welcome to Cor Malia. The center of our border, The Heart of Hope," Du Shar said.

Through unkempt hair, Bright felt the Wolf Rider's gaze burning through her for another moment, then she mounted and rode off beside Shar.

Sir Elaine issued them brief orders, mainly to sleep until fully rested, and sent them on their way.

"That was Ahn Alanna. The one that came up to talk to you," Leesee said, dusting herself off. Then the five of them began walking towards the forge.

"I would hardly call 'What is this?' much of a talk."

"Oh, that's just how she is. Ahn Alanna is Du Shar's second in command. She's always in charge if Du Shar's gone, and sometimes when she's here. She can be a little stern."

Dahni snorted.

"She's a great warrior. Probably the best one ever. Most of

us think she could even beat Du Shar, but she has never challenged her. Not once. They are very close. Some of the knights don't like her so much, but you couldn't name anyone else you'd rather have with you in battle."

"You, Pyper, Willow, Bright ..." Dahni started her list of names.

"Okay, but has she ever been in a battle that was lost? Ever?" Leesee asked.

Grudgingly, Dahni answered, "No."

"I don't think I should have made your list," Bright said to Dahni.

"You saved us! We would have been eaten by now if you hadn't smacked that goblin. Soon there would have been nothing left of us but goblin poo."

"No, the knights would have killed it before it got to eat most of us," Leesee said.

"Yup, you're right!" Dahni cheerily agreed.

Leesee and Dahni said goodnight and left as they approached a massive stone building. Smoke still curled from a couple of the many chimneys.

"This is The Great Forge. Willow and I stay here with my mother and fathers. The living quarters are around back, it's not as hot there."

"How many fathers do you have?" Bright asked.

"Five now," Pyper replied. "Mother just got a new one.

He's young. He's the one that Leesee wants to try."

"But one is your ... biological father, right?"

"I guess so, but there's no way to tell which one."

They came to a thick, reinforced door. Pyper pounded on it, and they waited. Shortly after the knock, a tiny window opened, and they heard a voice shriek. "My babies!" Then the sounds of bars being lifted and the door opened to reveal the heaviest-set elf Bright had seen so far. She appeared stouter and stronger than Pyper.

"My babies are back! Oh, my babies!" She ran out and hugged Pyper and Willow at the same time and took turns kissing them on the cheek. She finally let them go and tightened the simple linen robe she was wearing. A male elf dressed in a similar robe was standing back at a respectful distance. "Who is your new friend?" Sir Mahri asked Pyper with a smile.

"Mother, this is Bright, The Elvenstar. The Goddess named her. Bright, this is my mother, her name is Sir Mahri."

"Nice to meet you, Sir Mahri," Bright said.

"Stop it. If you are a friend of Pyper, it's just Mahri for you. Come in. You must be starving. Alred, would you be a dear and see to their bath. I'll wake the others. If they miss out on the stories, I'll never hear the end of it."

Alred gave Pyper and Willow a quick hug. "I'm so happy to see you back. You're not injured, are you? I see Lady Bright's eye, I'll fetch some ointment. Oh my! You both smell horrible. Was there a contest to see who could get covered in

the most blood? Willow, I'm afraid you won that contest."
Willow grinned as Alred ushered them down the hall. "Off to
the bath with the lot of you, then we'll all meet in the
kitchen."

Alred led them to a room with a large stone pool set level
with the floor. Water flowed in one side in a horizontal sheet,
and away through a gap on the other side. "Just throw all
your clothes against the wall over there. I'll see if I can get the
stains out. You ladies can find Lady Bright something to wear
after you bathe, can't you? I'm going for some ointment." He
left without waiting for a reply.

Willow and Pyper immediately began shedding their
clothes and throwing them in a pile. "Just throw everything
there. Alred will sort it out later."

They were scrubbing themselves when Alred popped back
in. "Lady Bright, I'll leave the ointment right … Oh! I am so
sorry!" He said when he saw the mark of the Wolf Rider.
"Please accept my apologies. Ahn Bright. No one told me. I
didn't know you were an Ahn. And here I am acting so
disrespectful. Pyper, why didn't you correct me the first
time?" He looked like he might cry. "Did I lock your wolf
outside? Oh no, I'll go let it in immediately."

"It's fine, Alred. She will be an Ahn soon, but not quite yet.
You haven't been disrespectful. You will hear all about it. Her
wolf is still at Kerridwyn's Pool."

"If you say so. I'm so confused. You'll find her something
suitable to wear, won't you? It's going to take me hours to get
all the blood out. Just call me if you need help. I can make
some quick adjustments if you need me to." He shuffled for a

moment, gave a quick bow, and then gathered up their bloody clothes and ran out.

"He's so sweet," Pyper said. "And he is very good with alterations. Just let him know if you need something taken in or let out."

"He is cute too. I can see why Leesee talked about him. He could have been a model where I'm from."

"A model what?"

"Oh, a … never mind."

"Mother will let you use him if you like. It might help you sleep. Shall I ask her?"

"No!" Bright responded a little too quickly. She added, "But thank you."

Bright was self-conscious about walking nude down the hall to Pyper's room, but they made it without passing anyone. They brushed their hair, leaving it unbraided, then excitedly went about finding Bright some clothes. Willow found an outfit that fit her well enough, although Bright had some reservations about the low-cut top revealing her mark, it seemed to bring about some embarrassing attention.

Bright realized how hungry she was once they entered the expansive kitchen and inhaled the pleasant aroma. Her stomach made an audible growl. Mahri and all five of her husbands were there and dressed for dinner. Bright was introduced and made welcome. Then they all sat around while Pyper told the story about all that had happened since she and Willow left. Bright did wish that Pyper had left out the part about being named by the Goddess and the Holy Quest to protect her given to all the Knights of the Realm. After they heard that there was an immediate attitude change and she was given more respect than she thought she deserved.

Once they had finished dinner and the story, they went back to Pyper and Willow's quarters. There were two beds. Pyper and Willow quickly disrobed and plopped into one. She started to get into bed when she heard Willow loudly clear her throat. Bright looked up to see Willow disapprovingly shaking her head and wagging a finger at her.

"Willow is wondering what you are doing getting into bed with clothes on? Do people do that where you are from? Here it is considered very rude. You don't know what you've been sitting in. Besides, it isn't healthy." Willow was nodding to indicate that is exactly what she was 'saying.'

"I'm sorry … Willow." She corrected her faux pas and went to bed.

Bright's sleep was interrupted on numerous occasions when Willow would awaken screaming at the top of her lungs. The first time it happened, Bright sprang out of bed, looking for goblins. Each time Pyper would console Willow, and the two of them would go right back to sleep. It took Bright much longer.

The bedroom had no proper windows. There were wide, narrow openings high up on the walls, but they didn't let enough sun through for her to realize the time. Consequently, it was nearly midday before Bright awakened to find herself alone in the room. She headed for the kitchen.

"She's awake. Willow, go get mother and Alred," Pyper said as soon as Bright entered the kitchen. Willow left immediately. Bright noticed that Leesee and Dahni were there, presumably waiting for her to wake up.

"What's going on? Am I late for something?" Bright asked.

"We thought you would sleep all day. Willow will get mother. Then you'll see. It's all very exciting!" Pyper told her.

"You're supposed to yell, 'Oh, my god!' when something is exciting or awful. Right Bright?" Leesee said.

"Well, there's no requirement to."

"You know what else, Pyper? Where Bright's from, cows and crap are considered holy," Leesee added.

"And shit. Shit is holy too. I heard Bright say it," Dahni contributed.

Bright smiled. "Okay, I'm going to say it just for you. Oh, my god! What's going on?"

Leesee solemnly approached her and whispered, "Sir Mahri is coming." As if that should mean something to her. Then louder, she added, "You should take off your clothes and stand on the bench."

"What?" Bright said just before the door flew open.

Alred rushed in with an armload of cords and measuring devices which he dumped on the table. "Oh my, oh my."

"Oh, my god!" Leesee shouted helpfully.

"Ladies, what did I tell you? Mahri will be here any second." He put his hands on his hips. "Why isn't she naked and standing on the bench like I asked? Mahri is very busy today."

Leesee turned to Bright. "I told you."

She protested as the girls tried to undress her. A distressed Alred kept saying, "Hurry up!" And then Mahri entered the room.

"What's going on here?" Mahri shouted. "Why isn't she prepared?"

"I don't know, Mahri. We tried, she won't do it. What should I do?" Alred was nearly crying again.

Mahri walked up to Bright and asked, "Do you know why they call me Sir Mahri?"

Bright hesitated then said, "Because you're a knight?"

"I am a knight, it's not a question. And I was a knight before I became a smith."

"I believe it." Bright was taken aback by her presence. This wasn't the same attitude she experienced when she arrived and met Pyper's mom. Now she was indeed talking to Sir Mahri.

"Last night Pyper told us that Kerridwyn herself gave the Knights of the Realm a Holy Quest. Is that true?"

"Yes. I heard Kerridwyn say that," Bright hesitantly replied.

"I am a knight. I am Sir Mahri. But you think because I am

a smith now, that Kerridwyn's words do not apply to me?"

"No."

"No? They don't apply?"

"I think she meant all the knights," Bright said, confused and wondering what she did wrong.

"Sir Mahri, she looks like she's going to cry," Leesee said.

Mahri softened. "I'm sorry, child. I think Kerridwyn's charge applies to me as well. In some ways, more than most. If we are to keep you safe, you need more than fierce warriors at your side, you need armour. I want to be the one to build you that armour. I want to be a part of the Holy Quest. One day I want to sit around the fire with my ancestors and tell the story of how I built the armour that helped to protect The Elvenstar. Now, do you understand?"

"Yes, I'm sorry."

"There's no need to be sorry, but you need to remove your clothing and stand on the bench."

"Told ya," Leesee said.

"Yup, she did," Dahni added.

Once an embarrassed Bright was standing on the bench, Mahri told her to stand straight and relax her arms. Immediately Leesee yelled, "Oh, my god! You're beautiful!" Then asked, "Did I do that right?"

Bright laughed a bit and said, "Yes, and thank you."

"She should have added 'holy shit!' Right, Bright?" Dahni asked. Bright laughed again.

Soon it was all business. Mahri taking measurements and calling them out to Alred to record. Every circumference and calibration was made twice. Once she had everything she needed from the waist down, Sir Mahri had Bright stand on the floor, and she took all the top measurements, to include her head and face. Mahri held up cards of differing colors and held them against Bright, a few she left out, the rest she returned to the deck.

Finally, Mahri told Bright she had everything she needed. She gave her a swat on the butt and told her to get dressed. She left the kitchen, looking at her notes.

"That took long enough," Du Shar said.

Bright jumped and asked, "How long have you been here?"

"Since you stepped on the bench. Get her dressed and ready, and meet me at my quarters." Shar was addressing her archers.

Leesee and Dahni quickly braided her hair, and together they left the forge, stepping into the brilliant afternoon sun. This was the first time Bright had seen the northern expanse in the daylight. She was a little shocked. Elves were moving here and there. Wolves wondered about, some were clearly unbonded Protectors. There were many buildings set among tall trees. Most of those were built of stone and thick timber, all had narrow, horizontal windows or openings very high up to guard against goblin intrusion. There were gardens and flower beds and streams. She thought the community appeared peaceful, beautiful, and vibrant. Not at all the military encampment, she envisioned.

As the duo led her through the village, they pointed out a long building in the distance they called The Great Hall. A paved Village Circle was found in front of The Great Hall. As they walked, Bright only saw one child playing under the watchful eye of a parent, and he protectively picked her up as they walked by. Burros pulled carts, and vendors shouted from stalls.

Finally, they arrived at a massive tree where Du Shar was waiting. "Welcome, Bright, to my home. You are looking quite Elven, I approve. This will be your home as well. You may stay as long as you desire," Du Shar said, then embraced her. "I understand your fear. I will not ask you to do anything that you cannot. Yet you will need to face your fears, and to overcome them."

Bright looked up and felt the grip of pure terror as if icy fingers strummed down the length of her spine. The tree was enormous. Long ladders rose to a small landing, only to have another ladder on the other side. And another platform after that with another ladder, and so forth. Until they ended at the massive branches that formed the dwelling itself. Bright was no expert, but the house must have been almost forty feet off the ground, after a straight-up climb.

"You want me to climb up there?" Bright asked.

"Yes, in time."

Bright stopped looking up, placed her hands on her knees, and vomited.

"Holy crap!" Leesee said and looked to Dahni for approval, who nodded sagely.

Du Shar held her braids back while Bright emptied her stomach. When she was finished, she was still shaking, and Shar simply held an arm around her until she regained some control.

They sat cross-legged at the bottom of the tree, and Shar explained the rationale behind their choice of dwellings. Bright learned that the ladders which spiraled up the tree served a defensive purpose. Many of the ladders were hung on metal brackets that could be detached and pulled up or dropped to prevent enemies from following them. Every ladder ended in a landing, with another ladder on the other side. There were lines to connect one tree to platforms on adjacent trees so they might slide from one to another. Most of their daily activities were conducted on the ground, but the trees made a safer place to rest, to sleep. Nearly every tree-dwelling had a stone building at its base where many activities, such as cooking and bathing, were performed. Although climbing to the residence was time-consuming, it was worth it for the safety it provided. Not to mention, it kept one's body fit and mind sharp. Getting down was much quicker and required almost no exertion. There were ropes, pulleys, and counterweights that allowed the elves to simply step into a loop, and jump off the platform to drop safely and gently to the ground. This same system was used to easily haul supplies up into their homes.

Shar explained that her dwelling was more elaborate than most simply because she was chieftain. It was a privilege of rank. A windmill placed in the upper branches kept water flowing into her home, while drains took the excess away. Her home was the largest with many rooms, including a kitchen.

"So now I need to know. Do you trust me? Do you trust me to keep you safe and unharmed?" Shar asked Bright.

"I do trust you, Shar. But that doesn't change the fact that I am so afraid that I might … well, vomit again. I am afraid that I won't be able to move. I might freeze on a ladder and not be able to go up or down. And I am afraid to let all of you see how afraid I am. Oh, this isn't making any sense."

"I understand," Shar began. "I was speaking the truth when I told you that I have many genuine fears. As chieftain, I have to overcome them. And as The Elvenstar, I am asking you to overcome yours. Let them be there, lurking. But take the right action in spite of them."

"I'll try."

"I want to start one step at a time. No ladders today. We will take the descent lines—up." Shar helped Bright to her feet. "Leesee, go ride a line down. Dahni, on my signal, will ride the counterweight down. We will need the extra weight with the two of us. My husbands know of the issue and will be there to help. One last thing, Leesee, don't try to be funny."

The two nodded and scurried up the ladders. Once they reached the top, Shar said, "Now watch Leesee."

Bright saw Leesee on a platform at the base of the dwelling. Leesee stepped to the edge and turned towards the tree trunk. She pushed off the platform with one foot, the other in a rope, and started sinking to the ground. At the same time, a heavy counterweight rose into the air. In seconds Leesee was standing inches above the ground.

"See? Easy," Leesee said with a smile.

Shar stepped up and placed her foot in the loop while Leesee held on to the rope. There were other loops tied higher into the line, a little above her head. Leesee stepped off as Shar took her place, but remained grasping the rope. Speaking to Bright, Shar said, "Come over here. Place your foot on top of mine. See those loops? Place one of your hands through it and then grasp the rope, just like I'm doing." Leesee helped her through the process. "Now take your other hand and wrap it around my waist, pull tight." Bright did.

Shar asked, "Are you ready?" Eyes wide, Bright nodded. "Then, keep your eyes on mine." Bright did, at first.

Shar waved, and Dahni leapt onto the counterweight. Slowly they began to ascend. Bright looked up, saw the platform getting closer, she saw Dahni descending on the counterweight. Jenny returned her gaze to Shar, and Shar kissed her.

"I told you to keep your eyes on mine, see what happens when you don't listen." Shar was smiling. At the same time, Dahni came by the other direction saying, "Fun, isn't it? Woohoo!"

Before she could think of much else, hands were pulling her onto a platform. She was being held between three men who were walking her up a stair, Shar close behind. They kept her close between them until they sat her into a comfortable chair in what appeared to be an average room. Then they walked off, and Bright found that Shar was seated on a stool close by.

"How are you?" Shar asked. "Was it as bad as you thought?"

"I'm ... I'm okay," Bright said.

"Just sit there for now. My husbands will bring you food and something to drink. Your friends will be up soon."

Bright looked around, the windows were covered so that she could not see out. "So I'm like ... way up there?" She gripped the chair. "How do I get down? Shar, I can't move."

"Shhh. You got here because you trusted me. You'll get down because you trust me. For now, just sit. Relax."

One of the men brought her a glass. It was the Water Sprite spirits. Bright took a drink without questioning what it was. And she relaxed, felt more confident. She finished the glass, and it was gently removed from her hand by the male.

Leesee and Dahni entered the room. Both with raised hands shaking their hips. "Oh yeah, Bright beat her fear. The Elvenstar can do anything!" They chanted. Du Shar's husband came back down the stair with another glass, intended for Bright, which Leesee snatched from his hand. "Thank you, Buckson." She drank half and handed the rest to Dahni.

"Buckson, you might want to bring the bottle down," Shar said.

"I think you are right, my love. Perhaps two."

Leesee and Dahni sat on the floor at Bright's feet while Buckson, Drew, and Rondal, Shar's husbands, brought food and drink. They talked of trivial and light-hearted things. They speculated on how grand Mahri's armour would look on Bright. And how spectacular she would be riding the Great White Wolf, Spook. They talked about food and flowers and inconsequential things. They spoke until the moon rose high above the trees.

Leesee and Dahni fell asleep on the floor. Shar stood in front of the chair and took both of Bright's hands. She looked into her eyes, and Bright looked back. Bright saw the thin scar, the one that started above her right eyebrow, ran down her cheek. She thought it somehow enriched her beauty. Like an old painting, the flaw enhanced the beauty and complexity of the piece as a whole.

"We have only a little way to travel, do not take your eyes off me," Shar said and started moving backward, pulling her up from the chair.

Bright felt the effects of the spirits. She felt confident, a sense of well-being, emotional warmth and empathy, and a willingness. A willingness to do what? Merely a general willingness, she supposed. At the moment, Bright was willing to watch Shar. To hold her hands and follow her.

They went up a flight of stairs. Bright noticed Shar's mouth, her full lips. Often downturned and serious, it made more of an impact when she smiled. Everything brightened.

Bright looked at the mark of the Wolf Rider upon her left

breast. Shar's mark wasn't swollen and angry but smooth and distinct. Bright wanted to touch it. To feel its smoothness.

A turn. More stairs. A door closed. Shar pulled Bright's corset laces free, and let it drop. Bright breathed in a deep breath, unrestricted. Shar unbuttoned the top, pushed it off her shoulders with warm hands. Deft fingers released her braids. Soon she was free of the rest. Relaxed and with the sensation of floating, she was laid down on the cool, soft bed. And Shar slid in close beside her.

Shar lay next to her, softly stroking her hair. Bright felt the warmth of Shar's flesh against her. Bright remembered how she wanted to touch the mark upon her breast. So she did. Softly she probed every edge. When she looked back up, Shar kissed her.

In her life, she had only lustfully kissed one other, Sariel. That was passionate and rough. This was passionate and soft. They kissed again and again, hands exploring without thought or conscious direction. Shar kissed her neck—it was electric. She moved down her chest, kissing continually. Shar's hands glided down her waist, her hips, and her legs, then softly back up the center of her thigh. Soft as a whisper, as powerful as lightning. Bright's heart raced. She could feel Shar's long hair slowly gliding down her skin, her breasts. Once the sensation reached her waist, she briefly thought of Sariel and supposed that she should protest. She breathed the word "Shar." That was all. And it didn't sound anything like a protest when she heard herself say it.

During the night, a strong gust of wind rocked the tree and made it sway and shiver. Bright gasped, then felt strong arms and legs around her, holding her close. She slept peacefully through the rest of the night.

Chapter 13

SIR RHAINE

As the sun began to rise, Bright found herself on the platform with the descent lines. Shar told her to keep her eyes on the horizon, and it helped. It also helped that they were holding hands. The loop of the descent line hovered a few inches off the platform floor. There were two loops affixed further up, for her hands.

"Leesee and Dahni will be waiting below. I assume they are not alone, Sir Elaine requested to help with your training. The rope will stop inches before the ground. The counterweight is set for a slow descent, there is no need to brace yourself. You grip the loops above your head, place one foot in the lower loop, then simply stand on the platform with the other. When you are ready, lean back and push off. Glide down, keeping your eyes on the horizon. You will slowly spin, but there is a horizon in every direction. Today I won't encourage you to enjoy the view." Shar smiled at her. "Your training begins now. Nothing will be easy from this moment forward. Begin this day by showing your sister knights a woman that will overcome anything. A woman they can trust to keep them safe, just as they are all sworn to defend you."

Shar helped her get her wrists through the loops. Bright gripped the rope tight. She placed one foot in the lower loop, her legs were trembling. Shar's firm grip on her waist guided her to the edge of the platform. Like the night before she kept her eyes on Shar's face. "Anything else?" Bright asked nervously.

"Yes. Try to refrain from screaming or showing any emotion. They are expecting that. Disappoint them. Free your wrists from the loops first, and grasp the rope. Support your weight with the rope and remove your foot. Then simply step down and greet your sisters like the whole event was commonplace. If you can do this … it will be an achievement that will set the tone for the rest of the day. There is only one other thing." Shar stood on her toes and kissed her. Then she whispered, "Stiffen your leg." And then Shar pushed Bright backward off the platform.

Bright saw the platform pass, the tree bark was a blur. Bright found herself leaning back more than expected. She had been holding her breath, but as she turned and saw the sunrise on the horizon, she began to breathe again. Orange and gold, it was beautiful. She spun back towards the tree and looked down, even though she was told not to. She saw the faces of her friends staring up, mouths agape. Seeing them actually made her smile. They helped her off the rope, which jerked upwards as the counterweight fell.

"Good morning, Sisters," Bright said. "Did you see the

sunrise? It was lovely." Bright was still trembling slightly. However, her friends couldn't see it.

"That's it? No screaming? Don't you want to vomit?" Leesee said.

"Not today."

"Well, that's disappointing," Dahni said with a pout. "We told Sir Elaine you would vomit."

Sir Elaine cut in, getting to the business at hand. "The first part of your training will concentrate on physical conditioning. Of course, conditioning takes time, and you'd collapse if we tried to do it all day. I have a schedule we will stick to that will encompass conditioning, interspersed with an introduction to the bow. What is left of the afternoon will be dedicated to the staff and other martial skills. In the evenings, we will talk about tactics and history. Leesee and Dahni will work with you on archery and conditioning, and I will take over the rest of your instruction. Warriors must be flexible, so expect deviations in our schedule."

"Sir Elaine spends a lot of time with the scholars. She's brilliant," Leesee said.

"She is," Dahni agreed. "I sure hope you're bonded this time, Elaine."

"Yup, this is her third try. You only get three," Leesee added.

"Let's talk about the schedule," Elaine said. "There's already been a change. You must meet with Sir Rhaine straight away. She's our bowyer. She has been ordered by Du

Shar to take measurements just as Sir Mahri did for the armour. Du Shar met with Sir Rhaine yesterday."

"How exciting!" Leesee exclaimed. "Let's go."

"I'm not going to have to stand around naked, am I?" Bright asked.

Leesee looked at her. "No. Why on earth would you? I've never seen anyone naked in the Bowyery. Whoa! Maybe we all should. I wonder what they would do. It would be sad if no one said anything."

The Bowyery was another large stone building, not as large as The Forge. Next to the building were neat stacks of lumber, curing in the sun. There were shallow pans filled with water where strips of wood were held between adjustable pegs to bend and shape them. Bright thought it was very much like an anthill with all the bustling activity. Elves moved about, carrying items in and out of the many doors, all propped open. Fletchers crafted arrows, while bowyers crafted their bows. Deep shelves lined the walls, so tall that ladders were needed to reach the goods at the top. Every shelf was labeled and packed with neat rows of boxes, envelopes, and crates. Some held lumber of differing types of wood. The craftsmen sawed, planed and glued on their workbenches. The aroma of cut wood and glue filled the air.

Sir Elaine headed for an ancient-looking Elf standing before a table displaying technical drawings and mathematical calculations. There were two other elves behind her, older but not ancient like Sir Rhaine.

"Sir Rhaine, Du Shar asked me to report to you with

Bright. She asked that Bright be measured," Elaine said.

Sir Rhaine looked up with cloudy eyes. She was balding, and what hair she did have was white and cropped short. Her skin hung loosely on a skeletal frame, even her ears were wrinkled. Her hands shook slightly. She ambled around the desk, often holding it for support. She peered closely at Bright as if trying to focus.

"So you are The Elvenstar," Rhaine stated. There was nothing feeble about her voice.

"Yes, ma'am."

"How is it that someone who is not an Elf, and not a knight, has earned the mark of a Wolf Rider?" Rhaine poked a bony finger into Bright's mark, causing her to gasp and wince.

"I really don't know," Bright replied.

"Kerridwyn said she was Elven now. I heard her," Leesee said.

"Is that so?"

"Yup. And if you don't mind, I'm just going to go now, and look around."

Sir Rhaine barked, "Leesee! There is no magic bow. Bows are crafted, they are science and art. There is no magic bow! Stop digging around my shop and getting everything out of order."

"Dahni told me there was one. A magic bow that you have hidden. And if I find it, I can have it!" Leesee said, and Dahni giggled.

Rhaine turned back to Bright. "Is that what you are looking for? A magic bow bewitched to instantly bestow upon you the skill others have worked for years, for a lifetime, to develop?"

"No, I want to train. I want to ..."

"Look around you. Do you think these young knights wanted to train? They had to. They worked and trained to survive and to ensure the survival of those they love and those they do not even know."

Bright did look at them, they appeared as stunned as she felt. And she noticed another near the door. Standing with head slightly bowed, looking up through long black hair. It was Ahn Alanna. She wore black face paint. Under her eyes and down the outside of her cheeks with four lines that extended from her upper lip and down her chin, giving her a skeletal visage. It wasn't meticulously applied, she did it with her hands, Bright could tell. This is why her face was shadowy and indistinct when she was first confronted two nights ago.

"Few knights are chosen for The Bonding. Those few worked harder than the rest, sacrificed more. Years of hard work, injuries and suffering brought them to the point where they would be allowed to sit around the Bonding Circle, and hope to be chosen. Hope to be bonded as a Wolf Rider of the Clan."

Bright noticed that the entire Bowyery was hushed, everyone was listening. Tears began to flow down her cheeks.

146

"Look at Sir Elaine. She does everything that is expected and more. Then she goes to her quarters to study. She studies the histories, the lessons learned from past battles, science, and more. Sir Elaine has been to two other Bondings. This is her third and final try. How do you know that the wolf you have taken was not meant for her? Or for Leesee or for Dahni? You cannot comprehend the heartbreaking loss one feels when walking away from the Circle without a bond."

Sir Rhaine began to stumble and leaned against the table for support. "Well, I can tell you. I was there once, a long time ago. I will tell you that the pain you feel at that moment—is just as potent hundreds of years later. LEAVE ME!"

Bright headed for the door. She could not stop the tears but was determined to make it out of there before she broke down completely. She nearly ran into Ahn Alanna, who did not step aside. Bright saw Alanna's contempt. She walked around, headed out the door, and started running.

Bright had no idea where she was running, she just wanted to get away. She thought she heard her friends running up behind her, so she sped up. Bright ran as fast as she could.

When they finally found Bright, she was lying face down on the ground crying into her folded arms.

Leesee cautiously approached her. "Bright?" They all sat down nearby.

"Sir Rhaine was very harsh. I want you to know she is usually cordial to everyone. I think she wasn't feeling well," Elaine said.

"No. Sir Rhaine is right. I don't belong here. I don't deserve armour or bows or all of you looking out for me." Bright sat up. "I don't deserve Spook." She looked up. "Elaine, I'm going to give Spook to you."

The Knights were visibly startled at this. "You can't give Spook to me. You're already bonded."

"Sure I can, I'll let you have him. We'll make it official at the ceremony."

"You're marked."

"I'll cut it off. I'll burn it off!"

"You'll die. Spook will die," Leesee said. "Your life and Spook's life are connected. There is no giving him away."

"I just want to go home."

"I understand," Elaine said. "I have only known you a short time, but I am sure that you have a lot of people depending on you there. And lots of friends that miss you. It must be hard."

Bright knew that wasn't true, but said, "Sir Rhaine is right. I'm soft. I have no skills, I have taken what does not belong to me."

"But what about what you've given us, Bright?" Dahni said. "You've given us hope. And a Holy Quest."

"And taught us when to say 'holy crap,'" Leesee added.

"Here is what I am thinking," began Elaine. "You could come back with us. Start your training ... and show Sir

Rhaine that she is wrong. Since you have arrived here, you have made friends with an angel, a huge pretty one. You have spoken at length with our Goddess. Bonded to the White Wolf, and without any real training, you attacked a goblin and saved our knights."

Leesee interrupted, "Elaine left out a bunch. You conquered your fear of trees, vomited like an ogre, got some great friends ... oh, and slept with the Chieftain. And, whoa, that must have been great! You moaned a lot. Dahni and I were trying to guess what she was doing to you."

"Yeah, you'll have to tell us," Dahni added.

"Boundaries! Can't we have some boundaries?" Bright said exasperated.

"Let's keep that one to ourselves. I wouldn't want Ahn Alanna to hear about it," Elaine said.

"What I am trying to say," Elaine continued, "is you could let us train you and know that you *do* belong here. You're our sister. And if I don't get bonded, I *want* to believe that it is because of you. That would fill me with pride. There have been many Wolf Riders, but few can say they were friends with Bright, The Elvenstar. Show everyone, show yourself what The Elvenstar is capable of."

"Okay. I'll try." Bright sniffed.

"Running was on my list of conditioning. We can cross that off the list. Good news, right?"

Chapter 14

TRAINING

It was a hard and long day for Bright. She was sore and exhausted. Leesee and Dahni had walked her back to Du Shar's quarters. Rend came up, sniffed, then walked back to a soft spot and laid back down.

Leesee said, "Dahni, go up and ride the line down, I'll get the counterweight."

"No. Thank you. Not tonight," Bright said, looking up at the ladder.

Trembling and jubilant after making the climb, Bright stepped onto the lower platform of the chieftain's quarters. Buckson met her and offered a hand in assistance.

"If I may say, Lady Bright, I am quite impressed."

"Thank you, Buckson," She said, quite proud of herself and wearing a triumphant smile.

"You will find them in the sitting room, Lady Bright."

"Them?"

"Du Shar and Ahn Alanna," He replied, patting her hand. Bright noticed the spear leaning against the railing.

The sitting room was up a short flight of stairs, no more than ten feet from where she now stood. It was where she nervously sat when she first arrived. Gallantly, Buckson placed her hand through his arm and led her up the stairs. Du Shar stood from the chair she used the night before. Bright thought it must be Shar's chair. Alanna stood nearby, staring through stringy black hair, as she always did. Bright felt a chill, a frisson that caused her goosebumps. Buckson must have felt her tremble, he gently squeezed her hand.

Shar stepped to Bright and gave her a quick hug. "I'm very proud of you."

"Yes, you found your way home. A great accomplishment. The second one I have witnessed today. The first was running from an old woman," Alanna spoke in her harsh whisper.

"Alanna!" Du Shar said.

The sarcasm hurt Bright and lit a spark of defiance. "Ahn Alanna, I am sorry you find me so disappointing. I wish I could be more like you, I am trying."

Ahn Alanna took two menacing steps forward. "You know nothing about me."

"I do. Leesee talks about you all the time."

"And tell me—the truth—what does she say?" She took another step forward. It took all the courage she had, but Bright did not step back.

"Lady Bright, may I offer you something to drink?" Buckson politely interrupted. Alanna glared at him briefly, then turned her attention back to Bright.

"No, thank you, Buckson."

"Very well then, I'll fetch you a glass of water," Buckson said and left.

"What does she say?" Alanna asked again.

"Alanna, what does it matter?" Shar asked.

"I don't mind. Leesee said you were the best warrior in the clan. Possibly ever. She said you had never been in a battle that was lost. That you and Du Shar were close and you had never challenged her. She said that there was no one else she would rather be with in battle."

"What else?"

"That's all I can recall, but there is one other thing."

"And that is?"

"I want you to stop pushing Leesee down. She doesn't show it, but I know it hurts her feelings."

Alanna stared at her. Bright could hear her breathing. Slowly Alanna smiled with her mouth, yet her brows remained furrowed. It terrified her more than anything she could have said.

"I agree to your request. You will take Leesee's place."

"Um, Hmmm." Buckson cleared his throat. "Lady Bright, here is the water I promised. Would you Ladies care for anything?"

"Yes." Alanna looked from Buckson to Shar. "Shar, may I use Buckson tonight?"

It was apparently a very unexpected request. Shar seemed lost in thought, but after long hesitation, Shar replied, "Of course, Alanna. Buckson, would you please go to Alanna's quarters?"

"Straight away, my love," he replied.

Alanna bumped Bright on the way past. Bright could see the platform from where she stood. Alanna grabbed her spear and leapt onto the descent rope, grasping it with only one hand. She swung out into the darkness and disappeared while the cable and pulley whirred.

Shar turned to Buckson, concerned. "Buckson, have a care. Alanna's in a fragile mood." *Fragile?* Bright wondered.

"I will be fine, love." Then by way of explanation, he turned to Bright. "I fathered a child once. My greatest achievement. Now I am frequently cursed to endure the tender affections of beautiful and powerful women." Buckson let out an exaggerated sigh. "We all have our burdens to bear." He said with a smile and a wink. Then he left to prepare.

Once he had gone, Bright asked, "Will he be okay? I don't think there is anything 'tender' about Ahn Alanna."

"He will probably be sore for a few days, but he will survive."

"Did you hear about what happened at the Bowyery?" Bright asked.

"Yes, I heard. I'm not happy with Sir Rhaine's behavior, but she has lived long enough to earn the right to defy me. I have a bow that will serve you well enough. Please put it in the past."

Shar continued, "You should know that I am very proud of you. You have accomplished much in only a couple of days. And, Sir Elaine says you are capable of running quite fast." She said the last part with a smile.

"Come, Bright. Let's get cleaned up. Your muscles must be in knots. Allow me to rub them smooth, or you will not be able to move by morning."

Bright lay upon the bed as Shar applied oil and massaged her back. The oil had a pleasant and relaxing fragrance.

"Shar?"

"Yes."

"Can I talk to you about last night?"

"Of course. Does it trouble you?"

"I've never been with a woman before. Or a man for that matter."

"Are you having regrets?" Shar asked.

"No. It's not that. That's not what I wanted to talk to you about. I was wondering ... that is if you wanted to ... I was wondering if tonight could be more about—well, more about you?"

"If that is your desire, yes."

"I may need some guidance."

Shar smiled, although Bright couldn't see it. "If there is a need, you shall have it. I think you can accomplish much on your own."

The next morning they met in the training grounds. Bright was made to do push-ups, pull-ups, and bent-over rows using metal weights with braided leather handles. All the while, Leesee and Dahni stood around her demanding more. Leesee was trying to explain that unless you do the exercise to complete exhaustion, your muscles won't build and tone. They always seemed to believe she could do more.

After a lengthy private discussion, they came back to where Bright was resting against a tree, trying to catch her breath. "Bright, was there someone in your world you really didn't like?" Leesee asked.

"What?"

"What was the name of someone you didn't like?" Leesee

repeated.

"I don't know. Why?"

"Come on, think about it. There must have been someone. Give me the name of someone you didn't like."

"You have to. Elven tradition," Dahni stated, and she appeared to be hiding something behind her back.

"Well, okay. There was a guy named Doug I didn't really care for. He used to say lots of hurtful things, and make fun of me," Bright admitted.

Leesee looked at Dahni, "Doug," she said.

"Bright, meet Doug!" Dahni said and proudly displayed a switch about two and a half feet long.

"And why do you have a stick you want to name Doug?" Bright asked.

"Because, when you aren't performing to the best of your abilities ... POW! ... There's Doug. Doug will motivate you to do your very best."

"You're not hitting me with a stick," Bright told them.

"It's a tradition. Besides, it's not me, it's Doug," Leesee said.

"An Elven tradition," Dahni added. "I thought you respected our traditions."

"I don't like this one."

"No one does," said Leesee, slowly shaking her head.

"No one does," agreed Dahni.

Bright met Doug one time that day, which caused her to yelp and knock out two more pull-ups.

While they were doing sprints, Ahn Alanna came by. She made Bright race her, allowing Bright a head start. Alanna caught her before the end and shoved her in the middle of the back, causing her to fall and scuff up her elbows. All she said was, "Too slow." And then walked away.

At archery training, Bright brought the bow that Du Shar had given her. Both Leesee and Dahni thought it was an excellent bow. The problem was Bright wasn't strong enough to draw it. Dahni promised to bring the bow she used as a child. They taught Bright how to string a bow, stressing that you only kept it strung if on patrol or before battle. Otherwise, it would lose its shape and power.

The quiver must be strapped on precisely the same way every time so that when you reached back, the arrows were always at your fingertips. They never let her pick up an arrow from a table or the ground. Only from the quiver. It developed a muscle memory they said, so that she could draw the arrow quickly every time.

The muscle memory drills were tedious. Exercises like drawing an arrow from the quiver and notching it properly. Leesee brought out a cord with black and red beads. She used it for counting and insisted that every movement be performed in slow motion—absolutely flawlessly—at least one thousand times in a row. No mistakes or she would have to start over. She wasn't allowed to even try it at full speed until she could accomplish this.

Training with Sir Elaine on the staff was a relief after hours spent with Leesee and Dahni. At least she could move around a bit. Elaine was incredible with the staff. She could make it float around her neck and body. She could spin it and release it into the air, only to dive and roll and catch it before it hit the ground. It was Elaine who had to slow down so that Bright could see what she was doing. The staff was a blur in her hands. Bright was able to impress Sir Elaine a little bit, having learned most of the basics from Sariel.

Inevitably, Ahn Alanna would happen by and find some flaw with Bright. It didn't matter how small. She would take every opportunity to humiliate Bright. It always ended with Bright getting shoved to the ground. When she found her sparring with Elaine, she would grab a staff and drop her to the ground so fast that Bright didn't even know how she did it. Then Alanna would make comments about how she was going to get her sisters killed with her incompetence.

In the evenings, they would meet at Du Shar's quarters. Sir Elaine would talk about history, Elven culture, battle tactics, and patrolling techniques. She would talk about the creatures of darkness in hushed tones as if speaking their names too loud would draw them out of the night.

"Let's talk about trolls," Elaine said. Leesee shivered. "Trolls are very tall, about nine feet. Some stories talk about ones even taller. They look thin and sinewy but don't let that fool you, they are exceedingly strong and fast. Very fast. For short distances, they can outrun a deer. They have thick, gray skin, and humongous flat noses. Have you seen a bat's nose up close? They are gross. Their ears are similar to goblins, they have very long arms, long fingers, and sharp claws."

"I'm afraid of them," Leesee said.

"Have you ever seen one?" Bright asked.

"Yes, once. We didn't get close. And we didn't attack it. I peed a little."

"As you know, goblins have rank, a hierarchy. They build strongholds, forge weapons and armour, and build armies. Trolls are usually solitary although the goblins have been known to press them into service from time to time. The worst thing about trolls is that they are very, very hard to kill. Entire platoons have been lost to a single troll. If your weapon penetrates their thick skin at all, their blood clots almost instantly. If for instance, many spears were to pierce a troll, the warriors would have to keep thrashing the spear around to keep the blood flowing. Arrows are almost useless unless you blind them. They can be blinded. However, their keen sense of smell and hearing keeps them going. Essentially you end up with an angry troll. Oh yeah, if Du Shar comes home, we stop talking about trolls. Listen to me, Bright, don't bring them up in her presence."

Leesee and Dahni were nodding, "That's very important."

"Why?" Bright asked.

"It's not for us to say," Elaine said. She looked at the archers. "None of us."

"Anyway, what it boils down to is that there are really only two ways to kill them. Cut off their heads, which poses a problem since they are so tall. To do that you will need to bring them down first. It's not easy. Or fire. Trolls are vulnerable to fire. Once they die, their flesh and bones will actually burn."

"So just drench them in oil and set it on fire," Bright said.

"And how do you drench them?" Elaine asked.

"I don't know, just pour it on them."

"When they see you, they attack. When trolls attack, warriors die. What you're saying is to walk up with a bucket of oil, which by the way you won't be walking around with on patrol, and pour it on?"

"How about have jars full of oil, and throw it at them?"

"Even if you managed to hit a rampaging troll with a jar of oil, how do you set it aflame?"

"I dunno, throw a torch?"

"Okay, so a troll is leaping around in a killing frenzy, you take the time to gather some dry wood, take out your flint and steel, and try to spark a fire? Then you need to make a torch. You can see that the logistics of setting them on fire is quite a problem."

"I guess you're right, but there must be a way."

"I hope you find it."

"I'll think about it," Bright said. "It bothers me."

Rondal brought in some food, and the conversation switched to less morbid topics.

Du Shar returned late and asked, "How goes the training?"

"I think it is progressing on schedule, Du Shar." Sir Elaine reported.

"That's good to hear. Thank you, knights. You all should know, I have to go check on the border villages and brief their captains. I have to see to the defenses. I'm taking Ahn Alanna and a platoon of Riders. We will leave at dawn and will be away for about a month. I'll head east first, then west all the way to Monlach, and be back at least a week before we leave for the Bonding Ceremony. For Bright, I am hoping there will be a Knighting first. But that depends on the four of you."

Leesee jumped to her feet and held up both hands. "I'll go, I'll go."

"I see you, Leesee. It's a small room. I'm taking the Wolf Riders; we have a lot of ground to cover. And I need your expertise here, with Bright."

"How will I know you're all right? How will I know you're safe?" Bright asked.

"I'll be fine." She told Bright. "The four of you can continue to use my quarters."

In the training yard the next afternoon, Elaine said, "Today we're going to do something different. Ahn Alanna is not going to stop bullying you unless you do something drastic. I thought of this long ago, but I was afraid to let her catch me teaching you. I'm sorry about that. Anyway, I am going to teach you how to counter when someone shoves you. It works just as well if an enemy tries to grab you or strangle you. The drawback is that it puts you on your back. But done right that can be for just a moment."

"Leesee will help me demonstrate. Leesee, you will be falling on your back, so be prepared." Leesee nodded eagerly. "Now Leesee is going to shove me, hard, just like Ahn Alanna has been doing to you."

Leesee shoved Elaine. Instead of resisting, she used that momentum. Elaine grabbed her upper arms and rolled back, placing a foot in her midsection. Elaine pushed up with her foot, and Leesee flew over. Elaine hung on and continued to use the momentum. In a flash, she was actually sitting on Leesee's chest, holding her fist poised for a strike to the face.

"There are many variations on this, and I will teach you. If you let them go, they will fall head first, and there will be a chance of serious injury. If you hold on, like I did, you can control their fall and put yourself on top for a blow to the head or throat. Ahn Alanna is a sister knight, so I want you to keep control. Let's not risk injuring anything except her dignity. However, I suggest a palm strike to the nose to keep her down long enough."

"Long enough for what?" Bright asked.

"Long enough for you to run away," Dahni said.

"Yes. That *is* what I meant. This is not a particularly difficult move, so if we train the rest of the afternoon, you should have it down. For us to take it from theory to execution, I will move to the next step. From now until Ahn Alanna returns, I will shove you from time to time, when you're not expecting it, of course. In time this move will become a natural reaction. You won't even have to think about it."

"If I run, she'll catch me."

"Move quickly, and you should have a good head start. Whatever the outcome, you have to do something, or she will not stop."

"Yeah, she hates you," said Leesee.

"Because I'm marked and not an Elven knight?" Bright asked.

"Partly. Mostly because you're sleeping with Du Shar," Dahni said.

"Oh," Bright said, then she thought about what that meant. Du Shar and Ahn Alanna must have been lovers. "Shit!"

"Yup," Leesee said solemnly. "Big shit. Dragon shit."

Bright quickly gained strength, and her endurance improved. Her muscles grew and toned. She was able to draw her bow, and target practice became her focus. The training grounds had ranges with targets placed all the way out to three hundred yards. There were towers at the beginning of the target range, and two found downrange.

Leesee began her instruction. "The targets really far away, starting at two hundred yards, you will shoot at, but the object is to get as close as you can to the center. Arrows won't normally penetrate armour at those distances. But it can help if there is an advancing horde. And you can always get lucky."

"I do expect you to be able to hit a target dead center consistently up to one hundred fifty yards. You'll need to raise the angle of the bow more and more as the distance increases. And you have to remember how much that is. It has to be done without a lot of thought, like an instinct. Takes a lot of practice. Then we'll move on to the towers and shoot the same targets at different levels. Or be on the ground and shoot the targets at an incline. That will be later. There's lots of math involved. Dahni can explain it better when the time comes."

"Math? I have to do math?" Bright said. "Oh, my God! I suck at math."

"You *have* to do the math," Dahni said. "Pretty much every Wood Elf is good with a bow ..."

"But few are its master," Leesee finished.

"Yes. And it's the details that make the difference. Like math," said Dahni.

"Like what math?"

"For instance, every time you take a shot from up high, like in a tree. You are firing at an angle. Every angle has a cosine. The cosine gives you the ground distance, that's the distance that gravity is affecting your arrow. The true distance will be different, longer. For instance, if you put a log between where you are in the tree and your target on the ground and measure it, that's the true distance, it's longer. So you multiply the true distance by the cosine, and that gives you the ground distance or the distance you would be firing if you and the target were on level ground. Switch places with the target and shoot at someone in a tree, and the angle is the same, so the ground distance is the same. And keep in mind that the angle of a drawn arrow is slightly different than the line from your eye to the target. Simple."

"No, it isn't."

"I learned the math, so can you. Leesee can sort of look at the problem and know the answer. She always knows the right answer, it just comes to her. She's weird that way."

"Really, Leesee, that's the only thing weird about you?"

Leesee thought a second, then said, "Yup, that's about it."

"Otherwise, she's perfect. And probably the most romantic woman I've ever met," Dahni said. "But don't worry about that now, we'll get into it later, then move on to the harder stuff."

"It gets harder?"

"What if a goblin is running down a hill at an angle? It changes things. And we haven't even talked about wind effects."

"Wouldn't it be easier to just shoot me now?" Bright asked.

"We'll get to that," Leesee said. "Don't be impatient. One step at a time."

"One step at a time," Dahni agreed.

"And put that stupid stick away!" Bright demanded.

"You mean Doug," Leesee said.

"Yes, and it's really disturbing you took the time to braid a leather handle for it."

"We wanted it to look nice. You get it as a gift when you complete the training. A reminder of the good times," Leesee said, looking a little hurt.

Every evening they met for supper and to study at Du Shar's quarters. One evening Bright excitedly pulled out some drawings she had been working on.

"What is it?" Elaine asked.

"I think it might be an arrow," Dahni said.

"Exactly!" Bright said proudly. "I've been thinking about the troll problem, and then it hit me … matches!"

"What?"

"Matches. You strike them, and they light. You know, where I'm from."

"They glow if you hit them?"

"Fire. They make fire! My little brother did a science fair project on how matches work. I had to help him, so of course, I ended up doing most of the work. It's really pretty simple. Sulfur, phosphorous, some powdered flint, and ground glass. The arrowhead is going to be a little heavy, at least twice as heavy as a normal one. It is essentially a cylinder about two inches long that has been cut into four open-ended prongs. The end of the arrow shaft fits into these prongs, but only enough to hold it in place. Dip the arrow in glue and ground flint, glue ground glass to the inside of the prongs, and then coat both sides in a paste of sulfur and phosphorous."

"What's sulfur and phosphorous?" Leesee asked.

"Chemicals. The apothecary may have them," Elaine answered.

Bright continued, "The arrowhead doesn't need to be forged for damage, it just needs to be sharp, maybe barbed, so it sticks in troll hide. We wrap an inch of cloth around the cylinder, just behind the arrowhead. When needed, we dip the tip in oil. Once the arrow strikes the troll, the force keeps the shaft moving through the cylinder. The glass and flint make a spark, ignite the sulfur mixture, and—POW—fire!"

"It won't work," Leesee said confidently.

"Why not?"

"I have no idea," Leesee admitted.

"I see what you're getting at. If the sulfur mixture works, I think it may be a good design. Worth a try," Elaine said.

The next day they brought the drawings to one of their friends, a fletcher apprentice named Kalia. It took a while before she caught on, but finally, Elaine convinced her to give it an attempt. Kalia wanted to try making the arrowhead with bamboo at first, just to see if it would work. There was no need to bother Sir Mahri with forging them out of metal if it didn't. She promised that she would accompany Sir Elaine to the apothecary the next morning.

While they were there, one of the bowyers Bright had seen standing with Sir Rhaine approached her. She asked to see her for a moment alone. She explained that Du Shar had commissioned a bow and that she had accepted the request. Bright was relieved to find that the measurements were few and there was no requirement to disrobe. She measured for height, length of draw between her bracing hand and the corner of her mouth, where she would hold the arrow. And finally asked her to grip a dowel that had been wrapped in clay to obtain a hand imprint.

A few days later, they learned that Sir Rhaine had found out about the measurements, and a massive argument took place between her and the other bowyer. The result was that Sir Rhaine confiscated her notes and the imprint. It didn't bother Bright much. She was growing quite attached to the bow Shar had given her. Bright would never be openly disrespectful, but she thought that Sir Rhaine was an old bitch.

Du Shar and the knights arrived a week before the Bonding Ceremony. Unfortunately, they knew this because Ahn Alanna showed up during target practice. Bright was doing quite well until she saw Alanna standing beside her, giving her that same icy stare through her long stringy hair. Bright grew more and more unnerved at her presence until she missed the target completely.

"I told you that you don't belong here." Bright heard the

hoarse whisper. "Now, you waste my arrows."

Bright turned just in time to see her shove. Bright didn't even think about it. Elaine had trained her to move instinctively. She used Alanna's momentum, added her own, and rolled back with a foot in her midsection. At the apex of the arc, Bright kicked up with her foot, accelerating Alanna and causing her to land heavily on her back. In an instant, she was sitting on Alanna's chest one hand grasping her corseted top and the other poised for a palm-heel strike.

Alanna's eyes went wide in surprise. Then they began to narrow, brows furrowing in anger as she began to focus on Bright. Bright didn't know what to do, she didn't want to hit her. So she raised her up and kissed her squarely on the mouth. Dropping Alanna, Bright screamed and ran across the training ground. Alanna sprang into a crouch and looked around, her gaze fell upon Leesee and Dahni. They shrieked in terror and ran off right behind Bright.

Alanna stood and dusted herself off. Elaine was standing nervously nearby. Elaine thought about running also. When Alanna turned to her, she thought about screaming and running. But she stood still. It wasn't appropriate for a senior knight to run around screaming.

"Did you teach her that?" Alanna asked Elaine.

"Yes, Ahn Alanna," Then Elaine added, "Not ... the kissing part."

Alanna turned to watch them disappear across the yard. "Then, you taught her well." She said, and walked away.

Chapter 15

THE TRIAL OF KNIGHTHOOD

Shar had other business and didn't arrive back to her quarters until late. The girls were studying an ancient battle. Bright ran to her, and they embraced. Bright was aware of the eyes on her, and she didn't care.

"I missed you," She whispered.

"And I missed you." She heard in reply.

Shar sat in her chair while Bright sat at her feet, often leaning her head on her leg.

"Sir Elaine, I need a report on the training. An accurate report."

"Du Shar, we have followed the schedule I briefed to you initially. There have been deviations, although they have been minor," Elaine reported.

"Is she ready? It has been months, and the Bonding

ceremony will be soon," Du Shar asked.

"Bright has grown strong in these few months. I have never seen another progress this fast. I believe she has the skills, it is not my place to say she is ready."

"What are you talking about?" Bright asked.

"The Trial of Knighthood. If your training is complete, there is still the trial, the final test," Shar began. "Every knight has been required to complete a rite of passage. Like your sisters before you, you will be charged to track and kill a goblin. Alone. You will bring back its right ear as proof. To pass the test, you must return with the trophy and tell your story around the fire. You will be accompanied only by a Second, a sister knight that is forbidden to interfere. She will be there only to observe, and return to tell the story of how you were slain in combat if you fall."

"I have to kill a goblin? By myself?"

"Like your sisters before you," Shar repeated.

Bright looked at her three friends. They were somber, solemn. She understood that they had all completed this test and lived to tell their story.

"If you are ready, you must then choose your Second. The person you trust to tell your story. This will be done at the time of the trial. If you ask it of me, I will go," Shar said.

"I will go," Elaine stated.

"I will go," Dahni said.

Leesee was looking at the floor.

"Leesee?" Shar asked gently.

Tears began to hit the floor. Leesee finally spoke. "I will not go. I can't tell the story of how you were slain. I couldn't speak the words. I would die defending you, but there is no way I will sit and watch it happen. I'm sorry, Bright. I'm so sorry." Dahni put her arm around her.

"There is no shame in this, Sir Leesee." Shar looked to Bright. "Are you ready for the trials, and Knighthood if you survive?"

"I've never killed anything before. I don't want to kill someone."

"A knight doesn't want to kill. They do it to protect those they love, and what is good in the realm. I will tell you that the creatures of darkness do want to kill, and they relish it. And if left unchecked, there will soon be no realm left. You only need to look to Willow, to see the effects they have. But it is your choice. It is the only way to become a knight ... to become Sir Bright."

"Du Shar," Elaine asked, "wouldn't she automatically become Ahn Bright?"

"I believe you are right, Sir Elaine. She has bonded already," Shar answered.

Bright thought about the Trial. She thought about how awful it would be. She thought about how much effort her friends have gone through to ensure she was prepared for this. She thought about Sariel, protecting the realm day after day, alone. She thought about Spook left back at the Pool of

Kerridwyn. Then she thought about Willow.

"I'm ready. Let's get this over with."

There was no cheering, no exuberant exclamations. Only a solemn nodding of heads. These warriors knew the cost of losing—and the horrible price of victory.

That night as Bright and Shar lay in each other's arms, Bright said, "Shar, if I don't make it back ..."

"You will return. You can't let your thoughts dwell on dark things."

"Still, if I don't return ... I want you to know that I love you."

"And I love you."

"Tell my friends that I love them too."

"Tell them yourself when you return."

At sunrise, a large crowd gathered outside the Great Hall, in the Village Circle. A bonfire crackled in the center. It would remain lit until the trials were over. All the knights were there, and many other villagers. Du Shar led Bright into their midst. She pulled the arrows from her quiver and left her only the small knife on her belt.

"Clan Du Shar," Shar began. "Today Bright, our Elvenstar, will face her Trial of Knighthood. Bright will soon leave. While today we are proud to call her Sister, she will return to us as Ahn Bright, a Knight of the Realm, and a Bonded Wolf Rider." The crowd roared, then quickly fell silent. It was a solemn hail. This was not the time for cheer.

"Sister Bright has chosen the bow. She will be given only three arrows. Sir Leesee has asked to be the one to present these arrows. May they serve you well."

Leesee slowly walked to Bright, holding three arrows. They were perfect, gleaming in the morning sun.

"I offer you three arrows. They are the best I could find." Her lip quivered, tears fell. Moments passed before she could speak the final words. "May they serve you well."

"Thank you, Leesee."

Leesee turned, walked calmly for about three steps, and then broke into a run with her hands over her face.

Shar continued with the ceremony. "It is our custom to choose a Second. The Second will not interfere, cannot interfere, but will observe, and return to the great fire, to tell the story of her battle, if so she falls. Traditionally the second is our most trusted friend." Shar turned to Bright. "You may choose your Second. She who you trust to give a faithful accounting of how you were slain."

Bright addressed the crowd without hesitation. "I choose Ahn Alanna."

Du Shar quieted the murmuring crowd by saying, "Ahn Alanna, step forward. Stand by your sister."

Ahn Alanna came to stand by Bright. Alanna glanced up at her, then lowered her head.

"May the Lord and Lady protect you. The trials have begun!" Shar thundered. However, no one cheered.

Ahn Alanna headed north at a jog, and Bright followed her.

Nearly an hour passed before Ahn Alanna slowed to a walk. They walked side by side for another half hour.

"Why choose me?" Alanna finally spoke.

"I knew you would speak the truth. If I do something stupid, which is entirely possible, I want it to be told. I don't want a sister that follows me to make the same mistake. You will tell the truth, you won't try to make it grand or something it's not. I'm hoping that lesson may prevent the death of another sister."

They moved on in silence. It was well into the afternoon. Bright was looking for goblin sign. Tracks to follow to her victim. She felt like an assassin. When that feeling would start to overwhelm her, she thought about Willow.

Alanna spoke for the second time. "The trees will begin to thin soon, then the land will become barren and desolate the farther north you go. Goblins will be found near the edge of the forest. Choose east or west. In this way, you may use the woods to hide your escape once you have completed the trial. If you are caught in the open expanse, you may find it hard to make your way back without being caught."

Bright thought, *Is she helping me now?*

The trees did begin to become less dense. Bright looked to the east. Then she looked to the west. She decided on the west and headed that way. Alanna had let her walk on ahead. Often she couldn't see her, but she trusted that Alanna was there, watching. Her task was to observe and not interfere.

Bright felt alone, and in reality, she was alone.

Bright walked as silently as she could, as she was taught. But she was no Wood Elf, she was human. Bright cringed at every misstep, every broken twig. Something inside her told her to be careful. She was afraid and had to keep moving anyway. It would be dark soon enough.

Something was bothering her, there was something she was missing. Then it became clear. There was the faint scent of smoke in the air. A campfire. She kept moving, and finally, she saw them. There were two goblins near a low smoking fire. Bright kept trees between herself and her prey. She knew she only had three arrows, and she just had to kill one. The problem was, there were two. She needed to be closer.

Bright moved closer, within 50 yards. She could hit the center of a target without fail at that range. She slowly picked up leaves and let them drop. There was a slight north to south breeze. She noticed a large tree about halfway to the goblin camp. Crouching, she slowly stepped to the side, temporarily exposed, until she put the other tree between her and the goblins. She was probably twenty feet from the tree when she froze. They were speaking loudly now. An argument.

She froze as one of them started walking south into the trees. If he looked back this way, the monster would see her. Luck favored her, and it disappeared into the tree line. It was now or never.

Bright covered the distance to the tree, notched an arrow, then sidestepped until the goblin was in view. His back was turned to Bright as he poked at the fire.

She knew that if she hit a lung, it would minimize the chance he would make a noise. So she aimed for the center of the back, then a little left, right below the shoulder blade. Bright released the arrow.

Leesee's perfect, silver-tipped arrow glided through the air. It struck home with a wet *thunk*. The goblin fell forward into the fire. Then it pushed itself back out, red embers streaming from its face and hands. It wasn't screaming but making gasping sounds. It reached around trying to grasp the arrow, but couldn't quite get hold of it. It was coughing. *Why doesn't it just die?* Bright wondered. But living things don't just die. Whether good or bad everything clings to life. Bright drew back hard and sent another arrow into its heart. Still, it fought on for several seconds, then lay still.

Her own heart racing, Bright wanted nothing more than to be back home. Not to tell this story, but to be held by her friends, by Shar, and cry. It may have been a goblin, but she felt terrible.

She covered the distance to the fire as quickly and quietly as she could. The goblin's body was still quivering slightly, and she felt sick. She grasped its right ear and pulled her knife. As she sliced the ear off, Bright noticed that there was a quiver of arrows and a bow nearby. This goblin happened to be an archer, just like her. Having something in common made it worse, she felt guilty before, and now that feeling had doubled. She finished cutting off the ear and put it in her pouch just in time to hear its partner crashing through the brush towards her, a wicked-looking axe poised to strike.

Bright notched another arrow, her last, and shot it square

in the middle of the chest. It fell but started to get back up. Bright stepped to her victim's quiver and pulled a large, crude arrow. She fired, and it landed next to the last. The creature collapsed.

They said I only get to take three arrows, does it count if I find more? Bright wondered. She decided it wasn't time to get technical, she pulled Leesee's arrows out from the dead goblins, but one broke. She put the goblin arrows in her quiver with the other two. Then she cut off the other goblin's ear.

Bright headed back east, hoping to find Ahn Alanna. She realized this was the first time she ever *wanted* to see Alanna. She had covered quite a bit of ground when she saw shadowy movement ahead in the twilight. There were many of the wet *thunking* sounds she now associated with an arrow striking flesh. And she heard a choking gasp. *Alanna!* She thought.

"Skin it!" Bright heard.

"Yes! Before it dies."

Then another voice, "No. Get the human! The Archon wants the human."

The shadows were moving closer. Goblins! The first arrow she grabbed was one of Leesee's. She let it fly. A shadow dropped. She notched a goblin arrow and fired. They kept coming, quickly losing their shadowy forms and becoming distinct. And terrifying. She shot again and again as they moved closer and closer. Still, one kept coming, it was almost upon her. She drew her last arrow, one of Leesee's, took aim and fired. The arrow pierced its side, it stumbled, yet it did not fall. It was nearly on her with a dagger in hand, and

Bright didn't know what to do. She couldn't think. She didn't move.

The goblin stopped suddenly, confused. It looked down at the spear protruding from its chest. It toppled over, and behind it, Bright could see Alanna on her knees, then she fell forward.

Panicked, Bright ran to Alanna. Her back was riddled with goblin arrows. Two arrows were near her left shoulder. Two were protruding from the right side of her chest. One in her hip and two in the right thigh, one of which was bleeding profusely.

Alanna lay face down, gasping. Bright couldn't roll her on her back, the movement of the arrows would kill her. She lay down beside her, turned her on her side and placed her arm under her head. She stroked the hair back from her face.

"Bright!" Alanna gasped. "Bright!"

"I'm here. Hold on. I'll get help."

"Bright," Alanna gasped again. "Thank you … for the story … even though it is yours. My ancestors … will be pleased." Then she closed her eyes.

"No!" Bright screamed. "No, no, no! You will not die, you will not die. You stay with me and live!"

Tiny blue lights filled the air, twinkling like fireflies. Then an intense blue light formed around Alanna. It surrounded her, it glowed within her, it grew in its intensity until it was blinding.

Chapter 16

THE STORY

Bright slowly became aware of the voices. Arguments maybe? She heard someone say, "I'm telling you ..." Then she coughed.

"Oh, my God! Oh, my God!"

"Holy Cow!"

Bright remembered the voices, familiar voices, but she couldn't place them. She couldn't move, couldn't see. As if being unable to wake from a dream.

"Bright? Bright!" She knew that voice too.

Something was repeatedly slapping her face. Not that hard, but it was annoying.

"Bright!" She remembered the voice now, it was Du Shar. Her Shar.

Fingers forced her eyelids apart. There was a sensation of sight.

More slapping and she coughed again.

"It's working. Dahni, go get Doug!"

She tried to form a sound and coughed again. She forced herself to try even harder. There was a sound, then she heard herself croak the words, "No Doug!"

There was a jumble of sound, hands forced her to sit up. She still couldn't see clearly, but someone was putting a cup to her lips. Water. A small amount went down her throat, and she coughed again.

Slowly her vision cleared. She could focus a bit. She focused on a cup someone was holding and tried to reach for it with shaking hands. It was placed on her lips, and she drank. She coughed again and realized that her head hurt, a throbbing pain.

Bright tried to look around. All was a blur at first, but soon she began to see. She was in the Great Hall, sitting on soft blankets placed upon one of the long tables. Elves were everywhere, the hall was packed with women and their men. There were even a few children, and they were all staring at her. *I hope I'm not naked*, she thought. She looked down and was relieved to see she was fully clothed. She saw all her friends. She saw Ahn Alanna standing nearby.

"Oh, you're alive!" Bright said to Alanna in a raspy voice. "I was so worried. What happened?"

"That," Said Shar, "Is what we have been waiting for a day

to hear. You are yet weak, would you allow Ahn Alanna to tell your story?"

Bright coughed again but nodded her head.

"Ahn Alanna, it is finally time for us to hear the story and conclude the Trials. Tell us what happened." Shar spoke, and the room went still.

Alanna stood on the table and began to tell the entire story. She spoke of how Bright stalked and killed two goblins. Intent on watching Bright, she was ambushed and filled with arrows. She told the story of how Bright stood firm and dropped the goblins one by one as they attacked, using their own arrows against them.

"In the end, throughout the entire battle, I slew only one," Alanna said. She took out a pouch and dumped the contents on the table—Goblin ears!

"Nine!" She proclaimed. "Nine fell before her, a feat never accomplished before this time. And if you think that to be remarkable, you have not heard the rest."

The crowd was still as Alanna stepped down from the table. She stood in front of Bright. "When I was ambushed, I took seven arrows. I was mortally wounded, only able to throw my spear one last time. I was dying. I couldn't breathe. The taste of blood filled my mouth. Bright lay down beside me. She held me. We were surrounded by blue sparks of light. The light filled me, penetrated and enveloped me. The next thing I knew was that I was healed and Bright lay still, next to me. I collected the trophies and carried her back. We laid her upon this table. And we waited. Now she has awakened and is with us again."

"These," Alanna threw seven wicked-looking barbed arrows on the table. "were buried deep within me. They are covered in my blood. And they are proof that Bright healed us, though I cannot say how."

There was something odd in that statement, but Bright's mind was cloudy. Alanna looked at her and actually smiled. "The healers have confirmed it. I am with child. Bright saved two of the Clan on that day."

"And now," Alanna looked over the crowd, "if any among you question my story, step forward." No one moved.

Alanna held Bright in her arms and said, "Thank you."

"I'm so happy for you," Bright told her.

The crowd remained silent. Shar broke that silence. "Does anyone dispute the story we have heard concerning Bright's Trial of Knighthood?" More silence, it was as if they were holding their breath.

"Alanna? Would you complete the ceremony?" Shar asked.

Alanna stepped up, rested the point of her spear on Bright's shoulder, and said, "Rise Ahn Bright, Knight of the Realm, and Wolf Rider of the Clan."

Now the crowd cheered. A deafening sound. Motes of dust fell from the rafters, sparkling as they passed through beams of sunlight. Long the cheering continued. Bright's friends helped her stand on wobbly legs.

"I believe there is a gift prepared," Shar stated.

Sir Mahri came forward. She placed a mail shirt over her; silver mail weaved so fine as to resemble course cloth rather than metal. They strapped on the plates. Golden plate armour with blue enameled inlays, featuring a White Wolf emblazoned upon the breastplate. There was a helm to match. Her friends helped her stand on the table for all to see. It was magnificent. Bright gleamed. The crowd roared again.

Once the cheering started to die down, Shar shouted, "Behold! Hear the words as I have heard them from our Goddess. The words many of us gathered here in this hall have heard from Kerridwyn herself." Shar paused, then said, "Behold Ahn Bright. The Elvenstar! Her spirit will shine as a beacon to all of Elvenrealm. She will give us hope during the dark times that will surely come. Bright is now and forever Elven. I bid you, welcome her."

The shouts grew even louder, longer. Many called out her name. Bright was overcome with emotion and still weak. Her friends helped her down. The cheering continued as she was led from the building.

Bright remembered leaving the Great Hall, but nothing after that. She awoke in Shar's bed. Drew was keeping watch. He asked if she needed anything. She said, "Coffee." but settled for tea when she saw his confused look. She still felt sleepy and sat on the edge of the bed.

A stranger entered the room. Someone beautiful. She sat on the edge of the bed and said, "Bright, are you well?" Bright recognized the voice. That harsh whisper was unique.

"Ahn Alanna? I didn't recognize you. You're so pretty

without the face paint." Bright said in a sleepy voice. "And your hair is braided."

"Don't get used to it. Now answer my question. Are you well? You have slept for the better part of two days."

"I feel okay. Still sleepy. I'll feel better once I get some tea. And maybe some food."

"Good. I'll help you get dressed."

Shar, Alanna, Elaine, Leesee, and Dahni sat around, watching Bright eat and talking amongst themselves. They mainly spoke about Alanna being pregnant and how wonderful it all was. Or they discussed light-hearted things. Bright was feeling much better.

"Buckson told me that he has asked to be Alanna's husband. He wants to be able to look after the baby," Shar told everyone. "Isn't that good news?"

"I haven't agreed to his request," Alanna stated.

"Why not?" Shar asked, surprised.

"I haven't had a chance to talk to you."

"That's not our custom. It's not my choice."

"You are my oldest friend. And custom dictates that it is still my decision to take him. I didn't want to make that decision without talking to you."

"I think you should. I hope you do. Buckson is an amazing father. You know that already, you've seen it for yourself. He will take care of you, and the baby will be well cared for. I appreciate you thinking about me, but this is best for the baby. Please accept his request."

"Very well."

"Do you have children, Shar? I will love to meet them if you do," Bright said.

Alanna hissed, "Bright!" as one would when admonishing a child.

Bright looked around with a mouthful of food. Everyone was looking at Shar. Everything went quiet.

"Did I do something wrong?" Bright asked. She looked to Shar who was staring at some point on the wall.

Shar signed and said, "No. You have done nothing wrong. I should have told you. I should have told you her story when we first met. I dishonor her memory, and I shame myself. I want to tell you, but I cannot."

Shar got up and went to leave. She paused near the ladder to the platform and said without looking at them, "Meet at the Great Hall in two hours." Then she left.

"You should not have mentioned that!" Alanna hissed. Sounding very much like her old self.

"Bright didn't know, Ahn Alanna," Leesee said.

"But you did! You should have warned her," Alanna said.

"Ahn Alanna, I can't tell her story. I wasn't there," Leesee pleaded.

Alanna considered this. "Bright, I will tell you the story some other time. I *was* there. It will not be mentioned again." Then Alanna left to follow Shar.

Bright pleaded to Leesee. "Please tell me what just happened."

"I can't. I'm sorry, Bright. I wasn't there." Leesee looked strange. Was it concern, sadness ... maybe fear? Suddenly, Bright wasn't so hungry.

Chapter 17

THE INTERROGATION

At the Great Hall, one of the long tables was filled with elves. Scholars and healers mainly. Some other members of rank were present as well. Du Shar sat at the head of the table, Ahn Alanna on the bench to her right. Sir Mahri was present, sitting across from Alanna.

"Ahn Bright, come on in," Du Shar said, sounding like nothing had happened. "I believe Sir Mahri has saved you a seat." She indicated the bench to her left. Sir Mahri began shoving and wiggling her hips, forcing the scholars to scoot down. Elaine, Leesee, and Dahni sat wherever they could find room.

"Proceed, Sister Jhenn," Shar said.

"The purpose of this conclave is to determine what happened during the trials of Ahn Bright. Here are the facts as we know them. Ahn Bright passed the test, no one disputes that. During the Trial of Knighthood, Ahn Alanna was mortally wounded, then healed by Ahn Bright, and no one disputes that."

Jhenn looked around. "These events are recorded as factual. However, the question is, *how* did Ahn Bright heal her?"

There was some low-level murmuring then Shar said, "Ahn Bright, I believe you are the only one that can answer that."

Bright was suddenly uncomfortable with all eyes on her. "I'm sorry sisters, I really don't know."

"Alanna, tell us what you know," Shar said.

"I know I was near death, my vision was beginning to fade, I saw sparks of light all around me, like embers from a disturbed fire, but they were blue. I saw the blue glow grow stronger, felt it inside me. When the intensity was almost too brilliant to bear, it was gone. And I was lying in Ahn Bright's arms, and I was healed. Ahn Bright did not move. I feared she was dead. I checked and found she was breathing, her heart still beating, and I brought her home."

"The events and the outcome of the events have been established. We are now trying to determine the 'how' of what happened. Ahn Alanna, your vision was fading. The blue lights may have been a hallucination perhaps? The mind does strange things from time to time." From one of the other healers.

"Perhaps, but how do you explain this?" Ahn Alanna stood and removed her clothing. She pointed out seven points on her back. Two near her right shoulder, both with matching wounds on the other side, exit wounds. Two on her back, below the shoulder blades. One on her hip and two on her thigh, one of which had an exit mark as well. These weren't ordinary scars. They were smooth and white. Many healers rose from their seats to inspect her wounds. Alanna dressed, and all resumed their positions.

"If those marks indeed represent the location of goblin arrow strikes, there are three of them that any one of which would have proved fatal. The one on her inner thigh alone would have severed a blood line and caused her to bleed to death," Healer Jhenn remarked.

"Bright, did you see these blue lights?" Shar asked.

"Yes, I did see them."

"What were you doing when you saw them?" One of the scholars asked.

"I was holding Ahn Alanna, lying next to her. I couldn't roll her on her back because of all the arrows. I did see the blue sparks, like lightning bugs. But then, I closed my eyes."

"And what did you do then?" Shar gently asked.

"Nothing, really. I was sad, upset. I felt so guilty that she might die, I knew it was my fault because I choose Alanna to come with me. I thought that I had led her to her death!" Tears were forming as she lived through the event again in her mind. "I screamed at her. I told her she couldn't die. I told her not to die. I just … willed her to live. That's all I remember." Sir Mahri put an arm around her.

An elderly, almost ancient scholar rose. "You have a strong

will, child. But this took more than will, it is a gift, a power. Where did you receive such a gift?"

"I don't know what you mean?" Bright said. "I arrived here with nothing. Everything I have has been given to me."

"This is a gift of power!" She persisted. "How did you come by this? Have you seen these blue lights before?"

"No, I haven't." Bright was getting a little put off. She started to think all elderly Elves were assholes. "I never saw blue lights before. I've seen the gold lights of Faeries."

"Faeries can't do this. I am very familiar with their effects, and it does not include ..."

"Wait!" Bright interrupted. "I have seen lights like these, one time, but they were green."

"When was that? When did you encounter these green lights?"

"I saw them around Sariel's friend when I first met him."

"Sariel has no friends that I know of," Shar said.

"Yes, he does," Bright insisted. "His name is Raphael."

"Does this Raphael have this power? And can it be bestowed?" The ancient scholar asked.

"I don't know," Bright said.

"The purpose of this gathering is to find out what you *do* know!" The ancient scholar shouted. Bright was really getting sick of this one's tone.

A younger scholar rose. "Sariel is a fallen angel. You are not referring to the Archangel Raphael, are you? And if so, could he have given you this gift?"

"Archangel? I don't know. I was told Sariel was a fallen angel. And I remember Raphael asked me to walk him to the gate. I remember now. He asked, 'May I give you a gift?' He placed a hand on my chest and told me green was his color, but blue was mine. I remember! Does this mean anything?"

"Sisters," The young scholar began. "If we are speaking of Archangel Raphael, he is known to have the power to heal."

"Known by whom?" The ancient scholar shouted.

In a soft and respectful voice, she replied, "By scholars, of course. By anyone who took the time to read the texts. Perhaps I could lend you my copies."

The room erupted in a cacophony of voices. The ancient scholar screamed at the youth, admonished her, while she sat impassively. Healers and scholars argued with each other, and each faction argued amongst themselves.

"Silence!" Shar shouted. "*I* believe that Ahn Bright may have received this gift of healing from the Archangel. And unless we are able to summon him here, we will have to accept it as our only explanation. The final outcome is that it does not matter where she came by this. In the end, it really doesn't matter. Because we all know it comes at a great cost. Ahn Alanna was near death, and she was healed. We are grateful. I am particularly grateful. But we nearly lost Ahn Bright in trade. It drained her of all her energy. It took nearly two days for her to recover and we were unsure if she would at all. The cost is too great. We cannot lose the Elvenstar. We will not try to use this gift and lose Ahn Bright in the process. The event happened, and now it is over. Go back to your homes." Shar concluded the meeting.

Bright and her friends gathered around Shar and Alanna. They talked for a short time and left the hall. Once they walked outside, they saw Sir Mahri standing with her arms crossed, waiting.

"Oh, no!" Leesee said, glancing around for an escape.

"Holy crap!" From Dahni.

"You!" Mahri shouted, pointing at Leesee. "What did I tell you? I said you couldn't break him! I said you had to be careful, didn't I?"

"I'm sorry, Sir Mahri, it was my first time with him. He was so pretty ... I got excited," Leesee whined.

"And you!" Mahri said, pointing at Dahni. "You were supposed to keep an eye on her, keep her under control." Dahni didn't reply, she sidestepped behind Bright.

"I said *not* to break him! It's been two days, and he still walks funny, he's bruised all over. There are *scratch marks* down his chest, they will probably scar! Patches of hair have been pulled out. His manhood is completely raw, it will be a week or more before I can ride him."

"I'm ... I'm sorry."

"And he says he can't move his thumb properly. What on earth did you do to his thumb?" Sir Mahri glared at Leesee.

Leesee opened and closed her mouth several times as if she were trying to find an answer. Then she bolted and ran as fast as she could. Mahri's gaze followed her retreat for a second, then landed on Dahni, who was peering out from around Bright's back. Dahni also chose to run away.

Sir Mahri turned her angry gaze on Du Shar. They looked at each other, then burst out laughing. After that subsided a bit, Mahri looked at Bright and Elaine, "If either of you tells them I laughed, we'll meet in the Trial Pit, understand?" They both nodded vigorously.

"Would you two give me a moment with Bright?" Shar said as she led Bright off without waiting for a response. She walked a distance away, far enough that the others couldn't hear.

"Bright, I know that Alanna is going to invite you to her quarters tonight. And you absolutely should go, but I'm worried about it," Shar said, apparently concerned.

"Why? What would she do to me?" Bright asked.

"I'm worried about what *you* might do to hurt *her*."

"Wait. What? We are talking about Ahn Alanna?"

"You heard me say she was fragile, she is. She has lost so many friends, she can't stand it anymore. She is the way she is so that people will stay away. Don't you see? If she doesn't make any friends, doesn't have anyone close to her, she can't lose them. But it's slowly destroying her. I'm the only one she has left. We have lost so many. Alanna couldn't take any more loss, so she has become the way she is. But I heard the way she told your story, and I think you may find that she will be quite different tonight. And if I'm right, I don't want you to be surprised, or do anything hurtful to her. Even if you really don't mean to. Bright, Alanna is my oldest friend and the best friend you could hope for. Alanna could challenge me and win in seconds. The only reason she does not do that is *because* I'm her friend and she loves me. Do you understand?"

"Yeah, I think so," Bright said

"Good."

Chapter 18

ALANNA

Alanna did request that Bright meet her that evening. Bright told her she would be there. After her bath, she stood looking at all the leather gear and weapons she usually wore now. She didn't feel like putting it all on. Instead, settling on a comfortable stola and belting it with a thin braided leather cord, leaving the weapons behind. Bright wanted to flee from war and battle for an evening. She thought she deserved an evening of peace.

Amica, Alanna's beast, barked loudly then walked up to Bright, tail wagging as she neared Alanna's quarters.

"Oh, look at you! You want some attention? Come here, let me scratch those ears." Bright pet the wolf and the wolf loved it.

"Bright," Alanna called out from above as she worked to play out the last of the descent line, "grab the line."

Bright shoved her foot in the loop and secured a hand-hold. "Okay, Alanna." Alanna let go, and Bright ascended to the platform. She felt grateful that Alanna's platform was about twenty feet lower to the ground than Shar's. Alanna gave her a hand at the top.

"Thanks," Bright said. Alanna was looking at her costume, so she added, "Yeah, I know this isn't very 'Elven warrior,' but I had to have a moment away from weapons and leather armour and everything. I hope you don't mind."

"Nonsense, you look lovely. And comfortable. I wish I had thought of it." Alanna actually smiled. It was a smile that went all the way to her eyes. There was no face paint. Her hair wasn't braided, but it was clean, brushed, and beautiful.

"Thank you for inviting me."

"You are welcome. Come."

They walked from the platform to the sitting room. Each level in a tree had to be built spiraling around the trunk, and each a little higher. Stairs connected levels by a ladder which rested solidly on the floor below but was not fastened to it; this allowed it to slide with the inevitable movement of the wind. The sitting room was the next level up from the platform, just like in Shar's quarters. Alanna's was smaller with only two other rooms and a small pantry instead of a kitchen.

In Alanna's sitting room, there were two short benches pushed against the wall. A large and thick rug of a colorful woven pattern covered the floor, with many pillows scattered around the edges.

"Please. Sit," Alanna said then stepped up to the pantry. She had already prepared a tray with fruit, cheese, and wine, which she brought down and placed in the center of the rug.

Alanna stood looking at Bright for a moment. Bright was just beginning to think something was wrong when she said, "Bright, would it be all right if I stole your idea? It's just that you look so comfortable."

Bright smiled and said, "Of course."

Alanna ran up the stairs and then more stairs. She called out, "Help yourself to the wine, I'll be right down."

Bright did just that. So far, so good, but she still felt like she could use a drink. This was all a little strange. She supposed it was also odd that she felt like she needed a drink. Across the veil, where she came from, she would still be considered too young for alcohol.

Alanna returned wearing a stola. "I'm back. I have to admit this feels so much better." Alanna sat cross-legged across from Bright.

"I know, right? I never heard of a stola before I came here. Now I love them," Bright said.

"I haven't congratulated you on your performance at the trials. No one has achieved what you did. Most, like me, take down one and head home. Nine. That is amazing." Alanna poured herself a glass of wine. "To Ahn Bright," she toasted.

"Thank you. But trust me, one would have been better," Bright said and took a sip. "This is wonderful. What is it?"

"It's blueberry wine. My favorite. I'm well-stocked because I drink it a lot, I'm afraid to say."

"Here's to my Second. Without you, I would still be wandering north," Bright toasted.

"That's not true. You'd have been eaten by now," Alanna said and then giggled.

Bright thought, *Did Ahn Alanna just giggle?*

"What was it like," Alanna asked, "on the other side of The Veil? Were you a powerful warrior there?"

Bright laughed, nearly snorting wine through her nose. "Sorry," she said, wiping her mouth with the back of her hand. "I was neither powerful nor a warrior." Alanna was still listening, so she continued. "I was weak, about as weak as someone could possibly be. I never even considered that I could ever become a warrior."

Alanna furrowed her brows in thought. "I find that hard to believe."

"It was a different world." Bright wondered why she used the word 'was.' "Full of scientific devices that were supposed to help you, to help you save time. We called them computers, cell phones, televisions, and other things. But they didn't save time, they consumed all your time. And what was left was meaningless and hollow. People walked around with their heads bowed staring at their cell phones. So much that it affected their posture. They were slaves to it. It all made everything meaningless. Real accomplishment gave way to the number of 'likes' you received on a post. No one read books anymore, they would rather wait for a movie so someone else could dictate what they should see. The government allowed poisons to be put in our food so the pharmaceutical companies could get rich selling medicine. Those drugs had side effects that caused you to buy more drugs. They designed genetically modified vegetables with no nutritional value. But you should know, I didn't see it clearly while I lived there, you don't realize what is wrong when you're in the middle of it. I didn't understand what was real and vital until I came to know Elvenrealm."

"Oh, my!" Alanna said. She looked shocked. "You make it sound like a nightmare."

"In a way, it was. When Kerridwyn brought me here, I finally woke up."

Alanna considered this. "I am not trying to be mean, but if this is true, why did the Lady bring you here?"

"She mentioned finding me because of a resonance, and some destiny thing. I really don't know what she meant. I guess I honestly have no idea why she brought me here." She looked at Alanna. "But I am glad she did."

"So am I," said Alanna. She sipped more wine.

"I have to say that, until now, I didn't think you *were* happy with me."

"I was being a bitch. I'm sorry," Alanna actually looked sorry.

"Don't be," Bright replied. "I wouldn't have worked as hard as I did if it weren't for you. You made me want to prove you wrong. You made me try harder at everything I had to do. I probably would not have been prepared for the trials." She took another sip of wine and said, "I wanted to be like you."

Now it was Alanna's turn. She laughed in the middle of a sip and nearly choked. When she finished coughing, she said, "No one wants to be like me."

"Then you just don't know. The worst thing I ever heard about you was, 'she can be stern sometimes.' Everything else is praise. You are the ideal. We all strive to be like you. Like you and Shar."

Alanna thought about this. "I am not the ideal. Shar is the example to follow."

"You could challenge Shar and beat her. That is what everyone says. Yet you don't."

"Shar is my friend."

"Yet if you did, she would support you as you do her. Because she is your friend."

Abruptly Alanna stood up and said, "There is something I have to do tonight. Wait a moment."

Bright waited and wondered if she had hurt her feelings. She knew she made many mistakes without meaning to.

Alanna brought down another bottle of wine, then left again, returning with a small iron cauldron, filled with sticks. She used a flint and steel to spark the tinder and a small fire formed.

"Refill our glasses, we will need it."

Alanna sat back down, this time next to Bright, and stared into the fire. Then she began.

"The Chieftain had a daughter. And Du Shar named her Tiah. She was beautiful and loved by all, and I was like a second mother to her. Shar and I spent all the time we could with her, and she became a skilled warrior at a very young age. She favored the twin daggers, like her mother. But she was skilled with many.

She passed the trials and in time was bonded to a fierce wolf, who she named Bay. We would ride the border and protect the villagers. She was kind to everyone, and they loved her for it. She was the bravest woman I had ever met. Her skill exceeded her mother's ... and mine.

One night we received word that a troll was attacking a nearby village. Tiah, Shar, four other knights and I rode hard to their aid. There was indeed a troll, and it had already killed most. By the time we arrived, it was riddled with arrows from the villagers, yet it ignored them. It was trying to tear down the door to a building. We could hear the screams of a child within. Trolls savor the flesh of children.

Tiah was the first to attack. She bounded from her mount and tried to sever a tendon in its leg, to bring it down. It kicked her hard, and she flew through the air. The rest of us attacked, but it was in a frenzy. Its claws raked our flesh. Shar tried to do what her daughter could not. She was caught and thrown. That is where she earned the four long scars across her back. But that is not all, her leg was severely broken in the fall. Our archer managed to take out an eye, and it went spinning, lashing out everywhere. I struck it then with my spear, I twisted and thrashed my spear in its flesh. Blood flowed but not enough. It pulled the spear from itself, and in an instant, because I did not let go, I was held aloft. Then it grabbed my leg in a crushing grip and flung me into the building. That is where I received these." Alanna spread her leg to display the four claw marks on her inner thigh.

"I was stunned, trying to regain my feet. Everyone that engaged the beast was flung away like leaves in a strong wind. We thought Tiah was dead, such was the force of the blow that sent her flying. But somehow she had made it onto the roof of that building. She flung herself on the troll and plunged both daggers into its neck. Blood gushed, then stopped. The troll reached up and raked wicked claws across her arms. Flesh tore away, but still, she twisted the daggers, and stabbed, again and again, one dagger then the next. Each time blood would spray, then subside. It reached behind its back and pulled hard on Tiah. Her armour flew away, and I saw ... ribs sticking out of her back." Alanna broke down and sobbed. Bright scooted close, wrapping her arms around.

"But Tiah ... she never stopped. It tore the flesh away from her legs, but she did not stop. Again and again, she plunged and twisted. Finally, it fell. We rushed in and severed its head. But we were too late. Tiah was dead. Bay was dead. And nothing has ever been the same."

For some time they cried, in each other's arms. Then Alanna said, "It is our custom to tell the story of a warrior's death. We must honor our fallen by reciting these events. But Shar cannot tell this story. And it shames her."

When Bright could finally speak, she said, "There is no shame." Bright wiped the tears from Alanna's cheek, then gently placed her cheek against Alanna's. "Had you perished, I do not think I could have told the story of how I led our greatest knight to her death. I would not have made it through the telling."

Alanna moved to hold Bright's face in her hands. They looked into each other's swollen eyes. Then Alanna kissed her.

Chapter 19

THE BONDING

Before dawn, Ahn Alanna rode Amica to the Village Circle with Ahn Bright mounted behind her. They were both dressed for battle. Alanna wore her face paint, her hair unbound. Du Shar, Elaine, Leesee, and Dahni were standing by with two others. It was time to leave for the bonding ritual. They waited on the rest of the coven and would travel at first light.

Shar, Elaine, Leesee, and Dahni greeted them with smiles and hugs for Bright. The rest held back, reserved and thoughtful.

"Bright, with all that happened at your trials, we forgot to give you this. You earned it," Leesee said.

Dahni proudly displayed the switch, now resplendent with a tassel of colored feathers. "Doug! Doug now belongs to you," Dahni proclaimed.

Bright hesitated, narrowing her eyes. Then she snatched the switch from Dahni's hands. "This!" Bright said displaying the switch. "This is an Elven tradition that I really don't appreciate."

"But it's a tradition," Leesee said.

"A very important tradition," Dahni agreed.

"What tradition is this?" Shar asked, curious.

Bright looked sharply at Shar. "The tradition of having a switch used on you during training. It's awful, right?"

"I'm not familiar with any switch tradition," Shar said.

Bright turned to Alanna, held up the switch. "I've never heard of it," Alanna said.

Bright turned to the archers, her brows furrowed and scowling. They could hear each of her deep breaths. Leesee and Dahni reflexively took a step back. Bright actually growled. The two held up their hands defensively.

"Holy shit!" Leesee said.

"Oh, my God!" from Dahni.

Then they both screamed and ran, Bright chasing right behind them with Doug held high.

Shar looked at Alanna. "Do you know what all that was about?"

Alanna just shrugged and shook her head. "I have no idea." They stood and listened to the screaming in the distance.

Shar assembled her coven of twelve Knights. Leesee and Dahni were the only ones who appeared eager and confident, although they frequently would fidget and rub their backsides. Bright wore a satisfied expression.

The others were thoughtful, nervous, and apprehensive. The Bonding was not something to be taken lightly.

"You all have achieved the title of Knight of the Realm," Shar began. "And in so doing, you have earned the pride and respect of every member of Clan Du Shar. *I* am proud of each one of you. You all know that you have nothing left to prove."

Shar continued, "To be a Wolf Rider is a choice. It is an honor that comes at a great price. All too often, we lose our sisters, and our wolves, to The Bonding. Long ago, it was called 'The Small Death.' Make no mistake, some of these pups may refuse to be bonded. They sense the risk, and they will serve as Protectors of the Realm proudly, without bond. Like the wolves, you may still make that choice. I challenge anyone who thinks there is shame in that, for there is none. If you are unsure, you need only stand. For you are all Protectors of the Realm and that is enough. Very few Bondings have passed without loss. For some, there will be great joy. Frequently, for all, there will be greater sorrow. A Bonded Knight is joined to their wolf at the soul. They live together, they fight together ... they die together."

"I will pause now. We will be silent and contemplate. If you are certain, follow me when I depart."

They stood, deep in thought, silent. When the moment of contemplation had passed, Shar turned and began the walk south with Alanna and Bright at her side. They traveled to the Pool of Kerridwyn. Nine followed. Three remained behind.

Most of the warriors were quiet on the march south. Shar had set perimeter patrols, but some were walking with Bright and talking, mainly about the Bonding, of course.

"Leesee, Dahni? You two have been unusually quiet," Bright said. "How are you doing?"

"Oh, we've got this. We're good," Leesee said.

"Yup, we'll be bonded," From Dahni.

"You seem pretty confident," Bright said.

"Because we know," Leesee stated.

"Yup, we know like we know," Dahni agreed.

"Bright, we have it set in our minds, right? We're keeping our thoughts focused. And we have a plan, a secret plan. And our wolves will be best friends, just like we are. It's already set. Done deal," Leesee said.

"Yup," Agreed Dahni.

Bright thought about it for a bit, then said, "I believe you."

It wasn't until then that Bright noticed that Pyper was walking in front of her, and Willow behind. They were still protecting her like they were on the way to Cor Malia. Something inside Bright resented this special treatment. She was Ahn Bright. She was a Knight of the Realm, a Wolf-Rider of the Clan. She needed no special treatment. What was all that work for if she still had to have babysitters?

Bright slowed, then stopped. So did they.

"Go on, I'll catch up soon," Bright said.

"It's okay, we'll wait on you," Pyper said.

"No, go on ahead. I'll catch up." Still, they waited for her to move. She did not.

"Do you have to pee?" Leesee asked. "Maybe we should all pee."

"I don't need you guys watching out for me. I can watch out for myself. I am an Ahn," Bright stated in a firm voice.

They all looked at each other, uncertain of what to do. Finally, Leesee admitted, "But we have orders from another Ahn. And you're the Elvenstar. We have the Quest, right?"

"Did Du Shar tell you this? I'll go talk to her."

"It was Ahn Alanna," Pyper said.

It wasn't until they made evening camp that Bright had a chance to catch up to Alanna.

"Ahn Alanna, could we speak?" Bright asked and started walking away from the crowd. Alanna nodded and followed.

"Alanna, I am an Ahn now. I don't need bodyguards," Bright told her.

"You are still the Elvenstar. The charge from the Goddess stands. It is our quest, you know that."

"So from now on, you plan on removing four Knights from all standard tactical formations, or from any defensive position, to watch over me. What will be the cost of that? How many sisters that are engaging the enemy while undermanned will die, so that I can be watched?"

Alanna stared at her, the way she always did. Only now it didn't unnerve Bright like it did before.

"Alanna, if I am truly an Ahn, I must be treated like one."

"We have a quest."

"I don't want to be part of a quest that puts my sisters in danger," Bright said, getting a little heated.

Alanna thought about it, then said, "*I* want you to be safe."

Bright softened, pushed the hair from her eyes and kissed her on the forehead. She spoke softly, "Whoever is with you, Alanna, is safe. One day I hope my sisters feel the same about me."

"I already do."

That night, Bright stared into the woods, she watched and listened. Alanna had assigned her sentry duty, just like the others. Shar approached and sat down beside her.

"I have talked to Alanna at length today," Shar said. Bright only nodded and looked at the leaves at her feet.

"Thank you for being kind to her. Thank you for treating her as a friend after all that she has done to make you feel unwelcome," Shar said and scooted next to her. Bright rested her head on Shar's shoulder.

"I see a little of my old friend in her now. I have been

concerned. She closed herself off too much after ..." Shar never finished.

Bright looked at Shar. "Shar, I need to talk to you about last night."

"Isn't that what we are doing? I am trying to thank you for being there for my oldest friend. I know she is finally opening up because of you. I love her dearly, as I love you. Let me ask you something. Do you believe that the heart only has enough space to love one person?"

It was an unexpected question. Bright thought and answered with a word, "No."

"Nor do I. Wouldn't that be a sad thing. If you could only love one. The reality is that the heart has an infinite capacity for love. It is that capacity that keeps us victorious in all things. Dark creatures don't understand this, they don't comprehend love. That is our strength, our power. And the only path to victory and peace."

"To know that you love me is a joy," Shar continued. "To know that you might love my friend is a joy as well. I like that feeling. The feeling of joy. Do you still need to speak of last night?"

Bright looked at Shar and only said, "No, I'm good." Then she kissed her, they held each other while her post went unwatched. And all was well.

No Bonding came without fear. A fear so intense and palpable, it hung on the air like a heavy dew. There was no more talk. All too often, this was a walk that some would not return from. Every warrior knew this, they knew that there was no solace to be found with their friends. Not now. Now was the time to look inside. This was the time to leap into the abyss and hope to climb out. There would be joy in the bonding, once the grief and loss had passed.

Du Shar and her knights entered the clearing that surrounded Kerridwyn's Pool. A Great Howling arose. All the wolves lent their voices to the choir, even Rend and Amica, they stopped to add their notes to the song. Du Shar and Ahn Alanna dismounted their howling beasts.

The Great Howling ceased. A dazzle of white sped toward the group. It ran straight for Bright. Spook couldn't stop in time and skidded into her, knocking her down. There was a blur of tongue and wet nose. Bright did not care, she sat up and hugged him while his tail wagged so furiously it shook his entire rear end. Spook whined, and Bright laughed. It was then that she realized there had been an emptiness, a hollow spot in her heart, which was now filled. "Oh, Spook, I missed you so much. Look how big you are!"

Du Shar walked into a clearing. Knights followed her. Sheep to the slaughter or warriors to victory, they followed. Shar pointed round about, and her sisters formed a wide circle. They lay their weapons behind them, for they would not help here. They knelt and placed their hands upon their knees, heads bowed. All except Leesee and Dahni. They knelt with palms up, arms open, heads held high. As if ready to greet their pup. *Probably their secret plan*, Bright thought.

Du Shar spoke. "There are few words given at this time. Some will be bonded as Wolf Riders of the Clan. Some will return to try again. Some may not return. May the Lord and Lady be forever with you. May you all return safely."

Du Shar left the circle. She found the largest pup. These were not the animals from across the veil. These were already averaging over 80 pounds. They were not dogs, they were not ordinary wolves, they were Great Wolves, Protectors of the Realm.

Once Du Shar entered the circle, the pup began to buck and squirm. She let it go, and it ran straight to Pyper. Pyper had only moments to hold the puppy, then the pain hit her. She screamed, over and over. Du Shar and the Ahns, Bright and Alanna, stood nearby. Everyone else remained in their place, but they watched their sister writhe in agony. They watched her and the pup fall still to the small death. They hoped she would awaken.

Pyper sat up and screamed. She cried out and howled in pain as Alanna and Bright helped her stand. The pup rose on shaking legs. But everyone was trembling now. She was led off, out of the circle. The young wolf followed.

Ahn Alanna chose the next pup, a female. It remained calm in her arms as she reached the center of the circle. She placed it on the ground, and it sat. It scratched its ear with a hind leg. Suddenly both ears perked up, and it ran straight for Sir Leesee. She held it tight in her arms. Even when the pain hit her, she hugged her wolf as long as she could. Bright ran to her side just as the spasm of pain caused her to lose control. Her body convulsed in agony, but she did not scream. Then she was still. Bright knelt beside her, hoping to see her rise, even if it was in pain. Leesee lay with open, unseeing eyes.

And they waited. Bright looked to Shar and saw the concern in her eyes. Bright began to cry. She reached down, to touch her cheek, then Leesee sprang up screaming and crying at the same time, startling everyone. Bright hugged her, and they helped her stand. Alanna led her from the circle.

It was Bright's turn to choose a pup. She went to them. A male looked at her, tilted its head, and one ear flopped down. It took some effort, but she lifted the heavy pup. As she entered the circle, she could see Sir Elaine, who was quietly crying, her shoulders shaking. Bright wished the puppy would go to her. Bright knew that this was her last try. Now she knew the courage it took to return to the circle for the third time. She felt a renewed respect for her friend.

She sat the pup down in the center purposefully pointing it towards Sir Elaine. As soon as she let it go, he ran, turned and knocked Sir Dahni over, stood on her chest, and licked her face. Dahni didn't hesitate to scream. The pain hit her fast. She went still fast, she and her pup unmoving in that moment of death. Mercifully, Dahni recovered just as quickly, and Bright led her away.

Bright met Du Shar outside the circle. Dahni rested on the ground, inhaling sharp breaths as the pain consumed her. Bright looked at Shar, "This is awful … I just want it to be over. I can't …" Then she broke down in tears, and Shar briefly held her. She felt Alanna's hand on her shoulder.

"It is a terrible thing. Much worse to watch than to go through. We must hope all continues to go well." Shar released her and went for the fourth pup.

This pup, the last male, hesitated a bit, then slowly walked up to one of the other Knights. And the awful cycle began anew. The Knight recovered, but Bright had been watching Elaine, her friend. It seemed her pain, from not being chosen, was somehow worse.

Bright pet the last pup, a female. She put her head close and softly whispered, "Choose Elaine." Then she picked it up and headed for the circle.

It was then that Bright noticed Sariel, standing at a respectful distance from the ritual. It comforted her to see him. She felt a need to be held by him, to cry within those strong arms. He nodded to her but did not smile. Bright took a breath and stepped to the center. Before Bright set the pup down, she whispered, "Elaine." She placed it on the ground so that it was facing Sir Elaine, who looked up at the last puppy.

It ran straight to Elaine. She held the pup and said, "I'm so happy." Then the pain consumed her, yet she did not cry out. Now all rose and gathered around, even Sariel. It was the last pup, and the ritual was complete.

All too soon Elaine went still as the small death took over. The pup went limp, still held within her arms. After a long moment, Bright shouted, "Elaine!" and knelt beside her. Yet she did not move. Bright looked to Shar, then Alanna, tears were beginning to form in their eyes.

"No!" Bright screamed. She shook Elaine's shoulder. "Wake up!" She shook harder. Elaine lay still. She was angry when Shar gently shut her eyes.

"No, no, no! Wait! I can heal her! I can heal her!" Bright placed her hands on her chest. "Come back, Elaine. Don't worry, I'll heal you." A few blue sparks appeared and quickly faded.

All the sisters were crying now. Shar said, "Bright, you have healed, but even you cannot bring back the dead."

"It's my fault," Bright said. "I made the pup go to her."

"That you cannot do. The wolf chooses," said Alanna.

"I don't accept this, she is not dead." Bright tried again to heal her.

"Bright, she has passed, I know this," It was Sariel.

"You don't know!" Bright insisted.

"Look!" Sariel said, pointing to an empty space nearby. Then he spoke, "You know me, I am your Dominion. Show yourself."

They all looked to where he was pointing, and an angel appeared, with a ghostly image of Elaine in her arms. There were no wings, and yet she was angelic in appearance. Brilliant, unemotional, nearly too beautiful to look at, she stood tall and stately in her white robes, gently cradling the spectral image of Elaine in her arms.

"Stop this!" Bright screamed at Sariel. "Put her back!"

"I cannot," Sariel said equally grieved. "Angels guide the dead, care for them, yet we have no power over it."

The warriors who had participated in the Bonding had removed their weapons, but the Ahns had not. Bright unslung her bow, and it was notched in an instant. Her arrow trained square between the angel's eyes.

"Put. Her. Back." Bright ordered the angel between gritted teeth.

"Bright!" Sariel shouted, shocked that she would threaten an angel.

The angel began to ascend very quickly. There was no doubt that the angel had seen Bright, heard her demand, yet her impassive expression did not change. This angered Bright even more. Bright would not hit her friend, spirit, or not. But she had no problem putting an arrow between the angel's eyes. She quickly calculated the steep angle, she estimated the fast rate of ascent, and she knew there was no wind. Bright released the arrow, and it flew true. Right before the point where its flight would have intercepted the ascending angel, it disappeared in a flash of light. And it took Elaine with her.

Bright collapsed to her knees, the bow fell from numb fingers. Her body so violently wracked with tears she shuddered, her sorrow so intense she tried to cry out, but no sound could break free. Sariel placed a comforting hand on her shoulder.

"Don't touch me!" She screamed and stood. "Don't ever touch me! I hate you! I hate you! It was my fault, but *you* let her go." And then she ran. She ran down the only trail she knew by heart. The one that led to Amalia. Spook followed right behind her.

Sariel looked about, not really seeing. His grief was evident. Her words had truly injured him. Even Shar felt sorry for him, and she hated Sariel.

"Let us go to your keep. Let us care for our fallen sister. I will speak to Bright after a time," Shar said to Sariel.

He didn't speak, but he nodded his consent.

Chapter 20

TIAH

Sariel plodded home. He was almost to the keep. All he had been able to think of was how much he desired to see Bright. He needed to tell her how he felt about her. He wanted to touch her. Now he found he was afraid to approach her, to even be seen by her. He hated who he was, he hated his obligations. His mood unintentionally manifested itself and mists rose about him.

Sariel heard the sound of the great beast, pounding swiftly along the path. He heard it slow as it hit the mists. Ahn Alanna emerged from the cloud with her spear at the ready. She lifted the spear once she recognized him. Sariel stepped off the path, leaned on his spear, and stared at his feet. He couldn't even meet her gaze. He grieved over the lost warrior, which is true. But mostly he mourned a love lost. Bright hated him, she had said it. And the worst thing was that he fully understood why. He had been helpless. He was Death, and sorrow followed in his wake.

Alanna slowly passed, studying him as she moved by. Sariel heard Alanna urge Amica into a run as soon as they were free of the mists and left him behind on the trail. Neither of them had said a word.

The keep gate was open. Alanna rode inside. She saw goats, so she dismounted and closed the gate. The door to the keep itself was also left open. Alanna felt uneasy in this place, she had never been here. There was never a reason for her to be here. Alanna called Amica to her. She urged him to find Bright. Amica sniffed and started up the stairs. He stopped at a closed door on the top floor. Alanna opened the door and found Bright lying on her side on the bed. Spook lay beside her, alert to their approach. When Spook saw Amica, he came down to greet the older wolf.

Alanna leaned her spear against the wall and walked around the bed. She sat beside Bright. Bright was alive, that was the main thing. Bright glanced at Alanna then looked away. Alanna didn't speak. What was there to say right now? She gently stroked her hair until Bright could cry no more. She quietly left once Bright had fallen asleep. Spook was already back up on the bed beside her. Alanna left the door open in the event Spook needed to get out.

Alanna heard noises at the bottom of the stairs and followed them into the kitchen. Sariel was there preparing a meal. At the moment he was chopping a large piece of boar into chunks.

Alanna leaned against the wall and crossed her arms. "I don't like you."

Sariel looked at her, then said, "Very few ever do."

"Would you like to know why I don't like you?"

"Not particularly," Sariel replied.

"I don't like you because Du Shar hates you," Alanna said anyway.

When Sariel didn't reply, Alanna asked, "Do you know why Du Shar hates you?"

"I assume that you are going to tell me." Sariel was dumping meat into a bucket.

"No. I am asking you why she hates you. What did you do to Du Shar? She is my friend." Alanna sounded threatening.

"I am not certain," he said.

"But you have an idea? If you do, you will tell me now."

Sariel sighed. He finished dumping meat into the bucket. "I have always loved Elvenrealm. I often observe this land from my own realm. I watch the modern world as well, but it does not keep my interest long. Once, not that long ago, there was a great warrior, she was fascinating. Strong and kind, I thought her the embodiment of all that was good. You knew her well. When she fell … I would not send another. I thought she had earned the right to be guided by someone who knew her and respected her. I am the one that brought her home."

"Tiah?" Alanna said, stunned. "You came for Tiah?"

"Yes. And I believe Du Shar sensed that somehow, sensed that it was me. As I said, I do not know for certain. But that is what may have happened. But remember, I am not well-liked anyway."

"Tiah," Alanna whispered the name as if to herself.

"Shortly after that, I chose to fall to Elvenrealm. No one could take her place, but I had to try." Sariel grabbed the bucket of meat and a bucket that was full of water. He headed up the stairs. Alanna followed him.

Just inside the door to Bright's room, Sariel placed the buckets of meat and water on the floor. It was for Spook. He paused a moment to look at Bright sleeping. Spook jumped off the bed and sniffed the roast boar as Sariel turned to go back down.

"There may be many guests. If you could help, it would be appreciated," Sariel said to Alanna.

Alanna stared after him as he walked down the stairs.

Chapter 21

THE PYRE

Spook began to bark, loud and rapidly. Bright sat up and saw him at the balcony window. It was dark, approaching midnight. He saw her and whined. Then Spook started into his barking again. Bright went to the window and saw Shar ride in through the dark mist. She quickly pulled the curtains, afraid she might see them bring in Elaine. She didn't want to see her like that. Spook looked at the closed curtains, then bolted out the door and down the stairs.

She noticed a tray of food with water and wine sitting on the desk. It wasn't hard to tell it was from Sariel. She felt terrible for the way she had treated him, but if he really was the Angel of Death, why didn't he stop it? Her hunger got the better of her, it always did. She sat down to get something to eat even though it looked like it had been there for a while.

Soon Shar entered and walked to her. "How are you?" she asked.

Bright just looked at her. It wasn't until she was near that she asked, "Is she really gone?" And she broke down again. Shar held her until she stopped crying and made her try to eat some more.

There was a knock on the door. Leesee and Dahni came in. Their wolves were with them, along with Spook.

"We wanted to make sure you were okay," Leesee said.

"Yeah, we wanted to cheer you up," Dahni added, then started crying.

"Oh, good job, Dahni," from Shar. "I'll be back, you three keep an eye on each other." Shar turned to leave the room, hesitated and said, "Bright, I do not like your male. That is no secret. But still … he could not have done anything. If you want to hate him, it's fine with me, but it shouldn't be because he couldn't stop death." Then she left.

Emotions settled, and Bright saw Dahni's wolf looking at her. When their eyes met, the wolf tilted its head, and one ear flopped down. It seemed so silly to Bright that she had to laugh.

"So ladies, introduce me," Bright said.

"That's Rhadia, his name means sunbeam," Dahni stated proudly. "You have to guess what Leesee named hers."

"Guess? I have no idea. Whatever means moonbeam?" Bright guessed.

"Nope. I named her Doug," Leesee said.

"Doug! No, you didn't."

"Yup."

"Where I'm from, Doug is usually a boy's name."

"I thought about it, and Doug helped you get through the training in record time. Doug helped you to do your best. So her name is Doug, and she'll help me do *my* best," Leesee said, obviously believing her logic was flawless. "Besides, I sort of like the name now. We'd say, 'Go get Doug' and you'd scream. Now I'll say 'Doug, get the goblins,' and they'll scream. When our enemies hear that the mighty Doug is coming, they'll tremble. "

Shar ran into Sariel at the bottom of the stairs. "We are going to make a funeral pyre down at the shore. Do you have objections?"

Sariel shook his head. "No. May I assist you?"

Shar appraised him for a moment. "We could use the help. And male, for what it's worth, I don't believe you have the power to stop death. No one does. I told her that," she said and walked out.

Alanna came into the room and informed the three that there were arrangements to be made that did not involve them. They were to consider themselves confined to the keep until she returned.

Leesee looked a little sheepish and asked, "Bright, do you have something else I can wear? I think that ... you know, when I died a little ... I might have pooped a little."

Bright smiled. "Trust me, I understand."

"Doug keeps sniffing my butt."

"Okay, I've heard enough. Follow me." Bright went to the wardrobe and pulled out three stolas. "Just throw your things here, we'll let the Dryads take care of them."

"You have Dryads?" Leesee asked as she stripped out of her leathers.

"I know we have at least one, but sometimes I think there may be more," Bright said, and added to the room, "Thank you."

"Yeah, thank you," Leesee said to the room. "Sorry about the poop."

They felt better after hours lounging in the pool. It was hard to remain in a somber mood watching the pups frolic in the water and snap at the waterfalls. By the time they returned, their clothes were clean and laid out on the perfectly made bed.

Bright checked the guest rooms on the third level. Lamps were lit, beds made with extra blankets. There were only four rooms so some would have to double-up, Leesee and Dahni could sleep with Bright in the vast bed she used.

It was twilight when they all started returning to the keep. The warriors had been at the preparations all day. Sariel came in first carrying a wood axe over his shoulder. He hesitated when he saw Bright, unsure of what to do. It was Bright that walked up to him.

"Sariel, I'm so sorry for what I said to you."

"You were hurt, you suffered a great loss, I understand."

"That is no excuse. I feel horrible."

"Please do not. You have enough sorrow. I was so happy to see you, I wish I could have done something. I would have if I could."

"I know that. I wish I hadn't blamed you. I told the pup to go to Elaine, I wish I hadn't."

"You did nothing wrong. The wolves go where they will, and no one can change that."

"Can we just ... start over?" Bright asked.

Sariel smiled for the first time. "Bright, it is so good to see you again. Look at you, the changes are amazing. You are truly Elven now. And an Ahn! Ahn Bright. I am impressed but not surprised."

"It's so good to see you." Bright hugged Sariel. "And it's good to be back home."

"This will always be your home, yet I fear you will be needed in Cor Malia."

"I suppose, but not right now."

"Bright, you should know that a rider came from Cor Malia. She spoke with Ahn Alanna and Du Shar. I know not what news she brought, but it seemed grave."

Ahn Alanna rode in as if sensing her name. She rode up to Bright and told her they should talk. They went to her bedchambers to have privacy. Alanna carried a large package.

"What news did the rider bring?" Bright asked.

"The male talks too much. However, it is a grim report. Are you prepared to hear it?" Alanna asked.

"What is it?"

"We lost another knight. Sir Rhaine is gone."

"Sir Rhaine? How?"

"She was very old. You know that. But she was found with two items. They both concern you. You should know that I have read the letter. Shar has, as well." Alanna handed her a letter.

Bright opened it.

I address this letter to Bright, The Elvenstar. First, let me apologize for the way I treated you when we first met. I do not like change. I believe the old ways are the only ways. I did not put any faith in the stories I had heard about you before we met. And I am often wrong.

I do not believe you saw me, but I was there in the Great Hall as we waited for you to awaken. You must understand that I have known young Alanna since her birth, and hold her in the highest regard. Alanna told your story, as you were still weak, and I listened to every word. I could see it in my mind, as the story unfolded. I heard the passion in her voice and felt as if I were there. Every word rang true, and it filled me with hope for our future because you had come to help us push back the tide of darkness. And then you stood, resplendent in your armour. You were still vulnerable and weakened by your effort to save Alanna. Yet I could only see the strength within you that few possess. You are humble and caring, and I was shamed by the way I treated you.

Then, Du Shar recited the words spoken by the Goddess. I heard those words, but it was not Shar's voice that I listened to. I heard the voice of the Goddess, whom I know. Many of us feel the same, we heard the voice of Kerridwyn. So you see, the Goddess spoke to me that day. And I listened. I knew what I had to do, what my part should be.

I set my most skilled bowyers to the task. I brought forth my best designs, used the finest materials I had saved. I watched over every cut, every move. Bone and sinew, wood layered and bonded, and silver cast. I spent every moment I had to create my greatest masterpiece. The culmination of my life's work. My gift to you. There is none other like it. I call it Fang. Perhaps one day you might think fondly of me and forget the fool I was when first we met.

Remember, no matter how fine, a bow is a tool. It is crafted. It is art. There is no magic in a bow. The magic can only be found in its wielder and her skill. You may need to remind Leesee of this.

And so I say to you, here is your bow. It is the best I could craft. May it serve you well.

Sir Rhaine

Bright was crying as she finished the letter. She placed it on the desk so that it would not be ruined by her tears. "Alanna, you must know. You must know that now I feel responsible for another death. Now I wish I had known her better."

Alanna's voice was sharp, scolding. "You are no more responsible for Sir Rhaine's death than you were for Elaine's. To think so is folly. But I will tell you what you are responsible for; you are responsible for inspiring an artisan to create a masterpiece. You have no responsibility in Elaine's passing. None. She wanted nothing more in life than to be a

Wolf Rider of the Clan. She would have been there even if you were not. She would have been chosen, no matter what words you whispered to the pup. You *are* responsible for telling your part of Elaine's story, of the remarkable warrior who became a Rider. Who now sits around the fire with her ancestors, her wolf at her side, and tells her stories. She is Ahn Elaine now. And I know she will be speaking of you."

"How can I tell the story, how can I make it through without breaking down in tears?" Bright asked.

Alanna tempered her sharp words by hugging Bright. She took her hands and said, "A short time ago you approached me, angered that you were not being treated as an Ahn should. It is the responsibility of every warrior to tell the stories of their sisters, the events you have witnessed. This is especially true of an Ahn. Shar has had to sit at the fire and tell the stories of so many warriors that I have lost count. I have done the same. There is only one story that Shar could not tell. But in truth, she should have told it. She should have told that story above all others. Did I not break down in tears? Your sisters will understand, we will patiently wait for you to continue. And we will know you cared."

Alanna's gaze grew in intensity. She said, "Tomorrow at dawn, you will either show your sisters your grief, or you will inspire them with stories about Elaine, whom you loved. You can also inspire them with the story of Sir Rhaine, whom I believe you now love. And you can show them this. And give them hope."

Alanna reached into a leather sack and drew forth the bow. She handed it to Bright who gasped when she held it.

It was exquisite in its beauty, perfect in symmetry. Bright ran her hands across the impossibly smooth surface. She studied the patterns in the wood beneath its polished exterior. Bright held the bow, which had already been strung, and the grip fit perfectly in her hand. It was an extension of her body. Two short, silver spikes protruded forward from either side of the handgrip. They were crafted as stylized wolf fangs, yet sharpened on the outer edges. If hard-pressed, the spikes would make a formidable weapon.

Alanna handed her an arrow. "I need to know who stands before me. Is it Ahn Bright, or the girl who once called herself Jenny?"

Bright notched an arrow, pointed at the wall and tried to draw the bow. She could not complete the draw. This bow held much more power than her other. Bright nodded to herself, or perhaps to the bow. She acknowledged that this bow demanded more. It gave more and demanded more of its wielder. Bright drew again, a full draw. She felt the tension and mastered it. She thought she could actually hear the bowstring sing as she pulled, reaching its highest pitch at the end of the draw. Spook heard it and sat up, watching. Bright released the arrow which embedded itself deep in the stone wall. Even Alanna's eyes went wide in surprise.

Bright stood, watching the arrow quiver in the stone. In a firm and unwavering voice, Bright stated, "I am Ahn Bright, Wolf Rider of the Clan." And Alanna hugged her tight.

There was also a bundle of arrows wrapped in a cloth. It was one of these that Alanna had given her, now embedded in the stone. A note from Kalia only said, "I offer you these arrows. They are the best I could craft. May they serve you well." One of the arrows looked very odd. It seemed similar to the one she had discussed with Leesee, Dahni, and of course, her dear friend, Ahn Elaine.

The next morning all were assembled before dawn. Sariel was there. Elaine's funeral pyre was built on the beach near the water's edge. It was tall, formed of dry logs placed one on top of the other to create a rectangle. Every space was filled with kindling. The wood had been soaked in oil. Somewhere inside this was the body of Ahn Elaine, and her unnamed wolf. Bright was grateful she could not see her, and she was thankful that she was not allowed to take part in its construction.

Bright was the one to speak first. She stepped in front of the group and said, "It is our custom to sit around the fire and tell the stories of our fallen sisters." Sariel thought, *Our custom? She is truly Elven now.*

"Today, there is a story that should be told before the flames are lit. And I will tell it if you will listen. You know Ahn Elaine spent much time with the scholars, her knowledge was great. She would teach me every evening. One evening she taught me about the trolls." Leesee shivered, then looked down at her crotch, grateful it remained dry. "She told me of their vulnerability to fire, and the great difficulty using that weakness against them. I thought about this a great deal, and one night brought out plans that I thought might work. Leesee and Dahni were there. Ahn Elaine ..." Bright paused to let her emotion pass. "... Ahn Elaine believed in the idea. We brought it to the fletcher apprentice, Kalia, and Ahn Elaine made her believe in it. Ahn Elaine spoke with the apothecary and continued the work. The problem, of course, is how to set fire to a troll in the heat of combat." Bright held up an arrow. "Ahn Elaine worked to make my idea a reality. And now, my sisters, witness that which Ahn Elaine has achieved."

Bright solemnly walked some twenty paces from the pyre. All eyes were on her. She set the arrow, drew and fired. It hit the center of a log, sparked and hissed, then Ahn Elaine's funeral pyre burst into flame.

The group gasped. They were amazed. Bright walked back wiping tears on the way.

For a time, all sat still, watching the flames. The sun began to rise over the cliff. Sunlight traveled in a line towards the keep, towards the pyre. It lit the land in its wake, the sea sparkled blue. And when it finally touched the funeral pyre, it collapsed, sending sparks high into the sky. Everyone wept for the loss of Ahn Elaine.

They all took turns standing and telling stories of Ahn Elaine, of what they knew, what they had witnessed. Du Shar began, and Ahn Alanna followed, then the rest stood in turn. Bright had asked to go last.

Bright spoke at length of Elaine. Of her brilliant tactical guidance, of how much she learned from her about

Elvenrealm. She even credited Elaine's martial training for helping her acquire Alanna as a friend. Through many tears and many pauses to find her voice, she told everything she knew.

She concluded with the words, "Elaine, we will move on without you because we have to, we will cry a little less each day, but we will never forget you."

After a pause, Bright began again. "Sadly, we have suffered another great loss. As many of you already know, we have lost Sir Rhaine. And I have something that I need to share with you. Sir Rhaine sent a letter ... to me. I would like to read it to you now."

Bright read the letter, although it was difficult to get through. The warriors sat patiently in their tears and listened.

"This," Bright held the mighty bow aloft, "is Fang. The bow crafted by Sir Rhaine. It is her masterpiece, a testament to her skill and vision. I would invite each of you to come, hold the bow, and marvel in her achievement. And remember Sir Rhaine."

Leesee was already on her feet. She reverently took the bow, wonder in her eyes. "The magic bow!" she whispered.

"Leesee, you obviously weren't paying attention to the letter," Bright said.

Leesee held the bow, ran her fingers across each surface. Then she held it aloft as if in salute and said, "Sir Rhaine." Then she gently kissed the bow. Dahni was already standing next to her, so she passed it on. Once Dahni had admired it, she saluted and kissed it in the same manner. Leesee's act had become the standard. Each warrior, everyone present, one by one, followed her example.

And so with the ceremony complete, they headed back to the keep. The tide eventually washed away the ashes, while the memories were kept forever.

Chapter 22

CELEBRATE LIFE AND BREATHE

The courtyard of the keep was filled with warriors and their wolves. Sariel approached the chieftain.

"Du Shar, may I have a word with you?"

"If you feel you must," Shar replied.

"I have cleared all the goblins the made it through the border. Every one that I could track. I would like to accompany you back to Cor Malia, to fight with your warriors on the border."

"You mean to be with Bright," she stated. It wasn't a question.

Sariel hesitated a moment, then said, "Yes."

"Have you asked Bright to take you as her husband?" Shar asked.

"No. I have not."

"You don't want to be her husband?"

"I did not say that. I asked if I could fight with your warriors."

"You should ask me," Leesee said. "I've wanted to try you out anyway."

"Leesee!" Bright said.

"What? If you don't want him, it doesn't mean he has to go to waste."

"I didn't say I didn't want him."

"Leesee would just break him anyway," Dahni said.

Getting frustrated, Sariel said, "What I asked was, can I accompany your warriors into battle?"

"Of course not. You're not a warrior, you're a male," Shar answered.

"I assure you, Du Shar, I am a warrior."

"No, you're not. And you are wasting my time." Shar stood firm with her answer and prepared to walk away.

"Du Shar," Sariel said in a clear voice. "it is your custom to be challenged by trial when there is a dispute. I challenge you now. Here are my terms. If I beat you, I am allowed to fight with your warriors."

Du Shar instantly lost her temper. Bright had never seen her so angry. "NO!" She shouted. "My sisters have to depend on each other. It is no joke, no trivial thing. Males take care of the household, the children, and their warriors. I will not jeopardize the lives of my warriors so you can have your way. Your terms are rejected."

"Those are my terms."

Du Shar walked up to him, even though Sariel was much taller, it was Shar who posed the more imposing figure.

"Then, here are my terms. *When* I win, if you yet live, you have to mate with me. And continue to do so until you give me a strong daughter. Those are *my* terms."

"I cannot," Sariel replied.

"Those are my terms. Counter terms dictated by our custom. If you cannot abide by our customs, then walk away."

"I cannot do this. I cannot accept your terms ... because I love another."

"I'm not talking about *love*, you idiot! I don't love you. I can't stand the sight of you. I want a daughter. I want my daughter back! Do you think I don't know who you are? You took her from me ... my Tiah." Shar was angry, her face red. And still, tears fell down her cheeks. "I knew the first time I saw you here, and I hated you. I knew it was you. Do you deny it?"

Sariel looked down. "I do not."

"You took everything from me. You think you know of our customs? Do you know what it is to be so overcome with grief, that you cannot tell the story of your own daughter? I have lived with that shame ever since. A mother should never have to tell her daughter's story." She fell to her knees. "A mother should never have to be the one."

Everyone stood in shock. There had been a challenge, so no one came to comfort Du Shar in her grief. She would remain alone until the trial was resolved. Shar slowly stood.

"Only a warrior can enter the pit for a challenge," Bright said.

"Bright! You are not helping," Sariel protested.

"Ahn Elaine taught me that only a warrior can face another warrior. Is this not true?" Bright said.

Alanna spoke up quickly. "This is true."

"But Sariel could choose a champion, correct?" Bright said.

Alanna hesitated before admitting, "This is also true."

Bright turned to Sariel. "You are not a warrior in the eyes of my Clan, and Du Shar is angry. You very well may die. I have the skill to challenge her. Do you choose me as your champion?"

"Bright, this is not what I wanted. I just want to help," Sariel said.

"The terms have been set. Now you must choose to fight with me at the border, or stay here waiting in the keep. Do you choose me as your champion?"

"I do not want this," Sariel said, but Bright continued to

stare at him without speaking until he finally said, "Yes, you can be my champion."

Bright handed her bow, quiver, and knife to Leesee. She took a staff from one of the warriors. Bright stepped into a clear area. She spun the staff. She released it into the air, only to catch it behind her. She made it appear to float around her neck, going from one hand to the other. Finally, with a roar, she slammed it into the ground in front of her and assumed a ready position.

"Bring the Chieftain a weapon!" Bright commanded, and another warrior scrambled to do so.

Bright spun the staff behind her, then readied it. She slowly walked up to Du Shar, who was looking concerned.

"Du Shar, the terms have been set. I am the champion and speak for the challenger. He will yield. He will try to give you the strong daughter you desire. *If* you allow him to fight alongside our warriors at the border."

"Bright!" Sariel protested again.

"Silence!" Bright commanded. "This does not concern you now." But Sariel thought it most certainly did concern him.

Du Shar looked at Bright for a long time. Her anger faded, her grief subsided. She reached up, placing a hand behind her neck, she pulled Bright close, so their foreheads rested together. Shar stepped away and said, "I agree. I accept your yield and your terms."

Everyone cheered, except Sariel. He stood, looking shocked.

Bright walked up to him, he had no idea what to say or even think.

Bright smiled. "Your terms have been accepted. You will accompany us to the border."

"Bright, those were not my terms. How can you expect me to do this thing?"

"I expect you to do it because you care about me. Even if you haven't said it. And I love Shar, she needs this. There is another reason ... I care about you, and I feel safe with you. I want you with me at the border. Are those reasons enough?"

"I cannot ... you know I cannot guarantee the outcome she desires."

"Then you'll just have to try again. Shar is beautiful. Is it such a difficult task?"

Shar walked up and grabbed Sariel by the upper arm and began to lead him into the keep. "Come with me you big, clumsy oaf. I'm going to ride you like a rabid wolf. Try not to cry. I hate it when men cry."

"I hate that too," said Leesee. Dahni nodded.

Sariel kept looking back as he was led away. Bright just smiled and waved.

"If Du Shar doesn't break him, can I try next?" Leesee asked.

"No! You're too rough."

"That's probably wise," Dahni said. "How about me?"

Bright turned on Dahni, hesitated, then said, "Maybe, I'll think about it."

"Hey!" Leesee exclaimed.

Bright thought it was strange how different things were here. What was going on with Sariel, whom she loved, and Shar, whom she also loved would have been a matter of distress to her when she lived beyond The Veil. That is if she would have ever had the opportunity to have loved someone outside her immediate family. She found herself hoping their time together would be something tender, a reconciliation of sorts. She wanted them to grow closer, to be friends.

But custom had its dictates, its edicts to follow. The ceremony for Ahn Elaine was for her, to honor her. The time after was set aside for those that survived. For them to celebrate life and move forward. Bright was lost in these thoughts and did not even notice that Alanna stood at her side, and they were holding hands. She looked at Alanna and kissed her, deep and passionate. "It's time to party."

Surprised at the kiss, Alanna just smiled and nodded. Leesee and Dahni had shocked looks on their faces.

"What? Holy cow! You two? Really?" Leesee said. Dahni continued to stare with her mouth agape.

Bright laughed. "How about this? Leesee, the wine cellar is down the stairs, bring as much as you can carry. Dahni, find some cups. Alanna and I will grab something to eat, and we'll all meet at the pool. Let everyone you see know about it."

Soon everyone was out of their clothes, in the pool,

drinking, laughing, and splashing each other. Wolves swam among them or chased each other around the keep. The front gate was barred, so there was no need for sentries. Weapons were nearby, but they did not need clothing to operate correctly.

Much later, as the sun was just beginning to set. A very tired-looking Sariel walked to the pool with a bottle of wine and a cup. He was sort of trudging along, exhausted.

He looked up at the mass of women filling the pool and froze. "Apologies, Ladies. I did not know you were here." He turned to go.

"Wait a minute!" Bright shouted. "Where are you going?"

"I do not wish to interrupt."

"Nonsense. Come and join us. You obviously came for a bathe anyway."

Sariel thought Bright wore a bit of a mischievous expression. It made him feel wary. He had just been through an 'interesting' ordeal, bordering on the traumatic, and felt like being alone. "Perhaps it would not be proper."

"Let me understand this," Alanna began, "You think yourself warrior enough to fight alongside us, but you're afraid to drink and bathe with us?"

"You have to bathe, or the goblins will smell you," Leesee said.

"Worse yet, we'll smell you," added Dahni.

"How can we trust someone that won't drink with us?"

Pyper said.

"Such a harmless rite of passage," Bright said, "to bathe and drink with fellow warriors. Don't let us lose faith in you so soon." She was smiling and wiggling her eyebrows.

"Harmless? I assure you all, I am quite consumed by fear," Sariel said, yet he was starting to smile at their banter.

"Come on. Come over here and sit by me," Bright cajoled.

Sariel sighed, resigned to his fate. He loosened the tie of his stola, and it dropped. He started into the water.

"Oh my God!" yelled Leesee.

"Holy cow!" added Dahni.

"That thing is huge!" Leesee observed.

"Yeah, how can you run with all that swinging around?" Dahni asked.

Sariel immediately spun around and started to back into the water.

"Nice butt," From Leesee again as Sariel hurried to the deeper water holding up the wine bottle and cup.

Near one of the waterfalls, Bright sat on a submerged rock ledge. Alanna was to one side sitting close with her arm around Bright's shoulder. There was a small space on the other side between Bright and Leesee. Alanna introduced everyone to Sariel. He filled his glass and took a long drink.

"Just so you know, that's the most dangerous one *you* will

face here. Leesee's what you might call a Weapon of Mass Destruction," Bright said, pointing to Leesee. Leesee looked up at him with a sweet, innocent smile.

"I find it hard to believe such a pretty and petite lady will pose such a threat."

Everyone laughed at that. Sariel was a bit confused since he thought he was giving a compliment. He took another drink.

"Where's Du Shar?" Leesee suddenly asked.

"I'm sure she'll be down presently."

"Is she okay? Oh, my God! Is she still alive? Did you split her in half with that giant thingee? Should I go see? If you hurt her, you will see how dangerous I can be. You'll be wearing your guts around your neck!" Leesee was actually getting concerned.

"I'm quite well, thank you, Leesee. But it warms my heart to see you care enough to disembowel someone for me." Shar was wading into the pool.

"Whew!" Leesee said. "I was afraid he split you open once I saw the size of it."

"Or maybe your eyeballs had popped out," added Dahni.

"I assure you I am well and quite intact." Shar made her way over to Alanna who was holding out a cup for her.

"Did he cry?" Leesee asked.

"Thankfully, no," Shar informed her.

"Why do I always get the ones that cry?" Leesee asked.

"You don't 'get ones that cry'—you make them cry. Leesee, you're too rough," Bright said.

Dahni looked at Sariel. In her most serious and thoughtful tone, she said, "Men are delicate creatures."

Everyone laughed at that, except Sariel who was painfully embarrassed by the whole ordeal. And starting to actually be a bit afraid of Leesee.

Dahni swam close and said, "Bright won't let Leesee ride you because she breaks men too often. But she said 'maybe' to me. She said she would think about it." Dahni stood there grinning up at him.

"Ladies, I beg you, is there any way we could possibly change the topic to something else? Anything else?"

"What would you like to talk about?" Bright asked.

Relieved at the chance, Sariel said, "I have been most anxious to hear what has been happening with you since you left. Would you tell me about it? I would like to hear everything."

"There are only a few times when a warrior must tell their own story," Shar informed him.

"Oh," Sariel said, disappointed.

"However, we will tell you about Ahn Bright if you desire."

"Yes, thank you. I very much would like to hear," Sariel replied.

Sariel sat with his arm around Bright's waist as she leaned against him. They all took turns telling stories about Bright and drinking. All the while, Sariel sat amazed by what he had heard. There was no longer any doubt in his mind why Kerridwyn had brought her to Elvenrealm.

As soon as they were finished, Bright said, "Music! We need music. Sariel, pleeease go get the lute."

Sariel complied with her request and soon returned with the lute. "I have one rule, please respect it. Don't get the lute wet."

He sat on the stone bench and checked the tune. "Can I add another rule?" Bright asked. "None of that mournful stuff you play so often."

Sariel played many tunes for them. He strove to keep them light and merry. The warriors had gathered near Sariel and danced in the moonlight. Faeries gathered in the trees nearby.

"Would you like to sing, Lady Bright? Truth be told I have longed to hear your voice once again," Sariel asked.

With everyone encouraging her to sing, she stood next to Sariel. He played, and she sang. They all enjoyed it. By the time it was over, most had decided to move off to the keep. Sariel and Bright remained on the bench.

"You put me in a very uncomfortable position today. I want you to know that," Sariel said.

"I know. Was it horrible for you?"

"I wouldn't say horrible, but it was not something I would

have done. Absolutely not. Why would you put me in that position?"

"Because I missed you. You make me feel safe. I couldn't bear the thought of you not being with me. I know it's selfish, the border is dangerous, and I don't want you in danger, but *I* would feel better if you were there. I said it was selfish. So," Bright added, "Who is it you are in love with? You said you 'loved another.'"

"I have lived far too long to fall into that trap," Sariel said.

"What trap is that?"

"The trap of prematurely expressing oneself."

"Yeah? I don't get it," Bright said.

"Have you ever been walking in the woods, and come upon a fawn drinking from a stream? She looks so beautiful that you freeze, afraid she will hear you and run away. You fear to draw another breath because you just want to take in the moment, and remember it forever."

"What does that have to do with anything? So you just made up some story about loving someone else to try and get out of sleeping with Shar? Or are you trying to make me jealous?"

"What do you want me to say? That I have loved you since I first saw you lying on the moss at Kerridwyn's Pool? That I have thought of nothing but you ever since? You want me to tell you that I would die a thousand times for another moment with you? Well, I will not say any of those things. I am too afraid to frighten you; afraid that you will run away from me. I am too afraid to lose this moment, right now. So here I am, standing in the trees, still holding my breath."

Bright momentarily went limp. Then she gasped in a breath and covered her mouth with both hands. "Oh, my God!" She began to tear up. "Oh, my God!" She repeated and began to cry.

"Bright, I am so sorry. I never meant to upset you," Sariel said.

Bright sat there with her hands over her mouth and tears running down her cheeks. She slowly shook her head.

"What can I do?" Sariel pleaded. "I am sorry."

"Breathe, baby. Just breathe, I'm not running anywhere." Bright threw her arms around him and said, "That's the sweetest thing I've ever heard in my whole life. I love you so much."

"I love you, Bright. Although you may have guessed that already."

They kissed and embraced for some time. As she lay upon his chest, Sariel said, "Bright, I would have come anyway, you know. I would have come to Cor Malia with you even without Du Shar's blessing."

"Probably, but you would not have been welcomed. I was also caught between two people I love. There had to be a compromise. Are you angry with me?"

"Angry? I do not think so. Perhaps a little. I feel … guilty, as if I have betrayed you. It is all very embarrassing, especially the way they all seem to think it proper to talk openly about such things. These are personal matters, very personal."

"You had better get used to it. Especially around Leesee, she has absolutely no boundaries," Bright said. "But please don't feel guilty, you didn't betray me. I betrayed you, I suppose. I tricked you into it. It seemed like things were going very badly, very fast. I had never seen Shar so angry before. I didn't want her to hurt you, and I didn't want you to hurt her. But I guess, either way, I messed things up. Did I ruin things between us?"

"Things have changed, but not how I feel about you. You ... seem very close to Du Shar, and possibly some of the others?"

"I am. I've never been with a woman before. Is that what you are talking about? Does the idea shock you? It would've shocked me not that long ago. I guess I've been with them long enough to accept that it's normal."

"I will confess to feeling ... well, jealous. I am sorry."

"Would it make you feel any better if I told you I have never been with a man?"

"Nothing would change how I feel about you ... but yes, I admit it does make me feel better."

"My affection for my sisters, for Shar and Alanna ... is that something you can get past? You know, something you can accept about me?"

Sariel smiled. "It would be difficult to lose you. That I could not accept. You have grown, changed. I accept that.

You may not know that among my kind, relationships with mortals are discouraged. It has been known to happen, but it is somewhat frowned upon. Raphael is about the only one you would talk to that would not have a problem with it. Perhaps that is one of the reasons why I often seek his guidance. He is an accepting sort."

"Whoa, that reminds me. Did Raphael give me some healing power or something? You heard the story, you know, about my healing Alanna? Did he do that? He said he gave me a gift while we were at the gate."

"I know not. It sounds like something Raphael might do. If so, remember that all such gifts have a price, even for angels."

"I slept for almost two days."

"Then use it wisely, if you use it again at all. In battle, it would leave you helpless."

"I know, right?" Bright grew thoughtful. "Hey, I have completely forgotten about something. After Alanna was ambushed, one of the goblins said to 'get the human, the Archon wants the human.' They meant me but, what's an Archon?"

"Archon?" Sariel repeated. "The word meant 'ruler' long ago. I have known of a few that liked to refer to themselves as such. I will investigate the name. This is distressing news. It means that they know about you, and have targeted you. They will try again."

"Well, that sucks. Better not tell Shar, or she'll keep me back from patrols."

"It *is* a good idea to tell the chieftain."

"No, it's not. Sorry, I brought it up. I didn't think it would be such a buzz kill. Talk about something else."

"There is one thing, a request really. But before I ask, I will say that I believe it to be an inappropriate thing."

"What is it?"

"It is about your mark. It is beautiful in its own way. I was wondering if I might touch it."

Bright sighed in frustration. "You know, sometimes you can take being a gentleman a little too far. It was sweet when I first arrived because I was frightened. But sometimes, maybe once in a while, you could just touch me. You know when someone likes you or loves you, they should just go ahead and touch you, or even kiss you. You don't have to always have to …."

Sariel kissed her. Then he kissed her again. And later he gently ran his fingers over the Mark of the Wolf Rider.

Chapter 23

BOUNDARIES

Bright yawned and stretched. It was beginning to get light outside. She looked across the bed with a sleepy smile. Leesee and Dahni were propped up on their elbows, waiting for her to wake up. If that wasn't enough, the wolves were watching too, their heads resting on the mattress. Currently, Rhadia's ear was flopped down.

"So? What happened last night?" Leesee asked.

"Did it hurt?"

"No, Dahni. We didn't do that. We kissed. A lot. It was all very romantic."

"You should ask him to be your husband. I see the way you look at him," Leesee said.

"I thought the men had to ask," Bright said.

"They get to choose, sure. But nothing says you can't ask,"

Dahni said.

"Hmmm, I hadn't thought about that."

"Are you thinking about it now?" Leesee asked.

"Yes, I'm thinking about it now," Bright said and hit her with a pillow.

They dressed and headed down. They would all travel to Cor Malia as soon as everyone was ready. They stuffed food in their pouches and filled their water skins. Soon they were headed north.

Sariel walked with Bright, Du Shar (who rarely acknowledged him), and Alanna.

"So Leesee says you asked Sariel to be your husband?" Alanna said. "What did he say?"

"Oh my God, Alanna!" Bright was mortified. "That is not what happened."

"I do not remember being asked that," Sariel said.

"I didn't ask him that! Doesn't *anyone* have any boundaries?"

"A warrior knows no boundaries," Shar stated in an officious manner, although she was smiling.

"So you didn't ask him. Leesee told me a lie?" Alanna asked.

"All of you do realize that I am right here, do you not?" Sariel asked.

"She probably said I thought about asking him," Bright said to defend Leesee.

"Yes, I believe that *is* what she said. Apologies," Alanna said. Then to Sariel. "So if she *had* asked you, what would be your answer?"

"That would be a personal matter, between Bright and me." Then he turned to Bright. "Were you thinking about asking me to be your husband?"

"I ... What? I think I ... I have to go check on Rend," Bright stammered then ran on ahead with Spook at her heels.

Shar looked at Sariel, "I think you have embarrassed her."

"Males can be so insensitive," Alanna stated.

Sariel just shook his head, then burst out laughing at the absurdity of it all.

They made no fire that night. Sentries were out while the group sat around talking.

"Du Shar," Sariel began, "Bright has remembered something important, and I believe it should be discussed."

Bright immediately said, "Sure, if you want your ass kicked."

"What is the issue?" Shar asked.

"It's nothing, never mind," Bright said.

"Your husband said it was important," Du Shar said, and Leesee and Dahni immediately scooted closer.

"Holy Cow! You already asked him, and he said yes?" Leesee asked.

"No. But now's a good time. Sariel, would you like to be my husband?" Bright asked.

"If you were not asking that as a distraction, I would answer," Sariel stated.

"Oh, Bright! Can I use him sometime?" Dahni asked.

"Sure," she said, staring at Sariel with her arms crossed.

"How about me?" Asked Leesee.

"Leesee, I would normally say no, but now it depends on what Sariel says next."

Everyone was looking at Sariel, who was looking at little Leesee with no small amount of fear.

"What is it, male?" Du Shar demanded.

"Nothing, never mind," Sariel replied.

"Bright, if it concerns you, then it concerns the Clan and our Holy Quest." Du Shar was firm.

Bright waited a minute, then sighed, "Oh, all right. Last night I remembered something one of the goblins said before they attacked me. You know, during my trials?"

"And that was?"

"Something about 'get the human, the Archon wants the human,' but they might not have been talking about me."

"What other human have you seen here?" Shar asked.

"It's no big deal."

Shar looked to Sariel. "Do you believe it is not important? For I believe otherwise."

"I believe it is of grave importance," Sariel replied. "It means that goblin kind knows of her existence and see her as a threat. It means they will specifically target Bright and seek her out in battle. Possibly to abduct her, but most likely to kill her."

"And you thought this was not important?" Du Shar asked Bright.

"I just remembered it last night. Look, I already talked about this with Alanna, I don't want any special treatment. I am an Ahn. Every Ahn, every knight, and every warrior is in danger. I'm no different."

"You're the Elvenstar. That's kind of different," Leesee observed.

"Leesee, can you ever just be quiet?"

"I don't think she can, Bright," Dahni added helpfully. "But she forgot to mention The Quest."

"I will think about this, everybody get some sleep. We'll set out before first light," Du Shar said. Then she moved and sat closer to Sariel. "Do you have any idea who this Archon is?"

"No. Not really, but there is something I need to investigate, although it seems highly unlikely. If I learn anything useful, I will tell you."

"By the way, Sariel, thanks a lot for bringing this up," Bright said.

"Please, Lady, do not be too angry with me. I swore to protect you before you were Bright and before there was a quest. Your chieftain needed to know."

Bright lay with Spook beside her. She was slowly stroking the fur on his chest as he lay on his back with his tongue drooping out of his mouth. When Sariel went to lie down next to Bright, she turned her back on him. Then she wiggled up against him, grabbed his arm and threw it around her. He held her tight.

Chapter 24

THE TRADE ROUTE

Back in Cor Malia things settled into a routine. Sariel accepted a bed in the Great Forge with Sir Mahri's husbands. Except for the occasional butt squeezes, she kept her advances to herself, knowing he belonged to Bright ... or at least she assumed that he would be her husband soon. He took to patrolling the northern border alone. He was often gone for days at a time. When he returned, he would spend as much time as he could with Bright. They walked holding hands and talked about anything that came to their minds. Bright spoke, for the most part, and Sariel listened to every word. Ahn Alanna had told Du Shar what Sariel said about her daughter, Tiah. After a few days, her attitude towards him softened considerably.

Bright stayed with Shar most of the time if she happened to be in Cor Malia. When Shar was away preparing defenses in another village, she remained with Alanna. Although many mornings found all three waking together. Even with the impending threat from the north, it was a happy time.

Wolves are essentially wolves, no matter how big. The pups grew and needed training, even though they were much more intelligent than a dog from across The Veil. One of the Ahns seemed to be gifted in this regard and held classes that they all attended together. They were taught all the basic commands, how to track, and how to fight. Often the new Ahns would walk through the woods, guiding their wolves by the neck with fistfuls of fur. This helped to prepare them for once they were big enough to ride. Dahni's beast, Rhadia, was the slowest to catch on. But when she tried to scold him, Rhadia would just tilt his head, and one ear would flop down. Whenever that happened, Dahni would forget about scolding him, and just hug him and kiss his nose. The trainer thought the cartilage in Rhadia's ear had been damaged early on in a puppy fight.

Bright learned that there were Aquatic Elves. They had a village near the sea far to the south-west. They weren't part of the Clan, but they would conduct trade with them. They traded pearls, dried fish, and spices for leather, hardwoods, and various other items. The apothecaries from both the north and south depended on trade with each other.

The trade caravans were heading west from Triborien and passing through Pagaetier. Each village would have sent at least two warriors. Cor Malia would send two or three with their traders. Since the trade route was relatively safe, Du Shar thought it would be an excellent opportunity for Bright to meet the villagers in Senisterum and those in Monlach at the north end of the Monlach Sea.

Shar made her way to the training grounds and found all four girls asleep in the shade leaning against their wolves, who were also sleeping. She walked up to Bright, nudged her foot, and said, "Training hard?"

Bright opened her eyes, smiled and yawned. Spook yawned, making an odd noise. He looked at Shar then stretched. Bright held up her hand and waved it around. Du Shar rolled her eyes at the young warrior but reached down and helped her to her feet anyway. Bright wrapped her arms around Shar and yawned again.

"I hate to interrupt. I can see you're busy," Shar said sarcastically.

"I know, right?" Bright said. "But I always have time for you."

"I was being sarcastic."

"I wasn't," Bright said sweetly.

"The traders from the eastern villages will be arriving soon. They will be heading to Monlach, then down to Tranquility by way of the Western Pass. We normally send a couple of warriors to protect the caravan, but it's more to make them feel better than any real need for protection. I was wondering if you would like to join them. There are many in the outlying villages that would love to meet The Elvenstar."

"Oo! Oo!" Leesee jumped up and had her hands in the air, startling Doug, who was looking around confused. "Can I go? Can I go too?"

Leesee's outburst had awakened Dahni. "If Leesee's going,

I want to go."

"I don't see why not," Shar said. "It doesn't look like any of you are doing much right now besides laying around going soft. Pyper can go as well if she wants to … if she ever wakes up. Willow is already worked into the patrol schedule so she will have to stay back. Get yourselves ready, the caravan will leave early tomorrow morning. Meet them at the Great Hall." Shar kissed Bright and walked away.

"This will be so much fun!" Leesee squealed.

They passed the Bowery and checked to see if Kalia had made any more of the fire arrows.

"Hello, welcome back *Ahn* Bright, *Ahn* Dahni, and *Ahn* Leesee. Congratulations are in order! Where is Elaine?"

"Kalia, she didn't make it through the Bonding," Leesee told her.

"Oh, no. Oh, my. I didn't know. I'm so sorry."

"As are we. We'll tell you the story sometime, but I wanted to see about those fire arrows. Did you happen to make any more? I used the one you sent me for the pyre," Bright said.

"Oh, Elaine would have liked that. Anyway, yes. I have about a half dozen more left over after the testing phase. We tried to use steel, but they were just too heavy. So I decided to stay with bamboo. I think it is okay since damage isn't their purpose. At first, they kept bending, and some wouldn't ignite. So I used a small spike, almost a nail, embedded in the shaft rather than use an arrowhead. It runs through a hole drilled in the bamboo joint and serves to keep it straight on impact. I've scored the spike to help it stay in place, you know, in the troll hide."

"It worked perfectly," Bright told her. "I think you should make more if you can."

"I'll inform my superiors, and we'll get to work if they authorize it. If they don't, I can always work on them in my spare time. How many do you think we need?"

"I think it would be good if all the archers had at least one. There is no way of telling who'll need it."

"Wow. Okay. That's a lot, but I'll see what I can do." Kalia had jars of oil handy that she was using for the testing. They scooped those up and headed home.

At Shar's quarters, Bright found Drew and Buckson cleaning the kitchen. "Hello, Ahn Bright," Buckson said. "Are you hungry? We can fix you something."

"No, thank you, Buckson." She started up the stairs, then came immediately back down.

"Where is Shar?" She asked.

"I'm afraid she's out again. She spends so little time at home these days," Drew replied.

"Can I get you to change your mind? We can make you some supper, it would be our pleasure," Buckson said it, but the others were nodding.

"Not tonight. But thank you," Bright said. "I think I will head to Alanna's for the night."

"Good choice. I have always found Alanna's company quite enchanting," Buckson said with a wink.

"Didn't she accept you as her husband? I thought that I would find you there."

"Alas, there are duties to see to in this household first. The beautiful Alanna has told me to take my time and ensure that Shar doesn't suffer from the transition. She is really quite considerate. I will sorely miss Shar and my brother husbands, but the excitement of a new child is too much for me to resist."

"I understand. I hope you don't mind me taking advantage of 'the beautiful Alanna' until you arrive," Bright said, giving him one of those winks he was famous for.

"Not at all! Where I am, you are always welcome. I will silently endure having two beautiful creatures prance around naked most of the time. I have grown quite used to it. I'm amazingly stoic where such things are concerned, really." He was wearing a broad grin.

Bright laughed. "I don't think 'stoic' is the right word for it, Buckson." She was still smiling as she rode the descent line down.

Amica greeted Bright with a quiet bark and after the appropriate amount of petting, allowed her to climb the ladders. She found Alanna sprawled across the bed, her right leg dangling off the edge. She had kicked off the blankets again in her sleep. As she undressed for bed, Bright noticed the four scars of varying lengths on the inside of Alanna's left thigh. She ran her finger across the one nearest her knee.

Alanna woke enough to see it was Bright, then made an *Mmmm* sound and lay her head back down. Bright gently stroked the scar, then moved to the next one up. Touching the top one caused Alanna a small spasm in her abdomen. A low moan accompanied it. Bright repeated the exploration from the bottom up but with kisses this time. The moaning gradually grew in volume.

The Caravan Master was from Triborien. He was older with hair more gray than brown. His skin tanned, wrinkled, and weather-beaten. He had been in charge of the movement along the trade route for about a half-century. He was also the first male Bright had encountered in a position of authority. As husband to the last Caravan Master, he knew more than anyone else about the route and how to move and account for the goods along the way. After his wife died, he just sort of took over, and no one thought anything of it. She found out that his name was Basil.

"Why's Cor Malia sending four warriors, *Ahns* ta boot, on this trip?" Basil demanded of Bright, peering up at her from under his wide-brimmed hat. "Are we expectin' trouble?"

"No, sir. Things were slow, and we wanted to see Tranquility," Bright answered.

Basil peered closely at Bright. "You're that Elvenstar gal, aren't ya?"

"Yes, Sir."

"Don't have any royal carriages for ya ta ride in."

"I wouldn't want that. I'll walk with my friends."

"*Hmmmph*," he said, then turned his head and spat. He had a cheek full of some herb he was chewing on. "Let's get a move on. We're wastin' light. Got a pub in Senisterum wit' my name on it, an' I mean to be drinking 'afore sundown." He started trudging west.

"That's Basil," Leesee said. "I like him."

The caravan groaned into motion with much creaking and coaxing of burrows. The largest two wagons were in the front, each pulled by a team of six. Those contained exotic woods found near Cor Malia and were the only wagons with four wheels, most were two-wheeled carts. No one rode in the carts or wagons, they walked alongside the burros, sometimes pushing the carts or helping the wheels turn over potholes on the trail.

Bright and Leesee walked a little ways ahead on the south side of the trail, while Dahni and Pyper took point on the north. The two warriors from Pagaetier took up flanking positions midway down the caravan while the two from Triborien brought up the rear. They left on a bright, sunny day, and the moon would be beginning to wax full that night. It looked like it would be perfect traveling weather.

The wagons and carts moved slowly, making for a relatively leisurely walk for the young Ahns. The wolf training had not been rigorous, so they were well-rested. They stopped for breaks and munched on pemmican and berries found along the way. By the time the sun was low on the horizon, they had entered the village of Senisterum. Senisterum was much smaller but looked similar to Cor Malia with stone buildings and tree dwellings. However, most of the buildings near the heart of the village were made of wood. The caravan came to an abrupt halt right on the trail, and the traders began making preparations to bed down for the night.

Bright and her friends approached Basil. "Lookie there!" He declared, pointing at a sign. "I told ya, didn't I?" Sure enough, there was a sign outside of a tavern with the words, *Basil's Break Tavern.* He gazed at the door and sighed. "Told ya there was a pub with my name on it. Come on in, first round is on me. Best part of the whole trip."

Basil burst through the door, put his hands on his hips and bellowed, "Ya drinkin' without me? Done tol' ya that wasn't allowed."

The tavern went silent, even the music stopped. Then many of the crowd lifted their cups and shouted back, "Basil!"

"Good evn'in, ya pack a drunken slobs," Basil said. "I brought our young Elvenstar wit' me this trip." He was pointing at Bright as if she didn't stand out anyway. Basil snatched a cup of mead from one of the passing serving boys, most likely ordered by another table. Basil gave him a pat on the backside as he went by. The boy rolled his eyes, knowing another trip to the bar was necessary.

The small tavern was already nearly full, and suddenly appeared much more crowded to Bright as most of the patrons stood and made their way to her. A young man in the corner started playing the lute while his partner began to sing. Soon Bright was surrounded by Elves who all began to talk or ask questions at once. She tried to be polite and answer their questions, but soon became overwhelmed. Before she realized it, she had been moved along to a seat at the head of the biggest table. Her friends were given positions at the table as well, while their former occupants stood close by. It appeared the rest of the tavern had gathered around. Tables and chairs were being pushed out of the way accompanied by loud, scraping noises. The wolves retreated under the large table to keep their paws and tails from getting stepped on.

Cups of mead appeared in front of the Ahns. Leesee and Dahni finished the first one in seconds. Questions came from everywhere in the crowd. Bright tried to be polite and answer one when ten more shot in. She was unaccustomed to this kind of attention and kept losing her train of thought. The musicians played and sung louder to be heard over the crowd.

"I'm sorry, there are too many questions ..." Bright began, then she hid her face in her hands.

"SHUT IT!" boomed Basil as he stood. "Shut it! Arv sawr more manners from an ogre. Ya two tarts in the corner take a break or git out." He was addressing the musicians. "Now we all want to meet young Miss Bright. But yer scarin' her. Here's what ye'll do. Ye'll shut it, and the Elvenstar will tell ya all about herself." Basil took a cup of mead from someone standing behind him and sat back down, looking smug. He looked at Bright and nodded.

Everyone was quiet and staring at her, so she began, "Well,

my name is Bright, but that was after Kerridwyn named me. When I arrived, my name was Jenny …" Bright began to tell them her story while Leesee tried to see how much mead Doug would drink from her cup.

At closing, the tavern owner insisted that the Ahns stay at her quarters. Leesee had already picked up the musicians and were heading to their home. She made them struggle, taking turns carrying Doug, who had too much to drink. Dahni followed to watch and prevent injuries to the young men, a task she was totally unqualified for. Later they heard the rumor that the lute player wasn't able to move his thumb properly. It took weeks for him to recover enough to play.

Chapter 25

MONLACH

They only picked up two carts from Senisterum, and they provided no additional warriors. The caravan moved out and didn't arrive into Monlach until the early morning hours of the next day. The good news was that they were not going to leave until the following day, so they had plenty of time to sleep and see the lakeside town. They spent the remainder of that night and most of the next morning at the barracks where most of Monlach's warriors were housed. Two of these were to accompany the caravan when it headed south.

They met Captain Domina, Monlach's Captain of the Guard. Bright thought she was the most muscular woman she had ever seen, on either side of The Veil. Bright found her to be a bit arrogant, but her warriors seemed to love her.

The next day they wandered around the town and spent time at the docks watching the fishing boats sail around the vast Monlach Sea. Monlach had many carts joining the caravan. They passed the apothecary shop and saw a girl loading a crate onto a cart.

The little girl saw them. "You're Bright! Aren't you? You have to be, I've never seen another human."

"I am," Bright said. "What's your name?"

"I'm Mariana," She said then promptly ran over and gave Bright a big hug. She was young, Bright thought she was very young, and she was quite different from the other elves. Her skin was dark, and she had straight blonde hair with dark blue eyes. "I wanted to be a warrior, like you. I wanted to be a knight one day."

"How old are you, Mariana?" Bright asked. "You are so cute!"

"I'm eleven. My mother says I have to be an apothecary, like her. But I always wished I could be a warrior and protect people."

"Well, you've got plenty of time to decide what you want to be," Bright told her.

She looked sad. "No. Now I'm too old."

"You're only eleven."

"I started training when I was eight years old," Leesee said.

Dahni nodded and said, "Me too."

"And when I was eleven, I was sent to Cor Malia to train. That was the best thing that ever happened to me." Leesee looked at Dahni and smiled.

"Yeah," Dahni said. "That's when we met. We didn't get along at first. One day we got into a terrible fight. We were all bruised up and covered in blood, but we kept at it until neither one of us could move."

"Then I crawled over to Dahni and kissed her," Leesee added.

"It was the most romantic thing ever!" Dahni said. "I think I'm going to cry just thinking about it."

Mariana's mother exited the apothecary with another crate.

"Well, I don't think you're too old. You can grow up to be whatever you want to be, Mariana. You can be a knight if that's what you want."

Glass shattered as Mariana's mother gasped and dropped the crate. Mariana shouted for joy and jumped up on Bright, wrapping her legs around her waist and kissing her, thanking her repeatedly.

"How could you do such a thing?" her mother shouted. Then she began to cry and ran back into the apothecary.

Bright looked over Mariana's head to Leesee and Dahni, who both wore a visible 'oh, shit' expression. "What? What just happened?"

"You just said she could be a warrior," Leesee said.

"And I don't think that her mother liked it. Not one bit," Dahni added.

"But it's not my decision to make."

"You're the Elvenstar. You said it. Now it has to happen," Leesee told her.

"Oh, no," Bright said. "Oh, shit!"

"Yup, big shit."

"We should get out of here before she returns with a vial of acid or something," Dahni said.

Bright peeled the jubilant Mariana off her waist and they left at a fast pace. She felt awful about the damage she might have caused with a few words.

They spent the rest of the day staying out of sight. The next morning Bright avoided the apothecary's cart. Pyper had been unusually quiet and keeping to herself. When approached about it, she only admitted that she didn't feel right without Willow and wished she hadn't come along on the trip.

Soon enough they were headed around the western edge of the Monlach Sea and down the Western Pass. The scenery was breathtaking with the Monlach Sea to the east and the Acies Mountains to the west.

They camped near the lake that night. Monlach had assigned another two warriors, and they all took turns with sentry duty. Basil prepared a cauldron of hearty stew. While Bright was enjoying the meal, Mariana's mother approached her.

"My name is Sara," she informed Bright.

Bright set down her bowl and stood. "I'm pleased to meet

you, Sara. My name is Bright."

"I know who you are. I just thought you should know my name, and the names of the family you destroyed. My husband is Paul."

"Please, I am so sorry I said anything. I was only trying to be encouraging. Mariana doesn't have to be a warrior. She will be a wonderful apothecary."

"It's too late!" She sobbed. "Mariana heard it from your lips. Now I have to send my little girl away. I just ..." She stopped, set her bowl down on the ground, and walked away.

Doug and Rhadia went to the bowl and started racing each other to see who could eat more first. Bright was no longer hungry and set her bowl down in front of Spook.

It was midafternoon when there was a commotion in the caravan. Bright looked back to see traders scattering from their carts. Leesee's sharp eyes saw it first, and she yelled, "Dragon!"

Bright notched an arrow and followed her aim. She saw it. It plummeted towards the earth at nearly two hundred miles per hour. Its wings were folded back, and it headed straight for the lead wagon. Bright froze for just a moment as she took in the sight of it. Leesee and Dahni were launching one arrow after another to no effect. Like a falcon, it kept to its course without deviation. She loosed an arrow but knew it would miss as soon as she let it fly. As she tried to recalculate the next shot, it was nearly to the ground. It had brought its powerful back legs forward for the strike.

Right before the monster was about to unfurl its wings to brake the descent, one of Dahni's arrows went wide and struck its wing right at the first joint. It went between the scales, through the thick skin and severed the tendon. The dragon intended to spread its wings to brake but only one unfurled. It twisted sideways and crashed heavily to the ground right on top of the lead burro of the lumber wagon, killing it instantly. The burro hitches splintered and the back wheels came off the trail, spilling the lumber everywhere. Three of the six burros got loose and ran towards the mountains. The one in the rear was still hitched, but terrified and trying to get away. Another that was hitched next to the one that was hit was making awful noises. It had two broken legs.

One of the dragon's rear legs was also broken and splayed at an odd angle. It hit with so much force there was an indention in the trail. Soft whining noises from the dragon could be heard between the braying of the injured burro.

Basil stomped over to Bright. "Well, what'r ya waiting for? Go put em out of their misery. Start with the poor burro."

"Um … what?" Bright said.

"Ya heard me. Put an en' ta the sufferin'."

"Be careful, Bright," Leesee warned.

"Um … what?" Bright repeated.

"They're waiting for you to put them both out of their misery. Just be careful. You know, in case the dragon isn't as hurt as it seems."

"Can it breathe fire?" Bright asked.

"Can it what?"

"You know, can it breathe out fire?"

"That may be the stupidest thing I've ever heard you say. Bright," Leesee replied. "how could they possibly do that?"

"I dunno. It's just what I've heard."

"Well, don't worry about that … can't happen," Leesee stated with absolute authority.

Bright walked over to the lead wagon with Spook at her side. The poor burro was in pain and would die given enough time. She was aware that the others were gathering around at a safe distance, watching her. She maneuvered around to get a shot at its heart. Once again, she felt like an assassin. She released an arrow which hit just behind its broken front leg, and in seconds it was dead, and the braying ceased.

She had concentrated on the burro. Now she looked at the dragon. Its body was as big as the wagon. The long neck and tail made it seem even larger. It was on its side with one wing pretty much destroyed. The other was somewhat folded. She could hear the soft whining sound now.

"Hey, Bright!" Leesee yelled. "Dragons *can* spit venom. No fire, though."

Bright just shook her head and rolled her eyes. "Thanks, Leesee."

Bright studied the dragon, unsure of where to hit it to end its life. She thought it was beautiful, in its own way. Metallic sky blue scales reflected the light of the sun. It was powerful, majestic. At least it should have been before it smashed into the ground. Its scales looked very strong, so Bright circled around to try to find a soft spot, maybe an eye.

Her boots crunched on the gravel, and it slowly turned its head around and looked at Bright. It seemed sad and definitely hurting. She realized it didn't go after any of the traders, it had attacked a burro. Bright felt horrible as she raised her bow and took aim at the poor dragon's eye.

"I'm sorry," Bright said and felt a tear fall down her cheek.

The dragon whined softly and closed its eyes for a moment, then it heard the singing of Bright's bow, Fang, under the stress of the draw. He looked back at Bright. Bright stood ready, then released the tension on the bowstring, realizing that this beautiful creature needed to live on.

"Look," she told the dragon, "I think you were just hungry. The burros are already dead, and we can leave them for you. But you have to promise us safe passage." The dragon just looked at her and moaned.

Bright put her arrow back in the quiver and stepped closer.

"Bright!" Leesee yelled. "What are you doing?"

Bright ignored her and stepped closer. "I can heal you, but you have to promise us safe passage, okay?" The dragon looked at her. "If I heal you, you can't attack us. Or spit acid or fire or anything. Are you okay with that? Is it a deal?"

She got even closer, and the dragon didn't move. She touched the metallic scales on its head, and the dragon made another mournful sound. Bright put both hands on the dragon, and blue sparks filled the air around her. The dragon, already blue, radiated and reflected her blue light from inside and out. Bright collapsed to the ground. Spook ran right up beside her and faced the dragon, his teeth bared and fur bristling.

The blue dragon folded its wings and lurched up, bringing its back legs underneath. Then it stood up on all fours. Bright was directly beneath it with only a growling Spook between them.

Long moments passed as the dragon looked upon the unconscious body of Bright. Everyone stood perfectly still, not daring to move. Then the dragon spread its wings and with a kick of its sturdy legs and the beat of wings, thrust itself into the sky. Bright wasn't visible at first as dust, grass, and leaves filled the air.

Her friends rushed through the cloud and found her, lying on the trail covered in dust.

It was nearly dawn when she woke up. Her head was on Leesee's lap, and her friends were with her.

"*That* was even dumber than the fire-breathing question." Leesee scolded her immediately. "What were you thinking? You could have been eaten." Leesee was so mad at her that she started to cry.

"I'm sorry." She mumbled and fell back asleep.

Bright stretched and yawned. She was lying on blankets on the lead lumber wagon. A good portion of the lumber had been removed. They intended to pick up the rest on the way back and sell it another time. Field repairs had taken place on the hitch, and four burros were back to work. Dahni and Leesee were walking beside the wagon. Leesee noticed she was sitting up and walked up close.

"I'm still mad at you," Leesee said.

"I know. Sorry."

"What were you thinking?"

"It really wasn't very smart," Dahni added.

"I guess it wasn't. It just looked so beautiful. I've never seen a dragon before, and it was just too sad to let it die. I felt sorry for it."

"It wouldn't have been sorry to make a meal of you."

"We could be looking around for Bright flavored dragon poop for your funeral pyre. How would that make you feel?" Dahni said.

"Like poop. But it looked like it was more interested in the burros than us," Bright said. "How long are you going to stay mad at me?"

"I don't know. A little while longer. You deserve it."

A couple of moments passed, Bright asked, "How about now? Still mad?"

"Yup."

Bright jumped off the moving wagon, nearly falling over.

Leesee steadied her and Bright gave her a hug. Leesee pulled away and punched her in the arm.

"Ow!"

"Okay, I'm over it now."

"Thanks," Bright said, rubbing her arm.

As they neared Tranquility, Basil told them all about it. The Elves of Tranquility were different; they spent their time on or in the ocean. They fished and dove for the treasures the sea provided. Some of their divers could swim down incredible distances. To such depths that it was rumored they could breathe underwater, but Basil assured them that was untrue. Centuries in the sun had changed their features; they were dark-skinned with pale, blonde hair. They wore tight leather clothing that had been oiled in such a way as to remain flexible and resistant to saltwater.

Tranquility Elves had no warrior caste. They lived in peace for the most part and spent their time meditating and pondering the secrets of the universe. They were governed by their priests. Tranquility was an egalitarian society, neither sex held dominance over the other. Although friendly and accommodating, they felt no need to be a part of the Clan. They recognized the authority of the God and Goddess and sought to follow their own path to enlightenment.

The landscape became a peninsula, and soon, the caravan pulled into the village. The homes and buildings of Tranquility were of wood, tall and circular with conical roofs. Those built near the ocean were raised on poles. Many were actually built on pylons over the blue water.

Chapter 26

CRAZY IS CONTAGIOUS

The caravan rolled into Tranquility. Bright noticed that the people were clustered in small groups. A particularly gorgeous young man wearing the blue robes of a priest detached himself from one of those groups and approached Bright and her friends, still leading the caravan. He had long, blond hair and a square jaw. Lean and muscular but not nearly the size of Sariel, he had the look of a swimmer.

"Greetings, Clan. I am called Jon. Welcome to Tranquility. Let me apologize for the confusion. There has been a disturbing incident."

"Hi. I'm Bright, and these are my friends. Leesee, Dahni, and Pyper," She said, pointing to each in turn. "What happened?"

"Ah! So you are the Elvenstar. I am so pleased to meet you." He took Bright's hand. "You are lovelier than I imagined. I heard about you, but those words do not do you justice." He continued to hold her hand.

"Um ... thanks. What happened?" Bright repeated.

"Ah. It is quite unusual. For the past three days, we have suffered raids from a troll. Each night a villager has been taken. Not too long ago, it was a child. Quite unfortunate. Would you care to join me for dinner tonight?"

Leesee crossed her legs tight and held her breath. She was determined not to pee herself. "Excuse me. I've got to find somewhere to pee."

"What? Dinner? No, what are you *doing* about it?" Bright removed her hand from his grasp.

"I was thinking about a poached sea bass. Some wine, of course. I am an accomplished chef, but that will be for you to judge. I look forward to our time alone together."

"What? No! What are you doing about the troll?"

"Ah. Life brings many lessons. Some are lessons of joy, while others may be of sorrow. We must learn from each one."

"Okay ... so what are you doing to stop the attacks?"

"The whole thing is most unusual. At the moment, the priesthood has gathered to meditate and manifest that the troll will depart the area."

"You're ... meditating?" Bright asked incredulously.

"Yes. Vigorously," Jon replied.

"How about killing it?" Bright asked. "Problem solved."

"That is not our way. We do not condone killing outside of the bounty provided by the sea. There are no warriors here."

"The Clan has many warriors. We're here now."

He stepped close and held her by the shoulders. "That you are here now, with me, is a wonderful thing. My home is on the water, the one with the blue pennants. It is shallow there so you can wade out with no problem. If you come by before dark, we can drink wine and watch the sunset together."

"Are you insane?" Bright was getting angry. "The troll took a child? Was it still alive?"

"She was alive when she was taken. It is all very distressing."

"And all you can think about is having dinner with me."

"Yes, your beauty consumes me."

Bright had enough. She walked away and gathered the warriors. There were ten of them in all. Since the troll had come every night, she decided to have three stay back to guard the village and the caravan. She left them two fire arrows and two jars of oil.

"Leesee, you should stay back. I know how you feel about trolls."

"Not gonna happen," she said. "Don't worry, I peed behind the wagon. I'm good."

Bright chose three to stay back, and the rest followed the

troll tracks back up the peninsula. At the foothills of the Acies Mountains, it grew rocky. They lost the sign and had to spread out until they found it again. The trail led to a path between two mountains and for a time they traveled quickly, wanting to destroy it before darkness fell.

The path became a narrow gorge, with steep walls lining the sides. Sounds echoed through the pass from up ahead. Bright opened one of the jars of oil, and the archers dipped their fire arrows. Cloth wrapped around the head of the arrow absorbed the oil; wicking action spread it. If they put too much on, they would risk getting the phosphorus and sulfur mixture wet, and it wouldn't ignite. They had four of these; Bright had two. Bright handed the rest of the jar to Pyper. Pyper and two warriors, each armed with oil, took the lead.

Pyper walked with her axe in her left hand, and the jar in her right, ready to throw. The path curved and there was an opening in the rock. It appeared to be a large crack between two slabs of granite. The footprints led inside.

Pyper crept up to the opening and peered into the gloom. She let her eyes adjust to the darkness and took another step. A deafening shriek came from within, followed by a raking blow from a clawed hand. One of the clawed fingers caught Pyper on the bottom of her jaw, while the rest gouged her chest with a ripping thud. Pyper was thrown back out of the opening, dropping the jar and her axe. She had another jar of oil on her belt. It shattered and soaked her hip in the fall.

The creature emerged and stood tall over Pyper with wicked claws upraised for the strike. Bright was startled, and her eyes naturally followed the creature's hand. Without thinking, she released her arrow. It struck the troll's hand and ignited, immediately catching the troll's attention. It grabbed the shaft and pulled. The shaft pulled free, but the arrowhead remained, burning the small amount of oil wrapped around the tip. The troll managed to grasp it and pull it out as two more jars of oil struck it in the chest, thrown by the warriors from Triborien.

The troll spun, and Leesee's arrow struck it in the back. The small fire caused pain, but the oil was on the front and didn't ignite. The monster spun back and jumped towards another warrior. Dahni's arrow struck it in the chest, igniting the oil. It howled and shrieked and danced about while the fire burned. It fell to its knees, howling in pain.

Pyper ran to the opening and retrieved her axe. The troll was still burning when she severed its head, and the howling ceased.

"Pyper!" Bright called out. "You're hurt. Let me ..."

That was all she could say before they heard another angry shriek. There was more than one troll!

"There's only one jar left!" Pyper shouted and headed for the opening.

"No!" Bright shouted. "RUN!" She grabbed Pyper by the arm and yanked her in the direction they had come.

Everyone ran except Bright. She stepped into the opening in time to hear another blood-chilling shriek. She looked inside. It took a moment, but she finally saw the jar lying on the floor. The troll's footsteps crunched in the gravel as it drew near. Bright aimed and shot her last fire arrow. It struck the jar, ignited, and the narrow passageway burst into flames. The fire illuminated the other troll. It was a female with sagging, pendulous breasts, much bigger than the first. It cried out in rage. Bright ran after the others, knowing the flames would die out all too soon.

Bright ran through the gorge as fast as she could, Spook ran just in front of her. By the time she heard it shriek again, Bright was nearly out of the narrow portion. She put on a burst of speed. Bright could hear the sound of it running up behind her, gaining on her, but she dared not turn to look.

The path had opened up, but Bright knew it would soon catch her. The others realized that Bright wasn't with them and arrows rained down into the monstrous troll behind her. It roared and slowed a bit. Bright could see Pyper running back towards her, axe in hand, her face grim. Spook and Pyper's wolf were charging right beside her.

"Go back!" Bright said, out of breath.

Pyper and the wolves did fall back, with Bright nearly on top of them, as they were all buffeted by a gale-force wind. There was a thud so loud that they felt the vibrations in the earth.

Bright went to her hands and knees and turned to see the magnificent blue dragon, its claws firmly planted in the troll, who now lay smashed and broken into the rocks. It roared and bit down, ripping off the troll's head.

Between heavy breaths, Bright couldn't help but release a

sound that resembled a hysterical laugh. She slowly regained her composure and stood.

Bright ignored the protests from the warriors behind her and walked towards the dragon. She breathlessly kept repeating, "Thank you," as she walked. The dragon released the troll head with a coughing sound and faced Bright. As she came closer, the dragon reared back, head high, and beat its wings a few times. Bright stopped.

It looked down at her and dropped to four legs. He stretched out his head towards Bright and sniffed. Bright held out her hands and slowly, the dragon rested his massive head between them. Bright kissed him on the muzzle, then rested her cheek against his.

"Thank you," She repeated, more clearly this time.

The dragon pulled back, studied her a moment, then turned and began to climb. When it reached the peak, it roared and sailed into the sky. The warriors gathered around Bright.

"Holy shit!" Leesee said, breaking the silence.

Bright turned to Pyper. "You're hurt. Let me help you."

"Oh, no you don't," Pyper said. She proudly looking down at her chest. "I only know of two other warriors that have troll scars. Don't you dare mess with them." She was actually smiling now, Bright thought it was the first time since the trip began. "I can't wait to show Willow."

"Let's get out of here," Dahni said.

"Not yet," Bright said. "I have to go check the cave."

"Oh, my God!" Leesee exclaimed. "I didn't say anything about the whole dragon kissing thing. But there could be more of them in the cave. Can we just go without doing something else, you know, crazy?"

"We don't know if the child is still there," Bright said. "It could be alive. I have to know."

"I'll go with you," Dahni said.

"Fine!" Leesee said. "Just let me pee first."

"Hey!" Bright said, pointing at her dry leggings. "How come you didn't pee yourself when the troll came out?"

"I dunno. Maybe crazy is contagious."

Chapter 27

VIGOROUS MEDITATION WORKS

A small crowd of people waited in Tranquility as the warriors approached. Dahni was carrying the little girl the troll had abducted; she had fallen asleep. Her parents cried out and ran to take her.

Jon walked up to meet them. Bright threw a troll head at his feet. He jumped back as it rolled across the ground, a disgusted look on his face. Spook thought it was a game of fetch and bounded after the rolling head. Jon looked back up just in time to dodge the other one that Pyper was carrying.

"Wel ... welcome back," he stammered, stepping over the second head. "I am relieved to see our meditation has solved the troll issue."

"Your meditation? Right," Bright said.

"Really, Bright?" Leesee asked, confused. "Meditation did that? I thought it was because we hunted them down, you know, and chopped off their heads."

"The dragon chopped the head off one," Dahni added.

"You're right," Leesee admitted.

"There was a dragon?" Jon asked. The villagers were listening.

"Yeah, a big one. Bright kissed it on the lips," Leesee said.

"Bright, does a dragon have lips?" Dahni asked. "I didn't get close enough to see."

Jon cleared his throat. "In any case, my offer still stands. I will admit to having spent most of the time you were away meditating on what will be a most memorable evening for the two of us."

"Oh," Bright said, tilting her head, and pushing out her bottom lip out in her best sad face. "That's not gonna happen. I know, right? Especially since you spent so much time *meditating* and all."

"But ... I am absolutely confident about this. Our evening will be quite memorable. I ask you to reconsider," Jon said.

"He is gorgeous, Bright," Leesee observed. Bright looked at Leesee, and her lips curled into an evil grin.

"Yeah. Jon, I think that's where you went wrong. You meditated for a memorable evening ... with *me*. I assure you I am very ordinary. If you were looking for memorable, you should have been meditating about Leesee here."

Pyper chuckled. Leesee looked thrilled at the prospect.

"I'll spend the evening with you!" Leesee said excitedly. "You're even prettier than Alred! It'll be fun!"

"Well ..." Jon began looking little Leesee over.

"It's settled then. You two run along. Leesee, make sure you make it a memorable evening for Jon, okay?"

"Oh, I will." Leesee took Jon by the arm. "Where is your house?"

Dahni looked at Bright, "I know what you just did. Should I go keep an eye on her?"

"No, Dahni. Let her go crazy with him. Batshit crazy." Bright was grinning ear to ear.

"That may have been the first truly wicked thing I've seen you do," Pyper said laughing.

"I know, right? Let's grab a blanket and some wine and sit nearby so we can listen to him scream."

Bright looked down, "Spook! Drop it! Drop the head. Good boy."

Chapter 28

PROPOSAL

They headed back along the trade route. At the lakeside village of Monlach, they found Mariana all packed and excited to go. Paul, her father, was unmistakably from Tranquility and had passed on his features to his daughter. Paul was concerned, but unlike his wife, proud of his little girl's decision.

"It was a good thing you did back in Tranquility," Sara told her. "You saved that child. You brought her home. Now I am asking you to do the same. Bring my little girl home one day. Keep her safe."

"I will," Bright said.

"That's not good enough. Promise me!"

"Sara!" Paul admonished.

"I can only promise that I will try. I'll do everything I can,"

Bright said.

Paul held his wife, consoling her as the caravan pulled away. Mariana took off swinging her arms and skipping, trying to keep up with Bright.

Along the way, Bright told Basil that it might be a good idea to trap a boar or two before the next trip. They could leave them tied up near where they encountered the dragon so that it would have plenty to eat and leave the burros alone. He liked Bright's idea and said that it couldn't hurt. Basil remarked that he hadn't seen the dragon before, he assumed it had been sleeping. It was rumored they could rest for decades or more at a time and who knows how long it would remain awake.

The barracks which housed Cor Malia's warriors were on the edge of town. Bright stopped by with Mariana. She intended to meet with Captain Meera, the captain of the guard for Cor Malia. Meera was a senior Knight, but not a Wolf Rider. Bright felt that she personally needed to ensure that Mariana was adequately housed and accepted into warrior training. She found the barracks bustling with barely organized activity. One of the sergeants told her that the captain was near the center of town, coordinating a response to recent goblin attacks. She left Mariana with the sergeant and headed on into town to find out what was happening.

Warriors, Knights, and Riders were forming into loosely organized groups. Sir Meera, in charge of Cor Malia's warriors, was busy briefing her lieutenants. Du Shar and most of Bright's friends were already present. Sariel had returned earlier from a patrol.

"What is going on, Captain?" Bright asked, interrupting Meera.

"Thank the Goddess you're here! I was expecting all of you two days ago. There are reports from many of the villages of goblin raids. There have been many casualties. I'm trying to send warriors out to secure the ones hard pressed, and fortify some of the others."

"When did this start?"

"Two days ago. The eastern villages all seemed to get hit at once. We just received word. Refugees are coming in as well. Not too many so far."

"They aren't usually this well-coordinated," Du Shar commented.

"What about Cor Malia? Has it been hit?" Sariel asked.

Captain Meera ignored him.

"Sariel has been granted Protector Status by the Goddess. He may speak," Shar informed Meera.

"So far there has been no activity here," Meera replied, looking directly at Du Shar.

"Why would the goblins attack only the villages, and not Cor Malia?" Sariel asked.

"Cor Malia is strong," Meera replied

"Or, they want to lure our forces away," mused Du Shar.

"Du Shar, allow me to scout to the north. If they are trying to lure forces from Cor Malia, then they will be forming their ranks farther north. We need to know," Sariel said.

"I'll go with you," Bright said.

"I need to go alone. One can get in and out without being seen. Your skill is impressive, but this task needs stealth. It would be difficult to keep Spook concealed in the wastes. He will be spotted a half-mile away."

"Take Dahni. You may need a runner to send word back. She is quiet, and her wolf will not be readily seen," Shar ordered.

"I could leave Spook here," Bright protested.

"This is a time for battle. I listen to the counsel of those around me and make a decision. Challenge me or follow me."

"Yes, Du Shar," Bright said.

"If they are indeed organizing, they may have pressed trolls into service. Bright, you and Leesee see if the Fletchers have made more of those fire arrows, get all you can and tell them to make more. Fill jars with oil and pass these out to the archers. When you are done, meet Ahn Alanna here."

"Alanna, assemble a small group of Riders prepared to respond if we hear any reports of trolls. Bright and Leesee will go with you. The wolves can handle the extra weight for a time. Switch them out when they tire."

"Captain Meera, send the warriors out as you have planned. But cut their numbers in half. I won't leave Cor Malia unguarded. At least not until we receive word back on what is happening in the north. Go!"

Everyone set to their assigned tasks. Du Shar stayed with Captain Meera, and her experience soon brought order to the massing warriors.

"Are you prepared for this?" Sariel asked Dahni.

"Yup, it'll be fun," She said, smiling and wiggling her eyebrows.

"I have something I have to do, it will not take me long. Would you find us some food and water for the trip while I am gone? We may be out for a few days."

"Yup, no problem. Just me and you. Alone for several nights. Got it." She was still smiling. Sariel suddenly felt uneasy.

Sariel walked until he found a place away from the others. He closed his eyes and thought of his friend, the Archangel Raphael. He visualized what it was like to be with his friend, his calming effect, his strength of character. Then he quietly asked for him to be present.

"Hello, old friend. I'm afraid there isn't much time for revelry at the moment. Are you presently vexed by more beautiful women? What perplexing problems you have. How is she, your golden-haired beauty? Jenny, I believe," Raphael said.

"She is well. The Goddess named her, she is called 'Bright' now. And she is Elven, Ahn Bright."

"HA! I knew she was special."

"Raphael, have you seen Abaddon, or have you heard where he may be?"

"Abaddon? No, and why would you ask? Why would you even want to find him? I don't believe you two ever got on well. I don't like the fellow at all, come to think of it."

"It may be nothing, but someone calling himself the Archon is trying to find Bright, probably trying to kill her. Abaddon has been fond of using that name in the past."

"I don't suppose you're ready to come back? No? Well, we need you, you have obligations and all. I'll see what I can find out about your Abaddon and send word if I hear anything. Take care, my friend. Apologies, but there are matters which I must attend to."

And then he was gone.

Ahn Bright had the attention of the senior bowyers the moment she and Leesee set foot in the Bowyery. Between her new bow, Fang, and her arrow idea, she had become something of a celebrity to them. A small crowd followed them around. She told them of Du Shar's orders and was led into the back of the shop where they found young Kalia.

"There are goblin attacks and rumors of trolls. Du Shar wants to see about making more of the fire arrows," Bright said.

"The elders didn't authorize the full-scale production, but I have a dozen more prepared."

A few of the elders were nearby, Bright addressed them. "Du Shar has ordered more fire arrows. They may be needed soon. Please give it some priority. The Chieftain is at the village circle if you would like to confirm it with her." The elders nodded and walked away. Whether to confirm the order or begin production, she did not know.

"Before you go, I would like to tell you something. Because of this arrow, I have been promoted. I'm no longer an apprentice. Fletcher Kalia. It is really because of you. Thank you."

"Congratulations, Kalia. That's wonderful," Bright said. "You should know that we have already used them ... against trolls. And they work!"

Leesee and Bright returned laden with jars of oil and the dozen fire arrows before the warriors had moved out. There weren't enough arrows to go around, so eight of the archers were given instructions on how to use them. Leesee and Dahni received a fire arrow, but Du Shar insisted that Bright keep two.

By the time Bright had caught up with Dahni and Sariel, they were about to head out. They had extra water, heavy cloaks, and leather sacks of pemmican, a food made from pounded meat, dried berries and fat. It would keep fresh for many months and could sustain a warrior indefinitely.

"You two watch out for each other. I want you to promise me you'll come back safely," Bright said.

"I promise," said Dahni.

"I will promise you that I will try," Sariel said. He gave her a kiss, then turned to go.

"Wait! I wanted to ask you something." Sariel stopped and waited.

"Would you be my husband? You know, like, if you want to?" Bright asked him.

He smiled. "Would this mean I have to stay home all the time and cook for you?"

"No. But I suck at cooking, maybe you could, once in a while? I love your food."

"I appreciate the compliment. The answer is yes, it would be my honor. It is my greatest desire, as well. You stay safe. I love you, Bright." Sariel started walking off.

"I love you, Sariel. Stay safe," Bright called after him. "Seriously, you two stay safe."

"Oh, my God!" Dahni said, walking beside Sariel. Her hands were pressed against her chest, and she was looking up at him with the sweetest smile. "You're Bright's husband. We get to mate! She already promised. Isn't it wonderful? "

"There has not been any ceremony that weds us as husband and wife."

"Um, yes. You already did it. Bright asked, and you accepted. POW! Ceremony complete. And I already have permission to bed you."

"Dahni, is that all you think about?"

"No. I think about killing goblins, mating with you, drinking wine, having sex with Leesee, she's so sweet. I think about Leesee and me raising a baby if one of us ever gets pregnant. We'd be perfect parents, don't ya think? I'm always wondering what Rhadia is thinking, I thought it would be delightful if he could talk. I just started thinking about sex with Kalia, you know, after we talked to her about the fire arrows a while back. I used to think about it with Alred, but all the crying he was doing with Leesee was a bit off-putting if you know what I mean. Du Shar said you didn't cry. Oh, now I'm thinking about Du Shar! Wouldn't that be fun?"

"Okay. Please stop. Did you ever think that once you found someone you truly love, you would wish to manifest those ... more personal affections with that person, and no other?"

Dahni thought about this for a while. Then she said, "That doesn't make any sense at all. Isn't that like saying 'I love blueberry pie,' so from now on I'm only going to eat blueberry pie? But there are so many good things to eat. Now I'm thinking about blueberry pie."

"Perhaps it would be beneficial if you started thinking of more serious issues."

"I don't think you're being very fair. Just because you are so serious *all the time*. In another couple of miles, I will be seriously looking for goblin sign, and when I find it, I'll be thinking about how I will kill them and hopefully survive. Each encounter is different, and one will be my last. I'll be thinking about Leesee and Bright and all my friends and sisters going off on their own patrols. I'll be wondering how many of them will come back, how many stories I'll have to listen to when I return. I'll wonder if you'll be telling mine, or having to look at Bright's face as I tell yours. So please forgive me if I don't want to dwell on serious crap when I don't have to. It's going to get real hard to think of pleasant things, the farther north we go. Let me think good thoughts, pleasurable thoughts, when I can because I may not be here tomorrow. Or worse, the people I love may not."

Sariel was surprised by this. He thought about it and felt that there was more to her than was visible on the surface. "I'm sorry, Dahni," was all he could think to say.

"It's okay. When you die, get eaten by a troll or something, do you go back to being an immortal angel?"

"Yes. And the obligations that come with it."

"Yeah, well, the rest of us aren't so sure what happens. It's scary for us. Unless you want to tell me all about it?"

"I cannot. There are different realms. We only serve as guides."

"Then, stop giving me a hard time about what I want to think about."

"Okay," Sariel said, then added. "But, I do not believe that the Universe would want to exist without you."

"That's so sweet." Dahni smiled up at him again. "Now you're thinking about being with me, aren't you? At least a little?"

"Perhaps a little. There was a promise, after all." Then he took off at a slow run.

"Really? Holy shit!" Dahni said, then ran after him. "Hey! Wait up!"

Chapter 29

PREPARE FOR BATTLE

Alanna had chosen Bright, Leesee, and three other Wolf Riders to form a quick reaction force in case there were any troll sightings or simply to go where they were needed most. They provisioned themselves and kept their traveling supplies ready to go. Next, they went about perfecting the defenses for Cor Malia. Sentries and forward scouts were emplaced, and the entire town was in a state of alert. Planks were set into stones in the walls to allow the husbands to fire arrows from the high, narrow windows. Children were kept safe in the trees with ladders and descent lines pulled up to prevent easy entry.

Alanna brought Leesee and Bright to her quarters for the night. Shar was in a neighboring village to the east, helping with their defenses. The other three warriors were quartered together, and town sentries knew where to find them in the event of an attack.

They all sat quietly in Alanna's sitting room while Buckson served them food and wine. None of the warriors had much of an appetite, but Buckson was insisting that they eat to keep up their strength and to ensure that Alanna kept their new baby healthy.

"Alanna," Buckson spoke quietly, "is there any way I can convince you to stay out of battle? I've already lost one child, and I don't know if I can bear to lose another. And losing you, well ... would be ... after all this time. It has been so long, and now we are finally together. Losing you again would be so hard to take."

"No, Buckson, I'm going," Alanna replied. "But you're not going to lose me."

"It might be a good idea," Bright said. "Leesee and I can take care of things. I want you to stay back. You have already been hurt once because of me."

"That was my fault. I allowed myself to be ambushed. It won't happen again."

Leesee drew in a shuddering breath. She looked up, and tears were running down her cheeks. "Something bad is going to happen. I can feel it. Something is coming. I'm worried about Dahni. She's out there without me."

"Dahni will be fine. She's with Sariel, and he will protect her," Bright said.

"I would die to protect her. I'm lost without her." Leesee said and burst into tears full force. Bright held her as she sobbed.

"Sariel may be male, but he appears to be a capable warrior. I am confident he will watch over her." Alanna said, surprising Bright with her uncharacteristic comment.

"Besides, Dahni promised to return. All Sariel said was that he would try." Bright said, trying to comfort Leesee, but all she succeeded in doing was upsetting herself.

"Bright, Leesee ... enough! If we continue to think bad things will happen, we may only succeed in bringing them about. Dahni will return. Sariel will return. We will win the battle. Then we will take it to them. Destroy them in their homes. This will not continue. We will give our children a safe place to grow and thrive." Alanna was stern. "Do you two understand?" They both nodded.

"Now, we are all tired. There is a long day tomorrow. Get some rest and consider that an order." Alanna reached out to take Bright's hand and lead her up to her room.

Once they were undressed and in bed, Alanna began to kiss Bright. Alanna felt they both needed a distraction. She knew that she sure did. There was no way she would ever get any rest in her current state. Bright welcomed the pleasant diversion and moaned at her touch. The door opened, and Leesee stood there, naked and unsure of herself. She appeared tiny, young, and vulnerable ... frightened.

"I don't want to be alone," Leesee said.

Alanna looked at her and said without hesitation, "You are not alone. Come here." She held out her hand, and Leesee crawled into bed with them. They found comfort in each other's arms. Soon all three were fast asleep.

Chapter 30

THE CAVE

"Goblin sign!" Dahni whispered.

"I see it," Sariel replied.

"They're heading east. It looks like twenty or more."

"We will follow."

They were well into The Desolation when they encountered the tracks. They had left the familiar forest far behind and now found themselves in a land of rocks and ravines, the only plants were low scrub bushes. In another two miles, they encountered more tracks, at least a day old, joining the others heading east.

"Look at this," Sariel said, pointing out a huge print.

"Oh my god!" Dahni said. "It's an ogre. The biggest one ever! How can one even get this big?"

"This is not good."

"Ya think?" Dahni said sarcastically. "I would have tried to take on the twenty with you, even knowing we probably wouldn't make it out alive, but this? There must be a hundred goblins … and this beast. We need to go back and warn the others."

"I need to find out where they are going and what we're up against. But you should go back and warn the others."

"I'm not going without you."

"That is why Du Shar sent you with me. You are my runner. Go back and warn the Clan."

"That's all I am to you? A runner? And you would send me back alone? It's already dark, and Sariel, I'm tired and afraid."

"You are here, under Du Shar's orders, to be a runner, to warn the others. But I would like to consider you a friend as well. We should find some shelter for the night. There is a ravine to the south, and I am hoping we will find a place to rest for the night. You can head back to the Clan in the morning."

"So … that's it? I'm just some friend you've made in the Clan?" Dahni pressed.

"I do not think this is the place for such a discussion."

"We'll be dead by tomorrow. When do you plan on discussing it?"

"I swear to you that I will do everything in my power to protect you … if you are willing to follow my instructions."

"And I swear to protect you. So there!"

Sariel sighed. "Let us find that ravine, okay?"

"Okay."

It was another hour when Sariel found a small cave hollowed out under a flat rock in the bend of a ravine. Once he declared it safe, Dahni went inside with their packs to make a place to sleep. Soon she heard low voices outside and crept out, her bow notched and ready.

Sariel was talking in hushed tones with someone she had never seen before.

"Abaddon is in Elvenrealm, Sariel. And he has not fallen. He is operating here while remaining a part of the angelic realm."

"That is blasphemy," Sariel said.

"Yes, and we are being watched." Sariel turned around and saw Dahni with her bow drawn, aiming straight at Raphael.

"Put down your bow, Dahni," Sariel said, but she didn't.

"Come on out, young lady. I would like to meet you," Raphael said. "Sariel, how is it you are always in the company of beautiful women? I am in awe of you. Now you've got me thinking about falling for a time."

Dahni released the tension on her arrow and crept forward. "Come on. I won't bite," Raphael said.

"Dahni, this is Raphael, my friend."

"How are you tonight, young Dahni?" Raphael said.

"I'm frightened. Why are you here?"

"So direct. No need to be frightened. Of me anyway. I have information that Sariel needed, that is all. I have the answer. Problem solved."

"How did you find us?"

Raphael chuckled. "That was easy. Well ... easy for me. You have others to worry about, but this area seems secure for now. I would strongly suggest you both return to Cor Malia."

"Are we going to die?" Dahni asked.

Raphael grew serious. "Well, I sure hope not. The world would be a less beautiful place without you. However, I don't see into the future, so you two had better have a care. Sariel, I must go. You have the information you requested. Now you take care of this young woman, or you'll be answering to me."

Raphael unfurled his wings, and with a snap, he was airborne and then he disappeared. Dahni stood with her mouth open, staring. "What is he, an angel? A real angel?"

"Yes, Dahni. He is, in fact, an archangel. I am grateful you did not shoot at him."

"Wow."

"Let us try and get some rest." Sariel headed into the cave, and Dahni followed. She stopped for a minute by the door, whispering to Rhadia. Rhadia laid down just inside the door. Dahni had spread out one of the heavy cloaks on the dirt at the back of the cave. Sariel had already laid down when she crept in and removed her clothing.

"What are you doing? You should remain ready to fight or flee."

"I need some sleep. That is what is important right now." She said and crawled in beside him and pulled the other cloak up over her legs. She snuggled up and lay upon his chest.

"Your archangel didn't say we would live through the day," Dahni whispered. "I would have felt better if he had. He thought we should go back. Sariel, I have a bad feeling about this."

Sariel put his arm around her to give comfort. He found that his hand was resting on the small of her back. He could feel the rise of her buttocks. "Dahni, you should head back at first light. I must see what is going on. Raphael said that Abaddon was here, and operating while still in the realm of angels. He is calling himself the Archon again. All that he is doing is forbidden. Perhaps I can convince him to return."

Dahni looked up. "He's another angel? A bad one? You're being stupid. He'll kill you."

"I can speak to him, one Dominion to another."

"What's he Dominion over?"

"Destruction."

"He'll kill you," Dahni stated again with certainty.

"He can try, but I am not so sure. That is why you should return."

"I'm not going back without you."

Sariel found that he was gently running his hand over the small of her back. He could feel the soft, short hair there. Dahni scooted up on top of him, straddling him.

"I'm not going back without you," she repeated. Then she kissed him.

Sariel pushed her back. "Dahni. You are sweet and beautiful. But you know I love Bright."

"So do I," she said and kissed him again.

"I remember the promise, but this is not a good time or place," he protested.

"We will die tomorrow. I am not Leesee. I have never been with a man before. That's not a story I want to tell my ancestors. And there is one other thing, you're the only man I ever wanted to be with." She kissed him again and felt his strong arms holding her tight. Then he kissed her. By morning, she would no longer have to tell her ancestors that she had never been with a man.

Dahni awoke first with a cold nose on her cheek. Rhadia whined softly. She shook Sariel and told him they needed to get ready. They dressed quickly. By the time Sariel looked out of the entrance, he could hear many footsteps coming up the ravine. The sun had not yet come up, so Sariel had them retreat to the back of the small cave while he knelt inside the entrance with his spear at the ready.

"Try to keep Rhadia quiet," he whispered.

Soon there was the sound of footsteps passing by with the occasional grunting and arguing. Goblins! A lot of them. Long minutes passed, and yet they continued to march by. Dust rose from their passage and choked them within the cave. Dahni had to stifle a sneeze. Worse, it was beginning to grow light. Another couple of goblins were in a heated argument when one must have struck the other.

A goblin fell right into the mouth of the cave, landing on his back. Others continued to march by, and one stepped on his legs. He yelped and scooted farther back into the cave. He rolled over onto his hands and knees and looked up, just in time to look Sariel in the eyes. Sariel plunged his spear into the soft spot between his clavicle and neck. Then he twisted the spear sideways and dragged the dying goblin into the cave. He had to put his boot on the goblin's shoulder to dislodge the spear and return to the ready, in case another saw him disappear into the cave.

The marching finally came to an end. Sariel waited until he knew there were no stragglers. He crept out of the cave into the early morning light. Dahni and Rhadia came out behind him.

"There must have been a hundred," she said.

"Yes. And they are all heading east. Dahni, you must go back and warn Du Shar."

"*We* should go back. Right now!" Dahni replied.

"I have to get to Abaddon."

"No. You don't."

"He is behind this. I need to convince him to return to our realm. If I can, his army will fall into chaos. I know you do not understand. So it is best if I go on alone."

"I'm not leaving you alone," Dahni said.

"Please, Dahni. Do as I ask."

"I don't answer to you. I answer to Du Shar." Then she added, "And I love you. I know you love Bright, and I accept that, but I had to say it anyway."

"Dahni," he said. "I do love Bright, but you mean a great deal to me, not just because of last night, you have always been kind to me. If anything happens to you, I will never forgive myself. And I promised to watch over you. Going back is not safe, but it is safer than continuing on."

"I already knew that I was going to die today. Leesee will be so mad at me for dying without her. Let's get going." Dahni stated then started heading east with Rhadia at her side.

"Dahni!" he called out in a harsh whisper, but she did not turn. He ran to her side.

Chapter 31

THE RISE OF THE ELVENSTAR

"Alanna," Buckson said, reaching over Leesee to shake her shoulder. "Alanna, darling, wake up."

All three girls were cuddling together with Alanna in the middle. She turned and opened one eye. "What is it?" She said, stretching and kicking the blanket off of all three. They all began to stretch and yawn.

"Alanna, Miss Willow, and Ahn Pyper are here. They say it's urgent."

They all got out of bed and made their way to the sitting room. Pyper stood when they entered while Willow was pacing back and forth with her arms crossed.

"What's going on?" Alanna demanded, being naked had not diminished her authority in the slightest.

"It's Willow. She has been helping the healers with the

wounded. One of them is from Triborien, where she was born. She seems to remember him. He was very old and severely wounded. He woke up and right before he died he told Willow that there were goblins there, in Triborien ... and a troll."

"Holy shit!" Leesee exclaimed. "I just peed. Sorry about the pee, Buckson." She ran back upstairs.

"Pyper, go get the others. They're all staying at Ahn Lissa's quarters," Alanna ordered.

"Prepare for battle!" Alanna cried out, more because she liked saying it than for the informative value.

Buckson grabbed her, he gave her a kiss on the cheek. "You be careful, don't get hurt."

"Don't worry, Buckson, this is going to be fun."

"Well, it won't be fun for me. I'm going to be worried sick until you return ... until you both return," he said, touching her tummy.

They dressed in short order. Alanna helped Bright strap on the armour given to her by Sir Mahri. Then Alanna was in front of the mirror with her hands in a jar of black paint. She closed her eyes and placed her paint-soaked hands over her eyes and down her cheeks. Then she took four fingers and starting on her upper lip drew lines down her chin. She was instantly transformed from beautiful to nightmarish.

"Do you do that for camouflage?" Bright asked.

"No. It is a ritual I do. It prepares my mind and body for

what is about to come. I see myself as a different person. Fierce. One prepared for battle."

"You used to wear it all the time."

Alanna thought about it for a moment. "Every day used to be a battle for me."

"And now?"

"And now, not so much." Alanna dipped three fingers of each hand in the paint. Her forefingers touched the bridge of her nose. She drew three diagonal lines through the corners of Bright's mouth. Then she washed her hands in the basin. "Look in the mirror. It's time to change from compassionate, kind Bright into something different. Gaze upon who you must become today. Today you must be ferocious. Today you are the defender of Elvenkind. Today you are the Elvenstar."

Bright looked at her reflection. The lines formed a frown of sorts and transformed her visage into something different. Something to be feared. Someone who had no choice but to defend those she had come to love. Bright saw the Elvenstar for the first time.

Bright strung her bow, slung it over her quiver and headed for the landing. She passed by Leesee and Alanna, grabbed the descent line with one hand and leapt over the edge, leaving her impressed friends behind. Alanna followed the moment the counterweight hit the ground.

They met Ahn Lissa and her two friends on the way to her quarters. They were mounted on their wolves with Willow and Pyper riding behind. Leesee jumped behind Lissa, and they headed east at a fast pace. Spook, Doug, and Bellum, Pyper's wolf, followed.

The wolves couldn't carry two riders without rest. Every half hour they would dismount and jog down the trail. Even with the speed of a mounted wolf, they weren't going to reach Triborien until the next day.

By midafternoon, they found fresh tracks. Alanna declared there were only six of them. They mounted and ran them down. Bright took down two goblins while mounted, and Leesee took out three. Amica knocked down the last one and Alanna planted her spear through its heart.

They had covered a lot of ground by the time night fell. Alanna took them south off the trail and posted sentries. If there were a troll at the village, he would have an advantage in the darkness, as if he didn't already have the advantage. They all were exhausted, and sleep came quickly.

Chapter 32

ABADDON

It was midday when they spotted the goblin camp. Dahni and Sariel knelt behind scrub bushes on a low rise in the land. From this point, they were less than a half-mile away.

"I don't see any sentries," Dahni said.

"If Abaddon is here, he is too arrogant to post sentries. Most are preparing to march south. You see that large pavilion? The huge tent in the center. I will find him there. He is fond of luxuries."

"You know how stupid that sounds. It's suicidal."

"If one of your sisters had lost her way, and you thought you could save her, would you try? I am not fond of him, yet he is a brother angel."

"Not the same. And no. If one of my sisters had been killing others, I would end her."

"You must return to Du Shar. She must be warned. If they are caught unprepared, many will die that could have been saved. The largest force has begun to march south, and there must be over six hundred. There is no time to waste."

"You're right. Let's head back now."

Sariel caressed her face. "No, Dahni. This is your task. I have mine." Her eyes clouded with tears. "Think of Leesee and Bright. They are depending on you."

"I am *so* mad at you right now." Tears fell as she began to cry.

"I understand." He kissed her forehead. "You will see me again, I promise."

"You promise?"

"I swear it to you. I never lie. I still have one trick left. I control the mists, remember. Even now."

"Don't forget that you promised."

"I won't. Stay out of sight. Head south until you are within the cover of the forest, then head back. And stay safe." Dahni hesitated a moment, then kissed him long and hard, and ran south.

Sariel waited until Dahni was out of sight. Then he stood and began walking to the goblin camp. As he neared the perimeter, a small group of six spotted him and headed his direction at a run. Sariel held up a hand as they approached. "I am here to see the Archon."

They glanced at each other, then one spoke. "I'll take him

your head."

Sariel was a whirlwind. His spear sang through the air. They were sliced, stabbed, and buffeted. In moments there was only one, busy holding back the blood flow from a severed hand. "Go tell the Archon that Sariel is here to speak with him." The goblin turned and fled back towards the camp.

Sariel took out his waterskin and took a long drink. Once it was empty, he dropped it to the ground. Then he removed his pack and continued walking. *If Dahni is right*, he thought, *this is a one-way trip.*

As he neared the camp the remaining two hundred or so goblins had lined up, shields at the ready. He was only a couple hundred yards away when he saw Abaddon flying towards him. He stopped and waited.

Abaddon landed gracefully and folded his wings. He was armoured similar to Sariel with a sleeveless vest that almost touched the ground. He had long, straight reddish-blond hair with bangs cut to keep it out of his eyes. Like Sariel, he was handsome, but in a boyish manner where Sariel was rugged and stern. "You're way too predictable. You know that, don't you? I knew you would come."

"You could have come to me," Sariel stated.

"Where is the fun in that? No, better to have you dancing to my tune."

"Abaddon, you interfere in mortal affairs while remaining within the angelic realm. This is forbidden. It is blasphemy and against our code."

"And what do you propose to do about it? Even the mighty Sariel must think twice about these odds."

Sariel gazed upon the line of goblins and smiled. "Perhaps you are right. It hardly seems fair. Shall I give you time to call back the others?"

Abaddon stomped a tantrum of rage. "You think so much of yourself, don't you? And eternally whining about your obligations. I have always hated you!"

"I am quite used to that," Sariel answered calmly.

"I am still in the realm of angels. You have stupidly become mortal and cannot hope to defeat me."

"And you risk banishment for it. Cease your meddling now. Leave Elvenrealm, and you will not have to fight me."

Abaddon laughed maniacally, his eyes wide. "I need only give the word to my host, and they will defeat you."

"I will cut through them and find you. Or you can leave the mortal realm. Or you could have some courage for once and face me in battle. Simple choices, really."

Abaddon grew thoughtful. He stood with arms crossed for a moment then lifted one finger to his chin and rubbed it a bit. "Do you remember our old friend from the realm, Behemoth?"

"Yes, I remember her."

"I tried to get her to come with me. She's so much fun

once you get her motivated, you know? And the size of her! The terror she incites. It makes destruction so much more satisfying. But she is lazy and started barking about the code. You two have much in common."

"There is a point to this?"

"Yes, of course there is. You see, anyone can simply destroy something, but it is my specialty. It is an art. One must elicit terror and the total loss of hope first. Otherwise, your efforts are amateurish. So I decided to find my own behemoth. And the funny thing is, I did! It was a marvelous bit of serendipity."

"You could make this very easy on yourself. I should warn you that you are beginning to bore me, and I never really liked you."

"You interrupted me! That was rude. So I was saying that I found my grand object of terror, which was no problem. But how to destroy all hope before I destroy everything else? That was the biggest problem. A real conundrum, you know what I mean. *That* was the real challenge. And then I learned about your new addition. Bright! The new Elvenstar. I learned she was brought here to give everyone hope. So I thought, what better thing to do than kill this Elvenstar! It was brilliant! What do you think?"

Sariel turned his spear and plunged it into the ground. "I think you should draw your sword." Sariel drew his blade.

"Oh, please. You're mortal. You don't have a chance against me. Besides, you haven't heard the rest." Sariel took a step closer. "What's amazing is, she's still a virgin! Can you

321

imagine the luck? You do know what power virgin blood brings with the proper rituals? Or maybe you don't. You were always so stuffy. After all, you had this young thing living with you and never touched her. What is wrong with you? I hear she is quite lovely. So here's the best part, as we speak she's headed to Triborien where I will have nearly a thousand troops. And she's traveling with only a handful of elves. I will take her to Splinter Peak and literally bathe in her blood. I'll be nearly invulnerable for quite some time. And all hope will die. Maybe that's the best part? What do you think?"

Sariel leapt the remaining three paces and slashed an arc with his sword. With a beat of his wings, Abaddon hopped back and drew his silver blade. He closed the gap and the air filled with the sound of ringing metal. Sparks flew whenever the angelic blades met. Abaddon used his wings to continually change his position, throwing Sariel into a disadvantage. Abaddon launched a flurry of attacks with Sariel hard-pressed to defend himself. Then Abaddon flew into the air and planted both feet squarely in the center of Sariel's chest. Sariel flew backward, rolled back onto his feet in time to catch Abaddon's blade with his own. In a test of raw strength, Sariel won, and as his sword shoved his enemy's aside, he sliced a bone-deep grove on Abaddon's face from his left temple down the cheek and through his lips.

Abaddon dropped his sword and bounded into the air, holding his face in both hands. He shrieked in rage and frustration. "Behemoth!" Blood flew from his lips as he screamed.

Sariel walked to his opponent's blade and stomped, breaking it in half. With a loud, earth-shaking roar, the pavilion canvas flew into the air. His behemoth had been curled up inside all along. It stood. It was an ogre the size of no other Sariel had ever seen. Hulking thickly muscled with no discernable neck, the beast had heard the call and was looking around. The palms of its hands had to be almost four feet across.

"Behemoth! Kill him!" Abaddon commanded from the air above Sariel. He was still holding his cheek with his left hand.

The beast looked around stupidly until it found the target. With a deafening roar, he ran towards Sariel, long legs covering the distance rapidly. Goblins lined up on the perimeter were scrambling to get out of its way. Several died as it stomped through the crowd.

Sariel sheathed his sword and picked up the spear. *Dahni was right*, he thought as it rapidly approached. When the monster was close enough, it leapt and slapped his hand down, as if Sariel were nothing but a bug to squish. Sariel barely managed to roll out of the way. The behemoth quickly got up on all fours, looking around. Then it cried out and grabbed at its left eye. When it removed its hand, Sariel could see an arrow, buried up to the fletching. Then two more hit the same eye.

Sariel turned and saw Dahni standing firm in front of the giant ogre. She fired one arrow after another. "Dahni, NO!" He yelled and held out an arm. "Run through the mist. Run NOW!" Thick mist spread from her position southward.

The exertion of creating that much mist made him feel momentarily lightheaded. The distraction gave the ogre time to reach down and snatch him up like a toy. He groaned from the pain of being squeezed from the waist down. He heard his own hip bones pop and snap. The behemoth brought him up and looked at him with his one working eye. Then he laughed.

Dahni screamed Sariel's name, but he didn't hear it. Sariel had chosen to become mortal for a time, and his world was filled with white-hot pain. His vision narrowed to a tunnel, nothing more. Everything else was going dark, but at the end of that tunnel, he could see the behemoth's remaining eye. Sariel launched his spear with all the strength he had left.

Mists were forming everywhere now. But the behemoth, now totally blind, roared in pain and stood above the fog. In a rage, he grabbed Sariel in his other hand and twisted, pulling him apart. Dahni saw everything as if it were a slow-motion event that she would suffer to relive for the rest of her life. She saw the two hands twist and pull him apart. There was a ball of light that streaked for the heavens like a comet. As the hands separated, entrails stretched between the two halves. And a red mist clouded the air in between. There were jets of blood from both halves.

The behemoth roared and stomped around. He dropped the pieces of Sariel's body and began to move blindly towards Dahni. Mists were starting to envelop Abaddon hovering above, although Dahni did not notice this. She turned and ran through the concealing fog, with Rhadia running just in front of her. She ran as fast as she could, as long as she could. She wasn't running to get away from the goblins or Abaddon, she was running from what she witnessed with Sariel. She had to gain some distance, or she would be overwhelmed by it. Dahni ran for a long time. Finally, she came to a lone tree and sat against it and cried. She had returned to help him but succeeded only in distracting him long enough to be captured. And killed.

After a time she remembered she had a mission. Mostly she remembered Sariel wanted her to do it. She stood back up and continued south. She had heard everything Abaddon had said to Sariel. Now she knew it was true. She no longer had hope. Her heart was once filled with it, hope and love. Now she felt empty, a hollow husk. It wasn't until she hit the trail with the wolf prints that she remembered Bright, Leesee and her sisters were heading into an ambush. She turned back east and started running down the path. Du Shar would have to wait.

Chapter 33

TRIBORIEN

The next morning they entered the village of Triborien. It was quiet, empty, there was no one in sight. A thin, gossamer mist spread over the ground, but it did not smell like smoke. The wolves growled at the eerie stillness.

"We're too late," Bright said.

"If there was a battle, where are the bodies?" asked Alanna.

Willow pointed, and Pyper said, "We should head to the center of town."

"I don't see any troll prints," Leesee said, sounding relieved. "But this is all very creepy."

Alanna stopped. She studied the ground. "Look at these marks. The prints have been brushed away. This isn't a good sign. Why would our people take the time to do this?"

Willow and Pyper were already heading deeper into the

village. They stopped for the others to catch up.

"Alanna, we should get out of here," Bright said.

"I think you're right."

Willow let out a small sound and ran towards the center square. The others ran after her. She stopped in the middle of the square and looked about as if confused. The wolves started growling, the hair on their backs standing straight up.

"Get out of here, MOVE!" Alanna shouted.

But it was too late. Goblins poured in from every direction. They came from behind buildings and from within them. Bright and Leesee launched arrow after arrow. For every one that fell, ten more were right behind. The goblins didn't even have weapons drawn. Wolves went for goblin throats. Willow didn't get a chance to unsheath her sword before she was overwhelmed and pulled to the ground. Alanna and Pyper managed to keep a circle free around them for a time. There were just too many pressing in. Goblins stomped over the bodies of their fallen without a thought. The green tide pushed in from every side; it could not be held back. In a short time, they were all pinned to the blood-soaked ground, including the wolves. Their hands were bound behind them and their feet as well. The wolves had all their legs tied together. All were bound except Bright. She was being held between two large goblins who were removing her armour and throwing it to the ground.

With a snapping of wings, Abaddon landed. His face hastily stitched together with thick black thread. Undoubtedly the work of goblin healers.

"Pick them up," Abaddon commanded, and everyone was raised to their feet and held there by goblins.

He walked straight to Bright. "So you are the mighty Elvenstar, the giver of hope. Well, well, there shall be none found here today."

"Who are you?" Bright demanded.

"Where are my manners? I am Abaddon, the Angel of Destruction. Or you may call me The Archon. No, no. No need to introduce yourselves. I know who you are. I know who you all are. Most of you, anyway."

"So if you're going to kill us, just get it over with," Alanna said.

"Kill you? How absurd. I'm going to kill your Elvenstar. And bathe in her virgin blood if you must know. But the rest of you? No, you will be released, relatively unharmed. Someone has to spread the word that your Bright is no more. Otherwise, everyone would simply wonder about it. Or worse, wait hopefully for her return. I can't have that now, can I? Her white wolf will remain with you so that when it falls, you will know the moment of her death."

"Okay, asshole. You want me, you've got me. Now let the others go," Bright said.

"Tut, tut. Such a tone. And I heard you were sweet and compassionate. Just goes to show you that you can't believe everything."

"Hmmm. You three," Abaddon said, indicating Lissa and the other two Ahns, "I don't know, so you are unimportant.

But *you*, little one. You must be Leesee. I know all about you. You like to treat men rough, don't you? Let's see, Miss Leesee. Hmmm. How about you, you, and you," Abaddon said, indicating three goblins. "I think it would be a marvelous idea if you all teach her what rough sex feels like on the receiving end."

The three goblins he indicated grabbed Leesee and started slicing off her clothing while she kicked and screamed.

"Stop it, you sick piece of shit!" Bright yelled.

"Why, I don't think you have a respectful bone in your body, Miss Bright," Abaddon said and backhanded Bright across the face.

"Now, you, I know. You're Ahn Alanna, the fierce warrior. You're not looking so fierce today, are you? And how's that baby of yours? Hmmm? You must be so proud."

"Why do you ask? Not man enough to father your own child?"

"Such an insult. I want you to know I am deeply hurt. Why you have cut me to the quick with that one. Whatever shall I do in reply?" Abaddon drew out a dagger and pushed it deep into her belly. He plunged it into the baby. Alanna screamed. She screamed for the lost baby more than the pain. "See? I can cut deeper than you."

"NO!" Bright shouted. She stomped on the insteps of one goblin, then the other. One tried to keep a hand on her, and she bit it. Once she broke free, she placed her hands on Alanna's wound, and instantly, a brilliant blue light burst forth.

The goblins regained their hold on her and pulled her away.

"Well, well," Abaddon said. "Let's take a look, shall we?" He yanked the front of Alanna's leggings down. "See here? You're all healed. Pity, she can't bring back the dead though. You know, your little dead baby?" Alanna spit on him.

"You are such a rude lot, really. So uncivilized," he said wiping the spittle from his face then licking it off his hand. "I wonder if I will get this healing power when I soak in your blood, Miss Bright. What a wonderful experiment! We shall soon see." Abaddon turned to face Pyper.

"And you must be Pyper. Don't worry, I've already destroyed you. I've taken away everything you love. You have nothing left for me to take."

"You'll have nothing from me," Pyper stated defiantly.

"Really? In a moment you will see," He walked over to Willow.

"Leave her alone! If you touch her, I swear I will kill you!" Pyper shouted.

"How bold. Willow, how are you on this fine morning?"

Willow giggled. "I'm good, love. But what happened to your face?"

"Willow?" Pyper said. Everyone stared at Willow, stunned to hear her voice for the first time.

"Oh, this? Angel blade, I'm afraid. It will probably scar,"

Abaddon said.

"I think scars are sexy," Willow told him with a seductive smile.

"If it was an angle blade, then it was Sariel that kicked your ass," Bright said with satisfaction.

Abaddon looked at Bright. "It was, as a matter of fact, Sariel that managed to get lucky with one strike. Now he is quite dead, I've seen to that myself. The Angel of Death falls to the Angel of Destruction. Pieces scattered for yards. No surprise there, surely. It was a nice way to start the day."

"You lie!" Bright screamed. She was growing weak, only her anger keeping her awake.

"Really? You know that isn't a trait of angels. Don't worry, you'll probably step through him on the way. Just look for a big puddle."

"You are a fool!" Bright said, her eyes closed, and her voice nothing more than a whisper. "Sariel is also the Angel of Protection and Vengeance. He almost beheaded you as a mortal, and you will fall when he returns for vengeance. He will protect me."

Abaddon appeared visibly shaken by this thought for a moment, then regained his composure and said, "Sariel will not break the code. He will not interfere in the mortal realm. Besides, I am a much more powerful angel." But his words fell on deaf ears ... Bright was already asleep, suspended between the two goblins.

Abaddon brought his attention back to Willow. "So you

find scars sexy? I think you are the sexy one. Forgive me if I don't give you a proper kiss. It's a fresh wound and all that. But you did a wonderful job leading the Elvenstar to me. I couldn't have done this without you."

"Willow? What's going on? What did you do?" Pyper demanded.

"What? You mean me talking?" Willow said coyly. "Abaddon healed me, he took away my fears. He soothed my mind and my rage. He found me while you were off playing with trolls in Tranquility." Willow leaned her head fondly on one of the goblins holding her.

Leesee screamed as she was bent over a fence and viciously sodomized. She screamed in anger at first, then in pain. Doug barked and growled, straining against her bonds.

"You see him as an angel, but to me, he is a God. He makes love to me like you never could, Pyper. It all makes perfect sense. We can't win against him. So it's our duty to serve him. I am his willing slave, and I love it. I love him."

"Well said, darling." He looked over at the knot of goblins surrounding Leesee. "Could one of you cover her mouth while you rape her? Really, the screaming is distracting."

"Willow, how could you?" Pyper cried.

"There! You see! I told you that you were already destroyed. Now, look at the tears. How lovely."

"It was easy. And I would do it a thousand times over for him. I love him with all my soul. And I will still be here, standing at his side when you all fall."

"Well, about that. You did your part very well. I want you to know that I appreciate all that you have done. But in the end, you did betray those you were sworn to protect. So I can only assume that you would one day do the same to me. Once a traitor, always a traitor. Really, how would I ever trust you when you so easily abandon your oaths?"

"No! No, this is different. I love you. I will serve you faithfully. You need me, I can help," Willow begged.

"Bind her and bring her to me," Abaddon said, pointing at Bright. "And if she dies or runs away before I have her, I will kill every last one of you. Oh yes, she had better arrive a virgin." Then he added, "You three keep showing Miss Leesee what a rough fuck feels like on the receiving end. Don't kill her, though. I want her to think about it. Make sure the others can watch, they need the entertainment to pass the time. I'm very benevolent. By the way, when I return it will be with thousands, they await my orders in the mountains near Splinter Peak. Do come by for a visit sometime."

Abaddon flew off, and soon the host followed with Bright securely bound. Bright's armour and weapons were thrown to the ground. Spook was struggling so hard against his bonds they feared he would injure himself. The fur on his legs was stained with blood. He bit at the ropes and thrashed about.

The goblins torturing Leesee had spent their seed and were lounging around drinking while Leesee appeared unconscious, still leaning over the fence.

Willow tried to squirm away, but Pyper rolled over until her legs pinned her down. "You're not going anywhere."

Everyone was softly crying except Pyper, who now looked hurt and very angry. Leesee was barely moving. If anyone tried to talk they got a kick in the side by one of the remaining goblins.

Finally, a goblin declared he was ready for another go at Leesee and mounted her. She immediately woke up and screamed. After a few strokes, there was a hollow *thunk,* and he slumped over her. One of the others checked on him and quickly noticed an arrow in the back of his skull. He turned around in time to catch one in the forehead. The other one scrambled as arrows started appearing in his chest and back as he spun around. Rhadia leapt for the throat of the last goblin and ripped it out before the arrows killed him.

Ahn Dahni stepped into the square, looking grim and vicious. She saw Leesee on the fence, blood and urine running down her thighs. She ran to her, pulling her off the fence and laying her gently on the ground. She pulled her knife and cut her bonds. "Leesee? Leesee? Talk to me. Please," she said, pushing Leesee's hair behind her ear.

Leesee's eyelids fluttered open. Once she focused, she started crying and held Dahni tight. Dahni held her and rocked back and forth. "Oh, Dahni. I missed you."

"I missed you too. Are you injured?"

"My butt hurts. But I'll be fine."

"You're crying, baby."

"I'm just glad to see you. I thought you had to break your promise. And I didn't want you to die alone."

"You made me promise we would die together. And here I am. You're the most romantic woman ever," Dahni said.

"I love you so much, Dahni."

Pyper loudly cleared her throat. "I am happy to see you too, but do you think you can cut the rest of us free? I can't feel my hands anymore."

Dahni gently laid Leesee on the ground and came over to cut the bonds. Knowing Pyper, she started with Willow.

"Not her!" Pyper demanded. "She betrayed us. Now the Archon has Bright."

"What?" Dahni said.

"We will tell you everything. Just cut us free!" from Alanna. Once Alanna was free of her bonds, she pulled her pants down and saw blood running down her thighs. It wasn't just from the stab wound. The baby was gone. She stifled a sob then spoke to Dahni.

"We need to collar Spook before you cut him free."

"Collar a Great Wolf?" Dahni asked.

"He's our best chance of finding Bright. He'll run after her if he's cut free. And if he is slain, Bright dies."

Dahni freed the rest, and they told her what happened at the village. Willow was begging and rambling nearly incoherently. Dahni told them what happened while she was with Sariel, although she only said that he fell to a giant ogre. She told them of all that she overheard from Abaddon. There was one common consensus, they had to go after Bright.

Spook strained against the leash, continuing to try to pull himself out of the rope until Alanna spent some time whispering to him. He was still agitated, but the struggling ceased.

Spook lifted his head and howled, long and mournful. He howled again and again, and all the wolves joined in his lament for Bright. It continued still, so Leesee joined the howling and Dahni followed her lead. The other Ahns merged their voice to the eerie choir. Their voices filled the trees with sorrow. Once it stopped, they could hear their grief echo through the forest.

Pyper cut the bonds on Willow's feet and led her to the town square.

"For what Willow has done to Bright, to our Holy Quest, and to all our sisters, I call for a Trial Pit. To the death!" Pyper announced.

"Pyper, no! I'm sorry. Believe me, I didn't think this would happen," Willow pleaded.

"You didn't think he would leave you behind, you mean."

"Pyper, you love Willow. Isn't there another way?" Dahni asked.

"Alanna, you are in charge here. I have called for a Trial. Is it a valid request or not? We can't take her with us, we can't let her go. There is no alternative."

"Pyper, do you really want to do this and live with it?" Alanna asked. "Her violations warrant it, we could all take part. Or you could just let me handle it. I lost my child because of her, besides the things you already mentioned. I won't lose a moment's sleep over it." Willow's eyes went wide in terror at the thought.

"It has to be me. I called for the Trial, now you have to judge whether or not my request has merit."

Alanna thought about it and slowly said, "It has merit."

"Ahn Dahni, if she tries to run, put an arrow through her," Pyper said, and Dahni nodded and notched an arrow.

Pyper cut the bonds on her hands and dropped Willow's sword at her feet. "Give your hands a minute to regain the feeling."

"Pyper, you can't beat me. And I don't want to kill you. Just let me go. You'll never see me again."

"You let him take your fear. You let him take your rage. You let him take your skill, and all that made you a great warrior. Now you are nothing. You betrayed us all. You are nothing to me," Pyper told her.

Willow considered this as she rubbed her wrists. She visibly paled. "I still have skill," she said but didn't sound convinced herself.

"Pick up your blade when you are ready. Show me your skill."

Willow picked up her sword and held it at the ready. Pyper just stood with her axe dangling in one hand. Willow lunged with the sword and Pyper batted it away with ease. Willow launched a flurry of attacks causing Pyper to grip her weapon in both hands to parry. She tried it again, but Pyper caught her blade and wrenched it from her hands. It fell clanging to the paving stones. Willow looked at her with eyes wide.

"Pick it up," Pyper softly said.

Willow picked up her blade and sprang into another frenzy of attacks that were parried until Pyper kicked her in the stomach, sending her flying back. Her head smacked the pavement hard. She was crying now and had lost her sword again.

"Pick it up," Pyper said

"No, I yield!"

"There is no yield! PICK. IT. UP."

Hesitantly, Willow picked up her blade and backed to the edge of the square. Dahni raised her bow. She lunged at Pyper and swung her sword with such force that when it missed, she found herself off balance and facing the wrong direction. Pyper didn't have to see her face this time. So she cut off Willow's head. When her body fell, Pyper collapsed weeping.

Everyone was silent, stunned. It was Alanna who finally spoke. "We have to go after Bright." Alanna picked up Willow's sword, rammed it between two paving stones and snapped it in half.

"Leesee, I think you should be the one to return to Du Shar. I'll send you with one of the Ahns," Alanna stated.

"Not gonna happen, Alanna. I have nothing but respect for

you, but I'm going to find Bright."

"You're hurt."

"We're all hurt. I'm going."

"Don't even look at me," Pyper stated with anger in her voice. "I'm going to kill him."

Alanna decided to send the other two Ahns back with orders to travel as fast as possible and get the news to Du Shar. They were told that if one fell, the other had to keep going. Dahni and Leesee found clothes that fit her in one of the homes. They hid Bright's armour. Leesee picked up Bright's bow and quiver. With only two wolves large enough to ride, they were going to have to run and travel through the night. There was no plan for how they were going to deal with such a vast horde of goblins. They only knew they had to try. There was a Holy Quest.

Chapter 34

RUNNING WITH THE WOLVES

Du Shar returned to Cor Malia to find all of her friends gone. She located Captain Meera who told her of the troll reported at Triborien, and that Alanna had taken her team there. She learned that Ahn Dahni and Sariel had not returned. Days had gone by, they should have come back by now, and the news troubled her. Finally, she ordered a full company to march to Triborien. She asked for volunteers among the remaining Wolf Riders to ride on ahead with her. They all volunteered, so she selected five and headed out. These wolves were mature and sturdy, as were their riders. They tore across the ground like wildfire.

Bright awoke with her head swimming in pain. She vomited on herself immediately. She found that she was tied to a crude wooden litter being pulled by two goblins. It was nothing more than two long logs with other, smaller branches tied across them to support her. The back of her head was bruised and bloody from banging against a support log. Another log in the small of her back caused a wave of agony every time they bounced over a rock.

She looked around, and goblins were everywhere. The smell of them assailed her senses. Dust filled the air, making it difficult to breathe.

"Stop," she croaked. "Please stop, and let me stand."

"Shut it!" yelled one.

"I have to pee, really bad. Please stop."

"Go ahead and pee," he said, and the other goblin laughed.

"My head is bleeding, my back is breaking, and I can't feel my hands or feet. If the Archon told you to bring me in alive, I'm not going to make it," Bright pleaded.

They looked at each other and stopped, talking in hushed tones. They dropped the litter to the ground causing another surge of pain. One knotted a thick rope around her neck while the other one freed her feet. Her hands were tightly bound.

"You'll walk then," he said.

"Thank you," Bright replied, and they laughed at her.

"Thank us when he slits your throat." They both thought

this was funny. "Now, hurry up and pee."

Bright had no choice but to pull down her leggings and pee in front of the two leering goblins. Once she was done, they yanked on her leash and pulled her into motion. It took all of her limited concentration to get her numb feet and legs to move, but it was a relief from the pain of the litter.

Standing, she could see more. There were other Elves, more prisoners, marching along with ropes around their necks and hands tied. There were at least twenty in the group she could see, but there was no way of knowing how many prisoners had been taken. There were hundreds of Elven folk in Triborien, and they found no bodies there. She looked back and could see that other goblins had picked up the empty litter.

Bright had to keep up with them. Whenever they felt the slack come out of the rope, they yanked on it, sending her tumbling to the ground, and scrambling to get up as they dragged her across the rocks. She looked for any opportunity to escape and found none. Her head swam, and she could barely think. Bruised, battered and feeling sick, Bright stumbled along. All her concentration was focused on putting one foot in front of the other. Panic swelled as she was swept away in a tide of green filth and despair.

By nightfall, they finally stopped. The group Bright was with gathered branches from the scrub brush and built a fire. Similar fires were scattered around the large camp. Bright found herself bound once again, hands and feet. She was laying on her side with her hands tied behind her back. She saw them pull an Elven woman from the group. The woman screamed and begged as they dragged her by her hair near the fire. Several goblins were busy taking apart the litter to form a spit over the fire. She cried as they ripped off her clothing. She screamed and choked as they raped her. Goblin laughter filled the air, cruel and heartless.

"Marinade her good, boys! I like my meat tender," yelled one, and they all laughed harder.

Bright was helpless to stop them. She could only lay there and cry. She cried as they tied the woman to the spit and set her over the fire. Bright shut her eyes, but her hysterical screaming could not be blocked out. It reached a frantic pitch then began to slowly die down. Bright could only sob for the poor woman. She feared they all would meet the same fate. She wondered how many children were captive. She could do nothing but lay there, heartbroken and exhausted, and cry herself to sleep.

Rough hands yanked Bright to her feet the next morning. The sun was beginning to rise. They untied her feet but kept her hands tied in front of her. The rope went back around her abraded neck. Something was going on, a commotion. She took the opportunity to pee, fearing they would not stop again soon. They gave her some dirty water to drink, and she did, she was too thirsty to refuse it. It appeared to her that a large group was breaking off and heading back south. All too soon, they yanked on her leash, and she trudged along behind her captors. She was led by the smoldering fire, charred bones littered the ground. She vomited up the putrid water.

Chapter 35

THE PROTECTORS OF THE REALM

Spook followed the trail unerringly. Not that it was a hard trail to follow, but Spook seemed to know exactly where she was located within the massive force. Alanna had spent a lot of time talking to him, and he had stopped straining on the leash. Spook seemed to understand his role leading them to Bright. And that he needed them once she was found.

They ran as much as they could, but the goblins were moving fast. They had longer legs and the endurance to keep up a fast pace for extended periods. After midnight Alanna declared they would be of no use if they were exhausted, so she had them rest for three hours, then they were back on the trail.

When dawn finally broke, the horde was still not in sight, but the tracks were fresh. They resumed a steady run. Leesee had slung her bow, in favor of using Bright's. She still believed it was a magic bow. She had already tested the draw and was amazed at the power it held. She too had heard the string singing to her as it went under tension.

The group approached a low rise in the land. The edge of a dry river bed. They stopped. The wolves growled. At least a hundred goblins were lined up on the other side of the gully.

"Stay here. Make them come to us," Alanna said as she bent to untie Spook's leash. "Spook, don't run off. We need you." Spook let out a short bark and bared his teeth at the goblin horde.

That was all the time they had. The goblins whooped and yelled and came running. Leesee and Dahni let their arrows take flight. They were magnificent in their accuracy. Goblins dropped, and others stumbled over their bodies. Ahn Lissa also carried a bow but did not have their skill. As their arrows began to deplete, she divided hers and placed them in their quivers. Leesee found that Fang could go through one goblin and into another. She sought out opportunities to use this to her advantage. Their callused fingers began to grow raw from the strain against the bowstring.

Yet still, they came. Leaping or stumbling over the bodies of their fallen. Leesee was out of arrows and had drawn her dagger. Dahni ran out seconds later.

"Dahni, Leesee, get behind us!" Alanna shouted as the goblins began to climb the rise on their side. They kept their slightly higher ground and met the goblin forces with fierce determination.

"Dahni, there's no one else I'd rather die with than you," Leesee said.

"I know, right? It's so romantic," Dahni replied as a goblin headed around towards her. She blocked its sword with her bow and slashed its neck with her dagger.

Pyper's axe chopped with precision. Alanna dropped them with her spear point or struck them down, her spear moving too fast to perceive. And Ahn Lissa's sword swiftly butchered enemies as they came. A mound of bodies piled up before them but the goblins were beginning to flank the small group. The wolves were all engaged trying to keep the flanks free of advancing goblins. They leapt, smashing enemies to the ground so they could get at their soft necks. But each of them knew it was no use. They fought with anger, fury, and determination. They fought for Bright and their Holy Quest. And for their fallen sisters. But it was not enough. Still, the goblins pressed in.

A tsunami of fur rushed by. It hit the goblin ranks hard, knocking them down and tearing into their awful flesh. The wolves had come! They heard Spook's howling and responded in force. The original Protectors of the Realm, those who were able to answer the howling, quickly pushed the goblins back from the hard-pressed warriors. Alanna, Pyper, and Lissa rushed forward to engage more, side by side with the vicious wolves.

The clanging of steel against steel diminished, soon it was over. The warriors had survived. Two Protectors had been slain and another wounded. Leesee bound its wound as best she could using her tunic. Pyper walked around, checking the injured goblins for signs of life. When she found them still breathing, she killed them. Dahni and Leesee scavenged for arrows. They recovered many of their own but would have to make do with goblin arrows, but there were only four archers to be found within the crowd. Those four apparently didn't get the chance to take a clean shot.

They were still catching their breath on the battlefield when Thor walked up to Alanna. Spook ran up to him, wagging his tail, his face and chest red with blood.

"I am delighted to see you," Alanna said to the massive beast. "I thought this to be my final battle." Thor made an odd yawning sound. "Great Wolf, they have Bright. And there are hundreds of them." Thor turned his head to the north and sniffed the air. A little over sixty wolves had answered the call. More were straggling in, too late for this engagement.

Thor barked. The thunderous sound startled Alanna. Other Great Wolves gathered around. Thor repeatedly barked at them. Then he lay down upon the ground and looked to Alanna. Leesee came up and threw her arms around his massive neck. She was crying in gratitude and thanking him repeatedly. Thor nudged her with his nose, sending her sprawling across his back. Several others were laying down nearby.

"Everyone! Mount up! They're going to let us ride!" Alanna yelled.

Leesee climbed onto Thor's shoulders and grabbed a fistful of fur. "Dahni, come on!" She held out her hand, and Dahni scrambled up behind and held her tight. The mighty Thor stood with ease and began heading north, Spook at his side. Alanna and Lissa mounted their own wolves with Pyper jumping onto another. Once the warriors had caught up to

Thor, he broke into a smooth, loping run. Dust churned in their wake.

Chapter 36

SPLINTER PEAK PASS

Du Shar had reached the village. She had already encountered the Ahns sent to warn her and brought one with her, sending the other back to alert Captain Meera. The eerie stillness bothered her more than if she had found it inhabited by trolls. Trolls she was expecting. This she was not. The goblin sign heading north was unmistakable, and there were too many to try to count. Over the top of these, were the prints of Elven warriors and their young wolves. There was still hope.

In the town square, Shar found Willow's body. She saw her broken blade, a deliberate act of disrespect. She ordered one of the Ahns to ride back to the marching company. She was to stay with them and guide them north as fast as they could march. Hopefully, they would intercept them in time. But there was little chance in that. Shar mounted and led the warriors north as fast as the wolves could run.

The goblin horde had begun to run. Bright could not keep up. She fell repeatedly and had to hold on to the rope with her bound hands to keep from strangling as they drug her along the gravel. Finally, one of her captors picked up her bruised and abraded body and slung her over his shoulder. She was sick and dehydrated. The goblin's body odor was overwhelming, and she vomited up the last of the dirty water. It ran down his waist, but he didn't seem to care. Then, mercifully, she passed out.

The Ravine came into view, a great gash that cut across the land. On the other side, rose steep mountains, known as The Crags. One peak rose above all of the others. A sharp and jagged shard of rock, as if it had been thrust upwards between, and through, one mountain peak like the point of a spear. Carved into this was the goblin stronghold of Splinter Peak.

The goblins panicked and began to sprint. Bright's captors scrambled to make their way to the front of the column. They had spotted the line of dust thundering up behind them like a storm. A storm of teeth and claws and death. They outnumbered their opponents more than ten to one, but the goblins had no way of knowing that for sure. They did realize that it would be unwise to be the last ones on the treacherous, switch-back trail that led down the Ravine, across the river, and back up to the Peak.

Spook could sense Bright ahead. He ran faster, so fast, his paws began to bleed. Soon he passed Thor who pressed onwards with renewed vigor. The entire pack could smell their prey and salivated in anticipation of battle.

Before they were three hundred yards from the horde, Leesee and Dahni began to let loose their arrows. The goblins were so tightly pressed that nearly every arrow found their mark. Confusion and panic spread within the ranks as goblins fell. Too late the goblin archers stopped to notch their bows.

The Protectors slammed into the enemy ranks like a hammer, sending green bodies flying through the air. Bones crunched between vise-like jaws. Goblins were picked up, crushed, shook back and forth, and thrown.

Leesee jumped off Thor and rolled across the ground. Dahni quickly followed. Leesee had spotted lifeless goblin archers and hurried to scoop up their arrows. She and Dahni planted themselves and began to fire into the crowd or at any goblins that headed her way. They made their way from one fallen archer to another, depleting their arrows then moving on.

Pyper and Lissa fought back to back, now surrounded by goblins. Alanna needed more room and was keeping a circle cleared around her. One large goblin picked up a dead comrade and held it in front of himself as a shield. He rushed at Alanna. She thrust her spear through the dead one and into the other, but not before the force brought her to the ground, wrenching the spear from her hands. Another was right there to take advantage of her position. He raised his sword for the killing blow and was immediately cartwheeled off his feet.

Alanna looked up and saw Du Shar kneeling behind him with both of her long, silver daggers at his throat. With a quick motion, the goblin was relieved of his head, painting Shar's chin, and neck in crimson.

"Just like old times," Shar said with a smile, then jumped back into the battle.

The other six Ahns were right behind and came to their aid. Their wolves fought by their sides. Alanna worked quickly to free her spear from the two goblins as Shar pressed her attack into another group of enemies. The goblins were stuck on her spear, and she screamed in frustration as Shar was drawn farther away into the battlefield.

"Leesee, look!" Dahni shouted.

Leesee followed her gaze and saw Abaddon flying towards the edge of the Ravine. They leapt over bodies as they ran forward. Leesee slowed once to grab a handful of arrows from one of the dead.

A goblin hit one wolf in the neck with his axe. The wolf dropped, and its rider fell as well. They were connected, in life and death. Spook was running between goblins now, dodging right and left but pressing forward. He was close to Bright, he could feel her.

Abaddon dropped down in front of Bright's captors. He was livid with rage. "You incompetent fools!" He screamed. "This will never do. Give her to me!" The goblin handed the limp body to Abaddon who cradled her in his arms, wings beating several times to get them both off the ground.

Leesee saw him rise. She drew Fang and took aim. She calculated the cosign automatically, she accounted for the wind. Finally, she accounted for the heavier arrow.

"He has Bright!" Dahni shouted. "Don't hit her." Abaddon spun in the air to head for the keep.

"I know exactly where to shoot, Dahni," Leesee replied. She set her arrow free. It hit him square in the middle of a butt cheek. Abaddon faltered in the air. He dropped down then beat his wings to gain altitude once again. Leesee notched another arrow.

"She's over The Ravine! If you kill him, Bright will fall!"

Leesee lowered her aim and looked at Dahni. Leesee shifted her aim directly at Dahni's head; Dahni's eyes went wide, and her mouth dropped open. Then Leesee sidestepped and shot a goblin in the eye. The arrow actually flew through Dahni's hair. It had been running for Dahni.

"Holy Shit! You could have just said to duck!" Dahni said.

"Yup, that would have been better," Leesee replied. Dahni just shrugged and smiled at her. They looked for more arrows and got back into the battle.

Half of the goblin force had made it onto the steep trail down The Ravine. They were scrambling to get by each other, and many were falling off the steep sides to their death. Another Ahn fell, and her wolf died with a goblin in its mouth.

Alanna saw Du Shar plunging into a knot of goblins, her blades glittering in the sun. Shar whirled and parried and cut with practiced precision. Shar danced and leapt. She spun and slashed, a pirouette of death. Alanna always thought it was a beautiful thing, to watch Shar in battle. Rend fought to stay near her. Alanna pressed hard to get to her side and fight together as they had done so many times before. When they were together, they were invincible. Now Shar was too far away, Alanna needed to be with her. Amica sensed Alanna's change of direction and knocked down goblins to get to her. As Alanna neared her old friend a goblin axe cut into Shar's thigh, almost to the bone. Shar dropped to that knee and continued to lash out with her daggers. Alanna screamed a warning as a goblin rushed up behind her with a spear. But the spear plunged through her, all the way into the ground.

Alanna screamed in fury and waded into their midst. She was a demon. Her spear lashed out with lightning speed felling goblins. Blood misted the air. The ones that could get out of her reach fled for the trail. The rest died where they stood.

Alanna ran to Shar. "I'm here. Don't worry, everything will be all right." But she knew it wouldn't. It was something you said, even when you knew it wasn't true.

Shar was kneeling, pinned to the ground. She coughed alarming amounts of blood. Blood flowed in spurts from the gash on her leg.

"I'm going to pull this spear out," Alanna said, but Shar shook her head.

"Alanna," she gasped. "I have … I always loved you."

"I love you too. Just hang on."

"Thank you ... for everything." Shar's voice was just a whisper now. "Take care of the Clan." Then she was gone, and Rend fell by her side. Alanna held her and wept uncontrollably. It was all she could do.

As the goblins fled down The Ravine, the warriors slowly gathered near the body of their beloved chieftain. And the wolves began to howl.

Chapter 37

PAIN IN THE BUTT

Abaddon landed near Splinter Peak's entrance and winced in pain.

"Take her!" he commanded a nearby goblin. "Bring her to the main hall. Healer!" he shouted, his voice echoing down the hallways.

He limped up the passageway until he met an elderly goblin. "Get this out!" he demanded, indicating the arrow protruding from his backside.

"Archon. That is goblin arrow. Is barbed and must go through. But it rests on bone, possibly through bone. If I pull it, it will rip out juicy chunks of flesh."

"Then you'll have to cut it out, you incompetent fool!"

"Yes, Archon. Come to my chambers. I get someone to assist you." The healer called another goblin over who helped the Archon walk. The healer went on ahead to prepare. Another goblin came their way down the passage, and Abaddon sent him to fetch the priest.

Abaddon entered the healer's chambers and was told to lie down on a bloodstained slab. "Archon, I will need to make two cuts, very deep, on either side of the arrow and try to spread flesh apart. Then I can remove arrow. You should drink this. It will lessen the pain."

"No, I have to have my wits about me for the ritual. It must be done immediately. I must be prepared. There may be unwelcome visitors from my realm."

"As you wish. The Priest is here, your majesty," the healer said, malevolence in his voice.

A goblin in black robes wearing a skull headpiece walked to his side. "Yes, my Archon?" he hissed.

"Prepare the ritual. I will bathe in her blood before another hour goes by."

"We are already prepared, my Archon. And the sacrifice is being made ready now," he hissed again with a smile. "I look forward to witnessing it."

The healer brought out a thin, blood-stained knife. His assistants on either side held two objects that resembled large forks with the tines bent back into hooks. He placed the blade approximately the width of the arrowhead, then moved it out much farther. He did not like being called a fool. He plunged the blade into Abaddon's flesh through his leggings and smiled at his screams.

"Hold him down!" the healer commanded.

He sliced back and forth as Abaddon gasped. He cut until he felt the metal of the arrowhead. Then he went to the other side and cut again. Abaddon banged his head against the stone slab until the wound on his face began to break open and bleed. The healer slowly sawed back and forth until he was once again hitting the metal arrowhead. Then he instructed his assistants to use the prongs to hold the wound apart. They pulled as their patient screamed anew. The healer twisted and pulled until the arrow was removed, stringing flesh behind it. He noticed that the arrowhead wasn't intact. A large piece had broken off when it hit bone. He shrugged indifferently and left it there.

"Now we just have to sew the whole thing back together. That wasn't so bad, was it, Majesty?" But Abaddon did not hear him. He had passed out.

Once he was done, he opened a jar containing a thick, black paste. He waved it under Abaddon's nose until he awakened, choking.

The assistants slid the Archon off the slab and helped him limp to the main hall.

Chapter 38

SPLINTER PEAK

The howling ceased, and Thor growled. It started low at first, deep in his throat. It was a sound that would not be satisfied until it ended chewing on the throat of another. Then he ran in the direction of the trail, and the rest of the wolves followed him. He bounded down the path. It was steep and cut back and forth with a sheer cliff to one side, and a steep drop on the other. It was only wide enough for one to travel safely. Once he caught up to the retreating goblins, he pressed his nose against the cliff wall and pushed forward. Goblins were forced off the edge by his sheer size. Any that managed to somehow make it by him were ran off the ledge by those that followed. Once he reached the bottom, he did the same thing on the way up to Splinter Peak. The few goblins that had already made it to the top were crushed, shook, and thrown over the edge.

The gates were shut by the time he was there. Another fifty or more goblins lay dead or injured at the bottom of the ravine. The other wolves ensured that they didn't stay wounded for long.

Thor scratched and barked at the gate.

Leesee wouldn't let Alanna watch as Pyper yanked the spear from Du Shar. They covered her with a cloak.

"My task isn't finished," Pyper said grimly.

"Du Alanna, you stay here. The Ahns will watch over you. We'll be right back," Leesee said.

"We'll be right back, Alanna," echoed Dahni.

Alanna grabbed her spear. She leaned against it as she stood. Her head was down, and her hair fell in front of her face. Slowly she looked up through her hair. There was murder in her eyes. All she said was, "Follow me."

They headed down the trail as fast as they could.

The priests tied Bright's hands and feet. Her hands were now bound behind her back. For the first time, Bright remembered the amulet she wore around her neck and cursed herself for not thinking about it earlier. She only had to hold it and think of an angel, any angel. She could just think of one. Sariel.

The priests began to cut away her clothing. One tried to make her drink something, she refused. They held her head back, then held her nose and forced it down her throat. She coughed and had a hard time breathing by the time they released her. It affected her almost immediately. She had been drugged. Her mind and vision clouded. She panicked and tried to fling the amulet around behind her, maybe she could reach up and grasp it. The priests picked her up and dropped her onto an altar. The Angel's Tear was now out of reach. Stones had been placed around the edges, and a large leather cloth draped over them. The Archon didn't want to waste any of her blood.

The older priest was instructing the others. Telling them that once she was suspended and her head was removed, they were to move her back and forth so the Archon would be coated in her blood. He said there would be consequences if one drop were spilled outside of the altar.

Bright laughed hysterically, then made whimpering sounds. The drug was beginning to take full effect. She could barely think, and her vision had become nothing more than fuzzy images. The priests tied another rope to her feet, and she was hauled upside down above the altar. This made her head spin, and she lost consciousness.

The warriors were exhausted, the steep climb up the trail

took its toll. They plodded along by the sheer force of will. Goblins somewhere above the main gate began to throw large stones at the wolves near the entrance. One caught a wolf in the back, breaking it. He thrashed about until he fell over the edge. Once the goblins saw the Elves heading up the switchback trail, they started directing their stones at them. This forced the small band to keep tight against the walls. They continued to slug forward, their legs protesting from the exertion. At the next bend in the trail, Leesee and Dahni let their arrows fly, and the stone throwing ceased.

Abaddon limped into the great hall between two goblins. He was wearing nothing but dirty and blood-soaked bandages around his waist and buttocks, he had prepared himself to bathe in blood. He was aware of a constant barking from outside the keep. This did not concern him. He was led to a podium containing a hefty tome. He opened it about halfway, turned a few more pages, and began an incantation.

The words he spoke were vile and blasphemous. The cacophonous sounds were so profane they caused him pain to pronounce them. But the goblins loved it. They grew excited and anxious. The spell was so depraved that Abaddon felt sick and had to choke back vomit. Yet he continued the foul recitation until it was complete.

Then he started limping towards the altar. There was a

flash, and suddenly Sariel stood before him, blocking his way to Bright. His wings spread wide. The priests moved behind him, and Sariel spun, drawing his sword in a fluid movement. A moment later their heads tumbled to the floor.

"You were warned," Sariel said.

"Warned? About what? Interfering with the mortal realm? Isn't that what you are doing now?"

"Yes, and I will answer for my transgressions. You will cease this at once, and return with me to Archangel Michael."

"Or what?"

"Or I will be required to tell him that I destroyed an angel."

"You wouldn't dare such a thing! You follow the code, you wouldn't break one of our most sacred rules for them, for these insects! You're bluffing! You'll be banished, or worse ... rebuked!"

"So be it," Sariel said and started forward.

"No! Stay back!" Abaddon yelled, scrambling to limp backward.

Sariel walked steadily towards him, his angelic blade gleaming silver from within. Abaddon was panicked, Sariel was closing on him fast. There was a pounding from the keep door. "KILL HER!" He shouted to his goblin minions. "Kill the Elvenstar! Kill her now!" Then he was gone. He had retreated into the Realm of Angels.

"Coward!" shouted Sariel.

The goblins only hesitated a few seconds. There were almost a hundred of them. Archers started notching arrows, as Sariel ran towards Bright, suspended over the altar. Bolts began flying, some missed but one hit her near the edge of her waist. Sariel leapt, beat his wings and landed on the altar. He wrapped his wings in a spiral around Bright. Arrows bounced off angel wings as if they were steel. But the rest were coming, and Bright was already hurt. Sariel could not think of any way to get her out safely. He knew he couldn't protect her for very long once the goblins reached the altar.

"Bright, I'm sorry, but I have to send you home."

Bright became somewhat aware. Perhaps because she heard his voice. Everything was muddled to her, but she said, "No, I have to use the amulet." It was still about her neck, dangling below her head, held in place by her chin and braids.

"Bright, my Elvenstar. I send you back across The Veil."

And then she was gone.

For a moment, Sariel stood within the protection of his wings. Then his soul filled with anger. Elvenrealm had lost Bright. He had lost the mortal he loved. The anger he felt turned into something he knew. Something familiar and warm. Vengeance.

Sariel's wings snapped wide like a thunderclap. "Behold the Wrath of Angels! Behold my vengeance." He thrust his sword above him, and a brilliant flash blinded the goblin horde.

The warriors had reached the ironbound gate. It was scratched but undamaged. They all pressed upon it, but it did not budge.

"Pyper, use your axe," Alanna commanded. Spook had gone berserk, barking, whining, and leaping about in circles.

Pyper pummeled the door with her axe. She concentrated on one spot of the thick, hardened wood between two metal bindings. Pyper hoped that they might reach through a small opening and unbar the gate. When she began to slow, they all took turns. Slowly they were making their way through the door.

Then the screams began. Alanna took the axe from an Ahn and began to furiously pound on the door. Wood splinters flew, but the screaming continued. She cried out in frustration. There was an indention forming in the heavy door, but they weren't through yet.

"Alanna, I don't think that's Bright screaming," Leesee said.

Dahni listened for a second. "Nope. Definitely not. Goblins, I think."

"My turn," Leesee said and took the axe.

The screaming started sounding farther and farther away. Leesee kept pounding the door with the axe. The wood gave way, only to reveal another iron band, reinforcing the door from the inside.

Then the screaming stopped. Leesee dropped the axe and slid down the door, crying. The others stood numbly, in the realization that they had failed. The realization that Abaddon, The Archon, had succeeded in taking their hope away. They were well past exhaustion, but all their efforts were for nothing. Even the Great Wolves were whining.

"Listen!" Dahni said.

They listened and heard the sound of footsteps. Footsteps moving slowly and deliberately towards the keep door. The warriors held their weapons at the ready. The archers notched their arrows.

The sound of footsteps reached the keep door and stopped. They heard the sound of the bars being lifted and thrown to the floor.

"Stand ready," Alanna whispered.

The door opened, and Sariel stood before them. Dahni dropped her bow. Her mouth opened and closed a few times as if she were trying to say something, but couldn't. Dahni ran to him and threw her arms around his waist. It sounded like she was trying to say something, but she was sobbing too loudly to understand. Sariel held her tight.

"There now, beautiful Dahni. Be calm. I promised that you would see me again."

Somehow she calmed. "You did. But I feel awful. If I hadn't distracted you …"

"Nothing would have changed. I knew that, and I still decided to go. So did you. You stood firm against the behemoth. You tried to save me. Put it all in the past. I am glad to see you are safe."

"Where is Bright?" Alanna demanded.

"I had no choice but to send her back across The Veil. I am sorry, but I could not have protected her otherwise."

"Then go bring her back," Alanna ordered.

"If it is within my power, I will do so. But for now, I have broken our code by my actions here. I must return to Michael for judgment. I know not what that judgment will be."

"I want her back. Promise me you'll bring her back," Alanna said with tears streaming down her face.

Sariel kissed Dahni on the top of her head. He went to Alanna and held her face in his hands. "I do not know what my judgment will be. It was a grave thing I did interfering in mortal affairs while in the realm of angels. Therefore I cannot make that promise. I will promise you this, if I can, then I will. Do you understand?" Alanna nodded.

"I believe that I have taken my vengeance on the goblins within this keep, but have a care, there may be some left. I know that many Elven folks are held within the keep as prisoners. You will need to search and find them all. Take them home." Alanna nodded again.

Sariel walked to the edge of the cliff and spread his wings.

"Wait!" Dahni shouted.

Sariel turned, and Dahni ran to him and jumped into his arms, wrapping her legs around his waist. She kissed him long and passionately, and he returned the affection. Then he gently set her down.

"I love you," she said.

Sariel smiled and said, "I find my heart is now big enough to love more than one. I love you too, Dahni." Then he turned, snapped his wings, and flew away. He flew straight up until they could no longer see him.

"Oh, my God!" Leesee said. "You bedded him, didn't you?" Dahni didn't answer. She continued to stare up at the sky.

Chapter 39

THE OTHER SIDE OF THE VEIL

A large man walked down the hallway. Powerful fluorescent lights glared against white walls washing out other colors. His booted feet trod purposefully over a white and black tiled floor. He was wearing a black long-sleeve men's duster jacket that nearly reached the ground and a fedora hat. He walked past gurneys, and nurses busy looking at clipboards. He walked past a nurse's station—she didn't even look up. Then he entered an elevator and pressed the button for the fourth floor. When the door opened, another nurse was there waiting on the elevator. She gasped at the size of him, then smiled coyly and let him exit first. He walked down the hall, turned and continued. He walked past a door then stopped. He backed up and pushed on the handle. Then he stepped inside.

A man was sleeping in a chair. A woman was standing by the foot of a hospital bed and a young boy, maybe twelve or thirteen years old was sitting in a chair next to the bed with a

369

thick three-ring binder on his lap.

"Tell me the story about your Bonding again," the boy said.

"I have told you many times. You have written it all down. Read what you have to me." The voice was barely a whisper. She sounded tired.

Sariel took another step into the room. The woman heard him and turned around.

"Can I help you?" she asked. "Are you a doctor?"

Sariel removed his hat. "No, ma'am. I am here for Bright." When he said that the boy stood up.

"Bright's here! She's the Elvenstar," he said proudly, pointing to the frail figure on the bed.

"Sir, we paid for a private room. *Jenny* isn't well. I'm afraid I'm going to have to ask you to leave."

"I understand your concern. Please be calm. I will only be a moment."

For some reason, she did seem to calm. "I'm Maureen, Jenny's Mom."

"I am very pleased to meet you, Maureen." Sariel stepped up to the bed. The young woman on the bed was emaciated, her arms skeletal. She couldn't have weighed seventy pounds. She had no eyebrows, and her head was covered in a bandana. She appeared to be asleep. However, Sariel knew she was only moments away from dying. Sariel knew death. He was death. There were machines in her room, but they weren't turned on—as if their electronic magic was of no more use.

Sariel took off his heavy duster. Maureen gasped. He was wearing some kind of armour, and he was immense and muscular. The man stirred in the chair. Sariel handed the jacket and hat to the boy. He said, "Here, you can have these. You'll grow into them soon enough. You must be Samuel."

"How did you know that? How did you know her name was Bright?" Samuel asked.

"I have known her for quite some time. She talked about you often. She missed you a lot." The man had awakened and stood up.

"I know who you are!" Samuel exclaimed. "You're Sariel!"

"You are a wise young man," Sariel said and sat on the bed.

"Who are you? What are you doing here? This is a private room. Get away from my daughter," the man said.

The woman, still acting polite, said, "This is Jenny's father, Bill."

Sariel stood back up and offered his hand. "I am pleased to meet you, Bill." Bill did not shake his hand. When he stood up, Bright felt the bed move and opened her eyes.

"Sariel? Is that you?" she whispered.

"Yes, my love. I have come for you."

Tears began to fall down Bright's cheek. She tried to lift her hand, and Sariel grasped it in both of his. "I missed you so much. I was hoping it would be you that came for me."

"I could not trust you with any other."

"I'm afraid I'm going to have to ask you to leave. I don't want you upsetting my daughter," Bill said.

"Dad, don't you know who this is? Did you listen to any of her stories? This is Sariel, the Angel of Death. This is Jenny's husband." Samuel looked at Sariel. "I knew it was all true, I knew it! I've written all of it down. The stories have to be told. It's the custom, isn't that right?"

Sariel reached out and put a hand on Samuel's shoulder and said, "You are correct, and I know that you will tell Bright's story well."

"So you're the one filling my daughter's head with all this foolish nonsense. You should be ashamed of yourself. I'm getting security," Bill said.

Sariel looked at her father. "You may not have heard the stories, as young Samuel has. I should let you know that this is Bright, The Elvenstar. And the Elvenstar never lies."

"Daddy!" Bright said as loud as she could. "*You're* upsetting me. I have been waiting so long to see him. Please let us talk."

Bright looked to Sariel. "It's been so long. It's been months. I have been trying to stay strong for you."

"I am sorry, my love. I have been forced into … obligations since I perished."

"Obligations? Oh, no. I'm so sorry."

"And I am sorry for …" He looked at her. "For all this. I thought I was saving you. I had no idea."

"That's because I never told you I was dying here, on this side of The Veil," she said and smiled. "A girl has to be a little mysterious."

"A quality you excel at. I think I finally understand why the mirror upset you."

"What happened? How is Spook?" she whispered.

"Most have survived. Spook is not well without you."

"Oh, no. Who didn't survive?"

"This is not the place to talk about that. I am here for *you* now. It is *your* time to leave."

"Does this mean that you have wings now?"

"Yes, I have wings now."

"Can I see them?"

"Of course." A sound like a sail billowed full by a strong wind rang out through the room, and it was filled, corner to corner, with beautiful white wings.

They gasped.

"Wow!" exclaimed Samuel.

"Oh, my God! You *are* an angel!" exclaimed Maureen. "Please don't take my little girl!" She was crying now.

"I love all of you," Bright said. "But it is my time to go. Go on with your lives. Be happy. My husband has finally come for me."

Sariel pulled the blankets from her. He removed the IV, lifted her easily, and cradled her in his arms. She managed to put her arms around his neck and said, "I am so happy."

Sariel turned to the wall behind the bed, and it disappeared. Only blue, sunny skies and white, puffy clouds could be seen beyond.

"Can we go home now?" Bright asked.

"For you, I will try," Sariel said. With a snap of his wings, he leapt into the sky. Bright's family watched them fly away between the clouds, and then the wall with the Venetian blinds reappeared.

Samuel ran to the window, spread the blinds wide and peered outside. He saw only the night sky. He turned and spied a large, white feather on the floor. He picked it up, stood there a moment then sat down, plopping the fat binder onto his lap. He turned the pages until he found a blank one at the end. He laid the feather down on the opposite page and started writing.

Bonus Sneak Peek at Book Two of the Elvenrealm Series

THE GOBLIN QUEEN

Uneven footsteps echoed down the cold, stone corridor, along with the occasional *clack* of a walking staff. He was in no hurry. There was only death here, and death did not bother him. Yet he hoped there was some life to be found within these caverns. Some small, yet somewhat significant life. He paused as he passed the doors to the great hall and savored the pungent aroma of rotting bodies. Making his way through the mounds of putrid flesh and body parts, he approached the podium placed some twenty feet back from the altar. He had to know. This was more important than finding any living thing.

Upon reaching the podium, he breathed a huge sigh of relief. The Tome was still there. No one had bothered to take it. That it might be missing was what he feared most of all. It was all he thought about ever since his forced departure. It had a title written in a language only his kind knew. It was one word ... *Blasphemy*. He caressed the book, and in that simple touch, he felt nausea swell; he felt the bile rise in his throat. It always had that effect. He smiled to himself and limped further into the stronghold.

He didn't think he had been gone all that long, yet time was such a tricky phenomenon. Judging time was often difficult. He hummed to himself as he walked. He came to a door. It should have been locked but appeared to have been forced open. There were stairs beyond, and he took his time climbing them. Another door stood ajar, and he walked into his former living quarters. His belongings were scattered, and he was sure some things would be missing, but the tome was still there, sitting safely on the podium, nothing else mattered. Well, one other thing still mattered, but that would be only a minor disappointment if he were too late.

He walked to a wall of stone and mortar. He spread his arms and pressed upon two stones at the same time. The wall swung open silently like a door. Stepping inside, he saw two figures lying on the bed. A mother and child. The mother was a goblin, although as their kind go, she was probably about as fair a specimen as could be found. Her red hair was wiry and generally unruly, as it was now. She had too much of an overbite with large, crooked teeth which had not been sharpened into points like the males of her kind were fond of doing. However, her other features were about as appealing as a goblin female could possibly manage. He had his pick of a thousand and had to settle for her. Now she looked way too thin. Her ribs and hipbones too prominent.

The baby fared much better, most likely at the expense of her mother's body trying to produce enough milk. He thought the child beautiful. It was about two years old … if he figured mortal time correctly. It had her mother's light green skin. Her hair was soft and straight with gentle waves and shined like red gold. Other than her skin, it was her ears that gave away her goblin heritage. Bat shaped, they stuck nearly straight from her head but were much shorter than her mother's. Most of her features, other than her slight overbite, came from him, she was his little angel.

He slammed his walking staff onto the stone floor. The report woke the mother with a start. The child yawned and stretched. Her mother saw him and weekly scrambled off the bed to prostrate herself on the floor at his feet.

"My Lord," she spoke, her voice harsh and raspy from dehydration.

"Greetings my sweet Surae. You have done well keeping our child alive."

"You have been gone for so long. I feared … for your safety," Surae said.

"You feared for *my* safety? Never a thought that you may starve to death, locked in this room? That is so sweet. Please rise." He flung a large satchel on the bed. "I have brought food and water."

"Thank you, my Lord," she said, eyeing the package.

"Please. Drink. Eat. It is a meager reward for your patience. And of course, your concern for my safe return."

Surae grabbed the satchel and emptied it on the bed. The child sat up and began rubbing her eyes with tiny fists. Surae grabbed one of the water skins and drank greedily.

"Slow down," he said. "You'll make yourself sick." Surae complied immediately. She snatched up some of the food and began to eat. "There, that's my girl," he said, and Surae smiled up at him with cheeks stuffed full.

The child made an excited sound; she held up her hands. He stepped near and picked her up. "Look at you! Regina, my lovely little angel. Your father's back. You didn't think I would forget about you, now did you?"

"Fa da!" she said, or something resembling it. He smiled and kissed her. She put her little arms around his neck.

"Regina, my dear, you're going to be daddy's beautiful queen one day soon. Do you know what your name means? It means queen. *My* beautiful queen. Together, we will rule this realm." She squeezed his neck.

"Soon, my child. Be patient. For now, you are quite overdue for a bath." Abaddon limped from the room, leaving Surae squatting over the satchel of food.

ABOUT THE AUTHOR

D. C. Bryant is the author of the *Elvenrealm* series and other novels.

His background makes him an unlikely author of fantasy, as he served most of his life as an Infantry officer, then moved on to become a Federal Agent. Later, Bryant spent several years as a professor at a major university. All this time, he did write, but it was dry and uninteresting stuff; memorandums, lesson plans, and operating procedures. D. C. Bryant led troops into combat during Operation Desert Storm and then went on to hunt down criminal fugitives.

People often ask him why he doesn't write stories about war or law enforcement. The answer is simple; to him, it feels too much like work. Upon retirement, he began to write the things that he had always wanted to write, unbound by the constraints of reality. Now he hopes that those authentic experiences will help bring Elvenrealm to life for readers. Elvenrealm exists.

Made in the
USA
Columbia, SC